THE LONG CON

THE LONG CON
Book One of the Fayette Bay Series

GEMMA NICHOLLS

Copyright © 2023 Gemma Nicholls
All rights reserved.
ISBN: 9798850076061

To Brandon,
for never allowing me to stop believing in myself. This book would've definitely been deleted a long time ago without you.

AUTHOR'S NOTE

While this story is not in the dark romance genre, it does touch on darker themes such as grief, violence, and death. There is on-page violence in this book, although I wouldn't consider it to be explicitly visual or gory. Please consider if these themes might be upsetting or triggering for you before reading.

CHAPTER ONE

Deep breath.

Silas glanced at the duffel bag on the seat next to him, its zipper threatening to burst open under the pressure from within.

How simple it would be for him to take the bag and run. Away from Desmond Rose's shop—away from it all. He bit the inside of his cheek as he contemplated the likelihood of getting caught after fleeing the country. With Desmond's men after him, he might not even get through airport security.

After another moment of hesitation, Silas let out a snort and swung the car door open to lift himself out, black duffel swiftly following.

Desmond's *shop* was no more than a bunch of shipping containers that he'd managed to put together to look like a garage. Every con man needed a coverup, and Desmond Rose certainly wasn't the brightest man around. The white exterior had a cheap sign above the door that read 'Desmond's Deals' in golden-red letters, and a few dusty cars parked out front that hadn't moved at all since Silas started working there.

He swaggered into the shop, swinging the bag back and forth down the dimly lit hallways until he reached his employer's office. The door creaked in agony as he pushed it open.

"There he is!" Desmond's voice was loud and dense and always came with the unwelcome stench of cheap whiskey and cigarettes.

Silas smirked and lifted the bag above the metal desk before letting it fall with a loud bang. Desmond grabbed for the zipper almost before the bag had even reached the table. Thick stacks of money exploded out, gasping for air.

Silas stood with his arms folded while his boss took a handful of cash and held it up to his nose. He took a deep, rattling inhale. A wicked grin pulled at Silas's lips as he considered the thousands of germs currently crawling towards Desmond's brain.

This was a performance Desmond liked to showcase every time Silas brought back the bounty from his missions. Personally, he didn't get the fascination. Most of the time the cash was covered in grime—occasionally mixed with blood. He certainly had no desire to know what that would smell like. But he let his boss do his little gloating ritual to christen his new money. The sooner that was over, the sooner Silas would get his cut.

Like clockwork, Desmond threw him a handful of stacks and quickly went back to counting the leftovers. Out of the hundreds of grouped notes that has been in Silas's worn duffle, he'd been thrown seven. Unsurprising. He inhaled sharply and grabbed his now-empty bag off the desk, tossing his meagre pay inside.

"So, go on," Desmond said as he piled his money in neat little rows. "Tell me how you did it, Mr Knight. How did you get them to believe that the necklaces were real?"

Silas's left incisor cut into his rigid tongue as he stared at the high wall of money between them. He was owed much more than the lousy pay barely lining the bottom of his bag, and he was too busy wishing that he'd never gotten out of his car to register the question.

Where could he have got to if only he'd kept on driving?

Another stack hit him in the forehead, breaking him out of his thoughts. It bounced into his hands. Desmond was already reaching out for him to give it back, but one swift glare from Silas had him withdrawing.

"Ah, you keep that one too, champ. You've earned it!" Desmond boomed, reaching into one of the desk drawers that made a horrifying noise as the rusted metal ground together. Silas tensed, ready to counteract whatever Des was about to pull out, just in case he tried anything stupid. If there was one thing he knew about his boss, it was that he was not to be trusted.

But all that surfaced was a pack of cigarettes and a box of matches. Desmond lit one and offered the box to Silas, who refused, and asked again, "Tell me how you pulled it off this time."

With one more lick across his front teeth, Silas kicked a metal chair backwards and fell into the seat, head rolling back so he was looking down his nose at Desmond. The right side of his mouth pulled up into a grimace as he thought of the pathetic men he had conned just this morning.

It was a simple trick—just another day at the office for Silas. He'd pulled off this joke so many times before that it had grown boring. How often would he see the same old sheep being tricked into thinking that fake glass gemstones were real diamonds, just because someone had told them so? Once he'd convinced one person to buy a piece of worthless jewellery, others had seen and lined up in the hopes that Silas didn't sell out before it was their turn.

Silas scowled to himself. It was pathetic.

"You know how it is, Des." Silas shrugged his irritation away and let his eyes wander around the room. It was poorly lit and the walls were unfinished, just like the floor. There was the metal desk, two steel filing cabinets where Desmond kept his research and earnings, and a tall, dead plant in the corner. It was a shame no one had watered it in time—the office needed a little colour added to it. The room was as grey as Desmond's hair and skin. "It's the same old story I tell you every damn time."

His boss took a long drag of his cigarette and leaned back in his filthy pleather chair. "Well, tell me again."

The stale, acrid smoke uncurled its way over the desk. With no ventilation in this humid sweatbox, it was an effort not to gag. Instead, he focused on Desmond's wrinkled, oil-sheened face and detested the power that he thought he had over him. That expectant, cocky look was enough to make him snarl.

Damn, he despised this place. He hated everything about it. The boss, the work, the idea of being someone's *puppet*.

But Silas knew his boss. Desmond would never let him walk away without an anonymous tip being sent to the cops, and the vermin had enough on him to send him down for life.

So, Silas would do whatever the slimy man wanted. For now.

One day he'd show Desmond who the real leader was, but that day had not come yet. He focused on the smoke tendrils dancing across the flickering ceiling light and pushed a piece of sand blonde hair behind his ear.

"Well boss, I was down by the park on Bluetine—you know the one with all the street food carts and the buskers—and I found my good friend Barney." Silas trained his voice to be playful, entertaining.

Desmond almost choked on his white spirit with glee, shifting to hunch over his desk as much as his protruding belly would let him. Barney was Desmond's favourite prey, feasting on his crippling gambling addiction. He spent the majority of his time in the casinos or betting shops around town, but his favourite was at Bluetine Park. It was a happy coincidence that Silas's favourite place to sell his counterfeit jewellery was opposite Barney's second home. They had struck up an unlikely friendship—or business transaction—almost a year ago when the small man had come out of the shop glowing in the success of a big payout. Silas had cornered him with his tray of goods, sparkling glass diamonds lined up in neat little rows on a velvet backdrop. There were rings, bracelets, and necklaces, some gold and others silver, but all featuring large, clear crystals.

Silas could practically smell Barney's innocence and managed to find out that he had a wife, and *wouldn't the lovely Marlene just adore a new bracelet or necklace on this fine summer's day?*

Why, she sure would!

Barney spent almost his entire winnings on a golden bracelet with small diamonds lining its full length, and off he went to surprise his wife. Silas didn't suppose Marlene was any more intelligent than Barney if she hadn't figured out that her new jewellery was fake, but he didn't care. After that day, Silas often waited to see Barney leaving the betting shop, either looking afraid and disgruntled or on top of the world.

"What mood was Barney in this week, then?"

"Not too good, poor fool."

It was the same almost every week. Barney just did not know when to stop. The longer Silas played this con, the more he saw just how much his senior gambling addiction affected the pathetic man. One week he'd be dancing on his way home, the next his ginger hair would be a matted mess, his clothes suddenly too small for his stomach but too big for the rest of his body. Silas found himself often being the confidant for Barney's troubles, much to his irritation, and he learned all about Barney's 'just one more' hubris.

Desmond smashed the bottom of his glass tumbler onto the desk, the cool metal wailing at the impact. "Then what happened?" he asked. Silas grunted at the insufferable, impatient beast before him, but continued with the story.

"Well, I called Barney-Boy over and we got to talking about his woes and his wife, and how she'd kill him when he got home. That she was on the verge of leaving his sorry ass anyway." Silas picked at his nail beds. He was droning, quickly becoming sick of his own voice. "And so, I showed him what was on offer today and I told him that whatever he wanted for dear Marlene, he could have."

Desmond hacked and spluttered on his drink. Silas forced the twitching corners of his mouth into a thin straight line.

"You did what now?" Desmond asked, still choking. Silas chuckled at the thought of those bleary eyes popping straight out of their sockets.

Baring his teeth, Silas leaned forward towards the man almost smoking at the ears. "Now, now, Des. Don't get your panties in a bunch." He was enjoying this a bit too much, but he didn't care. It was nice to see his boss squirm for a change. "It's all good publicity. Call it an advertisement if you will," he crooned. He tried to keep his expression bored but couldn't keep the wicked glint from his eye. Desmond snarled at his insolence.

Ignoring it, he continued. "There were at least six people there who saw how appreciative Barney was to get a piece of my gear. They didn't see him get it free of charge—just him admiring his new possession and saying how much his wife was going to love it before scurrying off into the sunset. Before I knew it, five of them had circled me, desperate to buy a piece of junk for their own loved ones.

And here we are." Silas gestured towards the stacks of money dramatically.

"Indeed, here we are!" Desmond chortled, the reminder of his new money seeming to appease him. Silas knew he could get away with anything, just as long as his unorthodox tactics paid for Desmond's next date with a new expensive woman.

Silas gave him a silent nod and stood up to leave. He grabbed for his now almost empty duffel bag that lay in a sad heap on the desk, but his boss grabbed it at the same time.

"Hang on a second, Knight. We need to go over the details of your new job."

"New job?" Silas fell back into the rigid seat, scrubbing at his unshaven face. He squinted suspiciously, waiting. Whenever his boss had a new job for him, it was almost always laughable. Honestly, Silas had no idea how Desmond had even gotten into conning people in the first place. He couldn't fool someone to save his life.

Desmond leaned back in his chair, sheer smugness painted across his face, and began to chuckle to himself. "Ho, boy! Is this a humdinger or what?"

He threw a thick beige file on the desk, the cover falling open independently. He handed Silas the first image from the top of the pile. It was a grainy picture of a businessman, early 60s, in a crisp suit with his hair gelled back. He was greying around his temples and had a few lines in between the eyebrows, but he looked well-kept. Some might even say handsome. Unsurprising—Desmond usually targeted people who were the exact opposite of him.

If Desmond couldn't look like them or have their power, he'd just have to take their money instead.

"Richard Morton," Desmond snarled as he continued to slide images of the wealthy man across the table. "Businessman and investor in…some company overseas. Earned all his cash from inheritance and luck. Hell! Old-money prick."

Silas said nothing, staring at his boss over the collection of images. A thin sheen of sweat coated Desmond's receding hairline. "So?" Silas asked, clenching his jaw. "What's this got to do with me?"

Desmond clasped his hands together and grinned grimly. The stuff of nightmares—Desmond Rose was enough to send young kids screaming.

Still examining the images, he twirled two of his fingers to indicate that he wanted this conversation wrapped up. Another picture slid over the table. This time it was an image of a young woman, perhaps in her mid-twenties, wearing a plaid tight skirt with a shirt tucked in. There was a loose bow around the collar and she wore an expensive-looking bracelet on the same wrist as an equally decadent watch. Her jet-black hair was incredibly curly, framing her face perfectly. It was somewhat tamed by a headband that matched the pattern of her skirt. She was walking down the street with a shopping bag that held a name he didn't recognise.

Desmond kept the pictures coming, each with the same woman in different outfits, walking down different streets, along the beach, in the local park. Desmond had been having her tailed for quite some time, it seemed. The last photo showed her face more clearly—her eyes so large that Silas thought they might just pop out of her head if anyone squeezed her too tight, her nose small and turned upright, and her full lips smiling.

"I'm still not getting the hint here, Des. What is it that you want done?"

Now puffing on a fresh cigarette, Desmond tried and failed to make rings with the blistering smoke. "That is Jessica Morton, the daughter of our good friend Rick. Word on the street is that he'd do anything for his only seed, and I want to test that theory."

Silas flicked through the pictures again. This wasn't the first time Desmond had ordered him to hurt someone for a payday, but they were usually older, grumpier men who had an easy-to-crack safe in their house. Something unfamiliar twisted at the base of his stomach.

"I'm not in the business of hurting women, boss," Silas said as he threw the stack of printouts back across the desk.

"Hurt her? Whoever said anything about hurting her?" Desmond scrunched his face up and threw his palms towards the sky in mock confusion. "We're just gonna take her. Borrow her for a bit, if you will, and see how long it takes to sell her back."

"Ransom? And what about when they call the cops on us and our whole operation gets shut down?"

"Oh, relax," Desmond drawled, rolling his eyes. Silas clenched his jaw tighter. "Rick and I went to school together. I got pictures of him that he'd never want out there. It was a stroke of luck that a little birdie let me in on the details of his offshore accounts. Trust me, this is going to be the easiest payday yet." He looked like a smug baby who had managed to sneak a sweet without his mother knowing.

"So, you want me to go get her, bring her here." Silas shrugged. "Then what?"

A chuckle. "Oh no, Silas. We need to infiltrate their family business before we can act on anything. I got the details of his less-than-legal business, but I need you to get the evidence." Desmond walked around the desk and stopped in front of Silas, perching against its corner. His eyes were wide with excitement. "You need to get inside that house and find the proof for the blackmail. Once you have that, then we can move onto the hostage stage."

Silas hesitated for a second, but then nodded. The plan seemed easy enough, and this wasn't his first theft. Hell, this wasn't even his first hostage job. "Anything else, boss?"

A glimmer of darkness shone across Desmond's eyes. "One more thing Knight, yes. They don't let just anyone into that manor of theirs—unless you're an investor with a big enough wallet. Our Jessica has never had so much as a playdate." He was closing the space between them, and Silas used every bit of his willpower to not shove the man away from him.

"How do you know that?"

"Don't worry yourself about the details," Desmond drawled, teeth grinding in a grin. "But I've heard she's a bit of a dark horse…I wouldn't underestimate her if I were you." He finished with a wink.

"What are you suggesting then?" Silas pressed, the heat of the cramped room suddenly making him feel incredibly nauseous.

Desmond was seemingly unaware of how many boundaries he was crossing in terms of Silas's personal space, and further ignored them by pointing his finger out and slowly reaching it to his chest. "You, my friend, are going to make her fall in love with you. Get her under your bad boy charm, get inside the house, get me the proof I need." He said it in an almost whisper as his yellow-stained finger jabbed into Silas. As soon as the jagged fingernail grazed the fabric of his T-shirt, Silas swatted it away. He was almost too revulsed to comprehend what Desmond had said as his boss crooned, "But I don't have all the time in the world, Knight. The sooner we can take Ricky down, the better. So, I'm giving you two months."

"Two months to make a woman fall in love with me? You're insane."

An evil twinkle flashed in Desmond's eyes. "Maybe. But it will be one helluva payday." He threw a folded piece of copier paper onto Silas's lap, detailing his cut of the profits. "How is your mother, anyway?"

CHAPTER TWO

✦

The door to Desmond's Deals slammed shut as soon as Silas escaped through it. The cool breeze was a welcomed refreshment to his skin, and he drew in a long breath of clean air. Purging the dust and dirt from his lungs, he shook his head and sauntered to the car.

As he slid onto the driver's seat of his small white car, he threw his bag down next to him. Silas gripped the steering wheel, taking a second to wonder if not running earlier was the right idea. He would've never had to work another day in his life with that money he'd secured from the earlier job. Would've never known anything about Jessica Morton.

With a grumbling sigh, he kicked the ignition to life. *One day.* The day would come when he'd get away from Fayette Bay for good, never caring for a final glance back.

But before setting off, he felt the urge to have another look at his target. Taking the thick folder out of his bag, he studied the images again. The dozen pictures of Richard Morton, then the ones of his daughter.

As he carved a line around her silhouette with his eyes, he thought of the ridiculousness of the task he'd been given. He'd certainly never had to make anyone fall in love with him before, although it wouldn't be difficult. Women came to him, not the other way around. He'd even had a hard time shaking some out of his life—the ones that got a little too obsessed with him after meeting in a bar the night before—so chasing women was never his style.

Hell, he couldn't even remember the last time he'd approached a lady first.

Looking at the close-up images of Jessica's face, Silas felt something flutter in his stomach.

Nerves? No, couldn't be. Silas didn't get nervous.

Intrigue was more likely, although he wasn't sure why he was so interested. He never usually cared enough to give his missions a second thought. Shaking the nagging feeling, he tossed the file into the footwell and ground the car into gear. The engine squealed in protest as he drove off.

He arrived at his apartment and parked in his usual space below it. The small entryway held a lift that had been broken since Silas moved in a decade ago, so he made the familiar trek up to his floor. The air was dry and had a faint smell of cheap disinfectant. He fiercely rattled his key inside the lock for several seconds before it gripped and allowed him entry into his living space.

It wasn't much, but the open-plan two-bed, one-bath flat gave him all the space he needed. It was furnished with neutral colours, and it was never considerably messy or dirty—Silas enjoyed a clean space. Perhaps it was to distance himself as far away from the likes of Desmond in his filthy little office.

He placed his key on the coffee table and fell into the comforting embrace of his emerald-coloured sofa—the only pop of colour in the entire apartment. Tipping his head back, he allowed himself the luxury of closing his eyes and letting his mind wander to nothingness for a moment or two, until slow footsteps interrupted his peace from behind his chair.

"Silas?" a tired voice questioned behind him. His eyes fluttered open again and he leaned to face the frail woman behind him. As soon as he locked eyes with his mother, his face relaxed into a weak smile, losing a lot of his usual hardness.

"Hi Ma, how are you feeling?" he asked her softly. She gave a small shrug, returning a watery smile as she inched closer to him. She was wearing a floral nightdress and her hair was wrapped in a silk scarf. Her eyes were exhausted and sunken, but Silas could still make out a sparkle that appeared whenever he'd return home.

Silas quickly rose from the chair and stepped around her. "Here, sit down. Have you eaten?"

Silas held out his hands and she took them graciously as they helped her lower slowly onto the sofa. Before Ma let go, she drew them to her crinkled lips and planted a dry kiss on his knuckles. "Nope, I just woke up."

It was two in the afternoon, but Ma tended to fall asleep before him and only wake up after noon nowadays. After falling ill five years back, she'd endured too many torrid symptoms to bear, from nausea to loss of consciousness, migraines lasting weeks and full-body tremors. The dozens of doctors Silas had carted her around to didn't have any idea of what was wrong with her.

Three years ago, he finally convinced her to go private. It was expensive enough just for a consultation, and Silas desperately needed to find a way to pay for all her treatments.

Enter Desmond Rose, and his mentorship that turned Silas into his most prized employee.

Ma's private practitioner had been able to diagnose a form of sarcoma in the vessel walls of her neck. The doctor shaved her head to disclose a tiny bruise-like lesion at the base of her skull.

Two years.

It had taken countless medical professionals two years to diagnose her, all because her hair covered this bruise that couldn't have been bigger than a penny. Overworked, underfunded public hospitals hadn't even thought to check in such an inconspicuous area.

They had been reassured that this speck of cancer was merely stage one and they had nothing to worry about, but a cruel CT scan had shown otherwise. A secondary tumour had been growing on the inside of Ma's skull, pressing deeply into her brain. After years of unknown diagnoses, it had grown too large to be anything but inoperable. A gut-wrenching mixture of chemotherapy and radiation blasts was their only option for prolonging her life.

Every treatment, every surgery was riskier because of Ma's older age and exhausted body. The doctor urged them to reconsider each new option, but Silas didn't want to hear it. If it meant she'd live, she was to have the treatment—and that was that.

Now, almost three years after the initial surgery and regular appointments for her different therapies, Silas could see the pain in his mother's eyes. She was giving up, and she tried so hard to mask her weariness.

But he still saw it, and he didn't think he'd ever stop blaming himself. He knew all too well that she was still fighting for him, not herself.

"I'll fix you something then, shall I?" He started towards the kitchen and looked through the cupboard in the hopes of finding something nice. He found a tin of Ma's favourite soup, butter beans and chilli, in an overflowing cupboard. Rustling came from behind him, but he took no notice as he popped the top off the tin with a can opener.

But as soon as that staggered gasp came from the sofa, Silas winced at his careless mistake.

"What's this, Silas?"

The rustling of the duffel bag continued, but he kept his gaze forward. "Just my pay, Ma," Silas threw back over his shoulder.

Well, he wasn't lying.

"Pay from what?" Ma's voice was small yet firm, like a mother reprimanding a son and demanding a confession for something she already knew he'd done. "Why won't you tell me about this job of yours?"

Prying. She'd been gently prodding the cloak he'd kept over his life this past year. Today, it seemed, she'd had enough of pulling the wool over her own eyes.

The soup was beginning to rumble around the edges of the pan, the beans attempting to get as far away from the heat as possible. He wiped the clean side absentmindedly. He was tired of the charade—she'd seen the counterfeit jewellery, the stacks of money at the bottom of his wardrobe, his bloodied clothes from a particularly harrowing night shift. It wouldn't take much to put the evidence together and come up with a near-accurate theory about what was happening. But she wanted an admission.

"Talk to me, Silas!" she pleaded, urgent and intrusive. He put down the dirty rag and took a few moments to himself, strong arms braced on either side of the erupting pan.

Whether he told her or not, she already knew too much to let it go.

He finally turned to see her wringing her stiff hands together, deep ridges forming between her eyebrows as she furrowed them. Her skin was almost grey, but her cheeks flushed rose.

"What does it matter, Ma? I got the money for your treatments, what else is there to know?"

She didn't reply. Instead, she remained staring at him with a look so pointed that it was him who had to break their eye contact.

"It's nothing, really. A guy makes me do his dirty work for him and I get paid for it." He shrugged and her eyes pierced into him. A rising bubble of panic knocked against his chest. "But I stopped, Ma. That was the last of what I was owed. Mr Rose added some extra as a little goodbye, a nice little thank you for my service. That's why there's so much cash in the bag—severance."

Ma's stare softened slightly, flicking her vision between him and the duffel bag that lay discarded on the floor. His body shuddered, and he chewed on the inside of his cheek while waiting for her to process his lie. Her eyes finally fluttered up towards him and she whispered, "Promise me?"

The tip of his tongue settled between his teeth, their sharpness cutting into muscle, as he nodded slowly. His eyes were fixed on the ground, but he glanced up through his fallen strands of hair to see if she'd taken the bait.

She had.

Satisfied, he turned back to the stove, dished up the overheated soup and served it to her without either of them saying another word. She nodded a stubborn thank you. Silas retreated to his bedroom.

☆☆☆

Silas had given his mother the bigger room when she moved in because she was sure to spend more time there than him, and the doctors and nurses needed the extra room for their equipment. Each passing month seemed to bring more callouts, the apartment always full of one professional visitor or another.

There wasn't much in the way of furniture, just a bed covered in beige sheets to match the light accent wall behind it, one nightstand, a chest of drawers with a small television positioned on top of it, and an old wardrobe looming in the corner.

He fell onto his neatly made bed, the weight of the stifling day collapsing onto him. If he closed his eyes, he'd fall asleep in a second. It took more out of him than it should've to roll over and get his laptop from the nightstand.

He typed the name Jessica Morton into the search bar and delved into the world of his new love interest. After twenty minutes of reading long pages on the business mogul's "angel" daughter, his head was pounding.

All traces of her, aside from the pre-approved blog posts and interviews on the Morton family, had been seemingly scrubbed from the internet.

And after far too long spent researching, all Silas had written down was that she was a twenty-six-year-old living at home in her daddy's mansion. Oh, and that the woman seemed to have a fascination with flowers and romance novels.

There were pages and pages of pictures, sometimes posed and others taken by the press, almost always wearing short skirts and tucked-in blouses, or summer dresses. She kept the colours light and vibrant to compliment her honey-brown skin. Her hair was often tamed by a headband or long ribbon, wild and unruly yet still so delicate.

As much has he'd like to, Silas couldn't deny the fact that she was…gorgeous. In a completely effortless way, she stole the show in every photo he saw, pulling the attention to her in even the most unflattering press photos.

Silas tried to remain focused, but his talk with Ma kept replaying in his head. By the time he'd finished his research, he'd decided that this would be his final job for Desmond. The back of his wardrobe was lined with tall stacks of money, more than enough to cover Ma's treatment for the next couple of months. Not to mention the cut he'd get if he could pull this final task off.

He didn't enjoy the con game as much as the others did, although he was damn good at it. After three years of back-to-back missions, Silas was done. *Wanted* to be done.

He'd get a real job, earning an honest wage and using Desmond's tainted money to top up his paychecks for the bills. How he was going to convince his boss to let him walk away was something Silas was not willing to consider at that very moment.

Desmond would be dealt with later.

Silas shook the thought of a promising future away, flicking through his notes. From what he could tell, the family were a bunch of homebodies who liked to minimise their outings as much as possible. Unsurprising, considering how many rooms the Morton Manor undoubtedly held. They probably had the resources to never leave the house again.

A few hours later, Silas found his mother still sitting on the green sofa, head lulled to the side and dreaming. Not trying to be quiet, he made them a simple dinner from leftovers found in the fridge. She still didn't stir as he waved the steaming bowl millimetres away from her nose, so he set up the TV table in front of her. He laid her food and fork on it for when she felt like waking up properly.

He sat down on the age-worn armchair to the left of her and turned on the television. The chair was lumpy and musty, and it had come from his mother's house when she moved in with him. She'd said it was her pride and joy yet had quickly taken a liking to his new sofa within a matter of weeks. He had been demoted to the battered seat ever since.

Flicking through the channels, Silas looked for a show that Ma would like in case she rose from her slumber to join him. He stopped on the channel that showed low-budget Christmas movies—she loved those—and ate his food in peace.

It was only when he was shutting his bedroom door for the night that he heard Ma finally mumbling back into consciousness. He smiled, certain she'd enjoy the film about a dog in reindeer antlers more than he had.

He fell into a dreamless sleep while thinking of the big day that loomed before him. After all—there was no time to waste when it came to his impending epic love story.

CHAPTER THREE

✦

Silas jerked awake from the obnoxiously loud alarm clock buzzing on his nightstand—7.30 am. He heaved himself out of bed, straightened the sheets, and got himself ready for the day. Making much more of an effort than usual, he dressed in a grey shirt and black jeans, brushed his hair through, and spritzed himself with a little of his expensive aftershave. The smell of fresh forests and spice filled the room.

He ate his cereal while leaning against the kitchen island. Ma's bowl was still unwashed on the table he'd set up for her the night before, the pasta untouched. He washed both bowls and left them to dry before swinging the door open and heading down the stairs, phone and keys in hand.

A wave of thick, balmy air engulfed him. He'd never been one for the summer—the stagnant air worsened the constant ache inside his head.

As he opened the car door and the trapped heat licked at his body, taunting, he reconsidered whether the money was truly worth it. Rolling the windows down immediately, Silas set off to his favourite coffee shop—the Twinkling Bliss.

The Twinkling Bliss café was a family-run business, clearly trying too hard to be an American-style diner. Red and cream panelling underneath the oversized windows surrounded the entire building. Above it was a small flat rented to someone for cheap, but the window was almost entirely covered by the Twinkling Bliss Café neon sign. The bulbs flickered incessantly, day and night.

The outside of the establishment was kept in remarkable condition, but it still didn't draw much of a crowd. Silas was often the only customer.

As he parked outside and approached the café, Maria swung the doors wide to invite Silas in. He winked at the owner as he walked past her to his usual table. The inside was similarly decorated as the outside—red, teal, and black patterns overused in the worst way. Tall seats lined the front counter. The rest of the space was littered with booth tables with green-blue benches. Silas liked the booth right at the end—it had the best view of Bluetine Park, and it was the furthest away from chatty waitresses.

Silas slid into the booth, palms sticking slightly to the table. Maria quickly followed him with a fresh pot of coffee and a white ceramic mug.

"Just as you like it, Sy?" Maria's voice was high and brassy, but she served him with that winning smile every morning. She was dressed in the same uniform that the servers wore—all black with a red chequered apron tied around her small waist—but she manipulated it so it fit her form perfectly. Her bleach-blonde hair was wrapped in a high bun and her face was brightened by a light layer of makeup.

She always looked effortless. Even on the tail end of a twelve-hour shift, when Silas stopped by both at the start and end of the day, she looked like she hadn't lifted a finger.

"Yeah, the usual please Mar."

The owner poured the steaming black liquid into the mug before him as he continued to read his book, not bothering to check if she made it right. He'd been coming so many years; Maria knew his coffee order off by heart.

"How's your mother doing? I haven't seen her in a while," Maria asked.

"She's doing okay," was all Silas said. Ma used to visit the café with him often, and she had become fast friends with Maria. But with her illness wearing her down so much, she hadn't left the house in months.

Maria gave him a gentle smile, squeezing his shoulder. "Tell her I said hi," she said, and he nodded before she walked back to the counter.

Once he was sure she wasn't looking over at him, Silas took out a crumpled piece of paper from his jean pocket. It was damp from the humidity, the ink running slightly. Still, he could just read the few words scrawled on it.

120 Ruby Boulevard

The address to the famous Morton Manor. Desmond had tucked it into his research file, but he needn't have bothered. No one could miss the largest mansion in Fayette Bay, seen from all corners of the small town. It was probably used as a guide for boats lining the harbour.

His deep dive into the world of Jessica Morton last night gave him a list of her favourite places to go, all within a few miles of the manor. The market just down the road from her family's mansion was open today, and Silas assumed it'd be a good place to start to engineer their meet cute.

Good—the closer he could stay to her father's files, the better.

Silas finished the last gulp of cheap, bitter filter coffee and raised his hand to Maria, who was leaning over the counter flicking through a fashion magazine. She waved back, and a brief passing smile ghosted his lips as he gathered his belongings, laid the money on the table, and left.

Walking straight past his car, he shoved his phone in one pocket, keys in the other, and folded his book to fit into one on the back. He fisted Desmond's note into a small ball and tossed it into a bin as he walked by.

The short journey to the obnoxiously large mansion felt like an eternity in the pulsating heat. Bugs hummed around him, intensifying every step. The unforgiving sun bounced off the light pavement, invading his eyes from every angle.

The manor was made up of all-white brick and had three rows of windows stacked upon each other. There was a ridiculous number of stairs leading up to the front doorway and a high white metal fence with golden spikes reaching upwards surrounding the perimeter. The rest of the land was covered in freshly mowed grass and a mirroring pattern of trees and shrubs lining the sides of the house. Two chimneys poked out from the roof, five dormer windows standing tall between them. There were at least three gardeners tending to the front garden, and he didn't doubt that there would be more out in the backyard, too.

Suddenly, it all made sense.

Richard didn't need this amount of money—no one did. Maybe there was a method to Desmond's madness this time.

Silas shook his head. The thought of agreeing with his boss for once left a sour taste in his mouth, so he picked up the pace and left the mansion behind.

Before long, he saw a handwritten sign that simply read MARKET in thick orange letters with 9 AM—2 PM added underneath. The first vendors were still setting up, so he stopped a few yards before the entrance and sat on a shaded bench.

His head thrummed, vision pulsing. Leaning his tender skull back on the soft wood, he let his eyes flutter closed. He took a few deep breaths—in, out, in, out—as he enjoyed the peace and stillness of the moment, trying to grasp as much energy as he could before the big charade commenced and his task officially began.

"Hey."

The closeness of the stranger's voice had Silas jolting out of his semi-relaxed position. He snapped his head to the left to identify the owner of the melodic voice and stopped dead in his tracks. Next to him sat a young woman, her midnight hair tied in a light green bow, rummaging in a handbag resting on her lap. She looked so unconcerned by him that Silas wondered if she'd actually said anything, or whether it had all been his conscience playing a trick on him.

It was Jessica Morton. *Wasn't it?*

Yes, he could tell by her honey-tanned skin, those rosy dimpled cheeks, the perfectly coiled hair.

Jessica Morton was sitting right next to him.

"Hi," he replied, casually straightening next to her.

She looked at him then, smiling politely. "Are you okay? You were looking a little peaky there."

Silas hummed an amused sound. "All good. Headache is all, but it seems to be fading now."

He looked down at her through the corner of his eye, but she was too busy rooting in her canvas bag for something.

"I get them too in this glorious weather." She motioned around her, voice playful and inviting. As if they weren't two perfect strangers. She pulled out a bottle of water and handed it to him. "Do you need a drink? I haven't opened it yet, I promise."

Silas hesitated before taking the bottle, twisting it open and taking a large gulp. "Thank you."

"Of course." Her voice was airy, sweet and soothing. It might've been improving his headache all by itself. "I'm Jessica, by the way."

"Silas—Silas Knight."

"What a lovely name," she mused. She sounded away with the fairies, full of wondrous adventure.

Silas cleared his throat. "So, what's a pretty girl like you doing all alone?" A rotting bench wasn't exactly where he'd planned their first meeting to be, but he'd roll with it.

Jessica cringed a little at the nickname, but that didn't stop a rosy flush from giving her away. "I enjoy my own company," was all she said as she stood up and brushed off her flowing green skirt. "Maybe I'll see you in there?" she said, pointing towards the large tent.

"I hope you will," he drawled, receiving one last gleaming smile before she floated off towards the market entrance.

Silas smirked to himself, resting his head back in its original position. This was going to be easier than he thought.

He took one last moment in his cool spot, making sure enough time had passed that it would take him a while to catch up with her. Once he was sure she was out of sight and engulfed in the white market tent, he pushed off his knees, brushed himself off, and followed.

CHAPTER FOUR

Stalls bunched together inside the market hall, forming a snaking line for patrons to follow from entrance to exit. Silas took a wicker basket from the entranceway and let it swing by his side as he walked briskly past each table. The smell of fresh produce overcame him, and he stopped by a random table to throw a few items in his basket.

Jessica hadn't gotten far, though. He slowed his pace as he walked towards where she stood, before a stall lined with rows of freshly cut flowers.

He smirked—he'd stumbled upon the perfect setup. He made a mental note to have Desmond reimburse him for the dying weeds he'd have to buy her later.

Strolling to the opposite end of the stall, Silas put on his best act to appear interested in the sickly blooms. Rubbing a yellow petal between his thumb and finger, he took a long-stemmed flower out of a bucket and turned to Jessica, but she was already eyeing him suspiciously over a flower of her own.

"Fancy seeing you here," he smirked, purposefully avoiding eye contact. A tactic he'd long since learnt drove women wild.

"Indeed," she drawled before pointing at the rose in his hand. "Buying for anyone special?"

"Only if you tell me your favourites," he said, and her eyebrows pinched. "I wouldn't want to get the wrong thing."

Jessica barked a light laugh. "You're quite the charmer, aren't you?"

"For the right woman, I can be."

She looked at him for a long moment before taking the rose from his hand and pinching it together with her own. "It's a good thing that you chose red roses then." She continued plucking other flowers from the buckets, crafting a bouquet of her own.

"You're a natural." Silas admired the bouquet of roses, lilies and sunflowers. "Are you a florist yourself?"

Silas knew the answer, but he needed to appear completely removed from any knowledge of the Mortons.

And judging by the small smile Jessica gave him as she handed the flowers to the vendor to wrap up, she appreciated the question.

"No, I'm not a florist. I just come here almost every week to make a new bouquet," she mused, almost to herself. "Flowers remind me of summertime and sunshine. Wherever that is, it's my happy place."

He looked at her sidelong. He wouldn't have expected a billionaire's daughter to be happiest in a stuffy market tent before a load of cut flowers. Not when she had all she could ever need at home.

And yet, there was something so intriguing about her answer. Something that made him want to stay and talk about flowers for a little longer.

The florist turned and handed her bundle of flowers back, now carefully swaddled like a newborn. The vendor's eyes glinted as he announced the price, eyebrows shooting up towards Silas in a silent challenge.

Jessica rooted around in her bag for her purse but, as he resisted the urge to snarl across the counter, Silas dropped some cash into one of the flower buckets and gently guided her away. The splashing water behind them was something to smile about, at least.

"Oh, you really didn't have to do that," Jessica protested, cheeks reddening as he let his broad hand linger on the small of her back while she put her money away.

"It was the least I could do, I had to repay your favour somehow." His charming demeanour reappeared as he tipped the cap of the water bottle towards her with a wink. She smiled at him, blushing brighter. He pointed at a sign reading COFFEE at the other end of the market and asked, "Can I buy you a drink, Jessica?"

"No, I couldn't possibly." Jessica's voice cracked with outrage, gesturing to the flowers in her arms. "Can I buy *you* a drink?"

He gestured towards the stall with a lazy smirk, letting her lead the way. She skipped ahead. The market had become busier during their floral exchange, but he only noticed as he tried to keep up with her. The petite woman weaved between the crowds like a swallow twirling through a forest of water reeds, while he was stuck behind trying to elbow his way through shoppers.

Old men with bent backs blocked his path while sniffing carrots and comparing the weights of watermelons. A dog walker allowed her pets to roam freely while she picked out the perfect toy, creating a barrier of dog leads in front of him. A group of middle-aged women nattered in a circle covering the width of the entire aisle. He gently pushed his way through the middle of their group, not bothering to mind their designer garments.

The loud whispers admiring the view as he walked away were enough to elicit an involuntary twitch of his lips as he followed the glowing light Jessica had left in her path.

It seemed that she had heard them, too. "Someone's popular," she goaded him with a whistle.

"Shut it," he growled back, the twinkle in his eye wicked enough to have her giggling and leading the way for him again.

"What would you like?" Jessica asked, gesturing to the chalkboards above them that were covered in swirly letters. Silas read a few, trying not to balk as he went.

Mazagran Mocha
Liquorice Latte
Cucumber Cappuccino

Each option sounded more disgusting than the last. The scent of each concoction mixed in the heavy air, smelling worse than the coffee Maria poured him each morning.

"Black coffee, please," he said to the vendor, who looked vaguely taken aback, and maybe a little offended.

Silas smirked—a challenge.

Jessica stepped between their tense stares. "He'll have a black coffee," she repeated, "and I'll have an iced lemon latte, please." Her affirming voice was still sweet enough to snap the vendor out of his hateful trance. That, or she was the first person to ever order his lemon latte.

The barista turned back to the row of silver machines, evading Silas's glare.

"Calm down, Macho Man," Jessica teased, amber eyes beholding something like flirtation as she pulled his own away from the quivering vendor.

Despite himself, Silas actually laughed, some of the tingling anger in his chest dissipating through his limbs and fizzling out his fingertips.

He took their tiny cups from the counter and passed Jessica's down to her. They began walking away, but not before he threw an exaggerated glare behind him towards the counter. Jessica snorted as she pushed him towards the market exit. He smirked at the sound as they burst out into the blazing sunshine. He wasn't hating this as much as he assumed he would.

Maybe the next two months wouldn't be so horrible, after all.

Silas discreetly dropped his basket before they followed the short line of outdoor stalls while sipping their drinks. Silas walked silently as Jessica marvelled at every single table they passed. But then a sign caught his eye, and he directed her towards the stall of rare books.

He beheld the towers of aged works in front of them as Jessica picked one up and flicked through it. "Do you read much?" she asked as he leafed through the stacks, searching. "I noticed you carry a book in your pocket," she continued, pointing towards the back of his jeans, "but it's all just a show for the older ladies, I suppose."

"Is that jealousy, Jessica?" Silas asked as her eyes lingered for a second too long. Her eyes went wide and she scoffed before dipping her face behind the book she'd picked up.

"I was trying to read the title, actually," she drawled, feigning a yawn. He considered teasing her some more as she tried to hide her blush within the pages, but he stopped himself, turning his attention back to the stall.

"What are you looking for?"

He turned to answer when he noticed the book in her hands. He pointed at the cover—a first edition copy of *A Christmas Carol* by Charles Dickens. "May I?"

She nodded and gave the book up, suddenly much more interested in his reaction. She cocked her head to the side, and he could see her out of the corner of his eye looking from his face to the book, back to his face, back to the book.

"You like Charles Dickens?"

"Just this one," he muttered as he angled the cover towards her, taking every inch of the novel in. Lifting the fragile cover, he relaxed into the timeless illustrations—ones he'd only ever seen online. A first edition was much too expensive for him to buy himself. With Ma's medical bills always looming over him, he'd never allowed himself to splurge too much in case an emergency required urgent payment.

He found the price written on the front page in light pencil—too much. He let out a soft grunt as he replaced it on top of one of the piles and took a step away. "Ready to go?"

Jessica nodded and followed him away from the white market tent, back onto the street near their bench. They fell into step beside each other silently, without much of a plan for where to go. He was considering the perfect conversation starter when she halted abruptly.

"Shoot!" she exclaimed, immediately flustered. He could see the panic rising on her face. "I left my bag!"

"Don't worry, I'll get it." He started towards the market's opening, which was now overflowing with hovering pests. "Stay here!" he shouted back over his shoulder.

The bag was easy to find, tucked between the coffee stall and its folded chalkboard sign. Silas nodded curtly at the vendor before he pushed his way back out into the open air.

Jessica was right where he left her, instantly breaking into a smile as he held her bag out for her to take.

"Thank you," she beamed as she looped it over her shoulder, and he tipped an imaginary hat to her. She started walking away from him again, and he fell into step beside her.

He nodded his head towards the path. "Where are we going, anyway?"

"*We*," Jessica said, accentuating the word, "aren't going anywhere. I need to get home."

His heart jumped, but he trained his expression into one of disappointment. "Leaving so soon, Milady?"

Her lips twitched at the nickname. "My parents worry if I'm out too long, and I have a very important date with my easel tonight." Jessica's eyes widened briefly as she rolled them, not trying to hide her disdain for such uninspired plans. Silas shot his eyebrows up, inclined to agree.

"You paint? What kind of things?"

"I do indeed. I'll try anything to take me away from reality for a couple of hours." She said it with a laugh, but he didn't hear any humour within the words. "I paint anything really—anything that makes me happy."

"Would you paint me?"

"Aren't you forward, Mr Knight?" She smirked, bumping her shoulder into his. "But I think you could make the cut, if you play your cards right."

"Will you at least let me walk you home?" Silas asked.

She thought for a moment. "Sure, that'd be lovely." There was a slight rosy tint to her cheeks as she walked ahead of him, leading the way. They filled the short walk with more small talk about the weather, painting, and Jessica's puppy.

"Her name is Ziva, she's a Golden Labrador. She's tiny, a little ball of fluff and slipper destruction." She made a crushing gesture with her hands to really drive the point home. The warm laugh that followed made him smile at his shoes.

Just before they reached the street the manor took up the majority of, Jessica stopped abruptly. "Everything alright?" he asked, turning back to her.

"Yeah…" She shifted on the spot. "I just—it's better if you're not seen with me too close to the front gate."

Silas sneered, glancing at and around the manor. There was no one on the grounds to spot them. But when he looked back at her, she had a look that made it abundantly clear she wasn't joking. He took a step towards her, but she moved around him.

"I can walk the rest of the way just fine," she assured him, tone much firmer now, laced with an odd coolness. He didn't try to argue. Instead, he lifted his hands to the air in surrender and gestured for her to pass. A tiny smile, woeful yet gorgeous, graced her lips as she did just that.

"Wait." Silas took her wrist in his hand before she slipped too far away. "When will I see you again?"

A teasing grin shot across her face. "I don't know, when will you?"

But before he had time to answer, Jessica wriggled free of his loose grip and pranced back towards the tall gates. He watched her all the way, a small smirk plastered to his face.

She was going to be trouble.

Silas walked back to his car, gave a quick wave to Maria through the café window and slid into the cab. He drove home in silence, but his thoughts rang loudly in his ears. He replayed the day over and over, Jessica consuming his mind.

Shaking her away, Silas turned his attention back to the mission at hand. He took stock of what he did right, what he could've done better.

And by the time he'd climbed the stairs to his apartment and was hidden safely behind his closed bedroom door, Silas couldn't help but groan at how much trouble he could already feel himself slipping into.

CHAPTER FIVE

✦

By the time Ma emerged from her room for the day, the sun was blazing through their balcony door and casting a warm light over the furniture. Silas made her some buttered toast and told her about his morning as she nibbled the quartered pieces, leaving out any detail that would do more harm than good.

He told her about the market, Maria's message and the café, and the choking heat. He'd gotten his hatred of the sun from her, so she physically shuddered at the thought of leaving the comfort of their air-conditioned apartment. He'd invested in the unit when Ma first moved in, explaining the cost away with the generosity of the hospital.

As he told her about Jessica, he couldn't miss a knowing gleam flash across her face. "What?" Silas asked with mock annoyance, stopping his story short.

"Nothing!" She replied in a high-pitched tone, feigning innocence. "You just seem happier today, that's all."

He scoffed and rolled his eyes, but she was right. He did feel happier. Lighter, even. *Giddy*.

Stop it, his inner voice rumbled in warning. *This is a job—nothing else.*

Changing the conversation before he could overthink these new emerging feelings, he told her about the book he'd found at the market. Ma almost squealed—they'd been looking for it for years. She didn't enjoy collecting books as Silas did, but she loved Christmas and everything about it. Every December, she'd put the Christmas channel on the television and hide the remote. No one was allowed to change it until mid-January—at least. He'd long given up counting how many times he'd seen each version of *A Christmas Carol*.

"Let me see it, then!" Ma said with such excitement that he hadn't seen from her in a long time. A welcomed surprise.

But he had to shake his head and avert his gaze as he said, "It was too expensive, Ma. Next time."

"What? But what about that pay from Mr Rose?"

Silas coughed to cover his scoff. "We need that for your treatments, Ma. I couldn't justify spending so much on a book when we don't know what tomorrow will bring."

Ma hung her head, whispering a defeated, "Silas…"

But he didn't want to hear it. Not when the start of his day had been surprisingly enjoyable. "Look, Ma. Let's just forget it—I'll pick up the next one I find." Never mind that it took him years to find today's copy. "Maybe I'll take Jessica on my search, like some sort of lucky charm."

He knew his diversion had landed when Ma's eyes sparkled, instantly forgetting the book and flaring with excitement. "So, she's a girlfriend? Oh Silas, please tell me this is a girlfriend?" She took his hands in hers, gripping them tightly like she needed to hold onto something or else she'd fall out of her seat.

He burst into laughter before he could stop himself. "No, she's not my girl, Ma. Just a very lovely lady I met today."

A few more questions and prying comments came, but he shook them off as he descended into his bedroom.

But as Silas entered the small room, he forced his smile to drop. He loved seeing Ma as animated, as lively as she had been, but this was one thing he didn't want to let work get in the middle of. As nice as his morning had been, Jessica was a job—one he would not allow feelings to ruin. Silas didn't catch feelings, especially when Ma depended on his payment. He wouldn't allow anything to jeopardise her health.

The rest of the day passed slowly, and Silas tossed and turned for hours before finally drifting off to sleep, the events of the day cycling through his head, replaying against the soothing darkness of his eyelids.

☆☆☆

The few hours of broken sleep Silas had managed to steal left him feeling groggy and miserable. As the sunrise illuminated his room, he wanted to throw his pillow over his head go straight back to sleep. Perhaps he would have done, if it weren't for the incessant buzzing coming from the nightstand. He already knew who was bugging him this early—Desmond Rose.

Early bird catches the worm, Sy!

I hear your girl is going to be at Roseding Point this morning—fancy a dip?

Get outta bed, you lazy fuck! Time is ticking…

There were several more colourful messages from his boss, but Silas deleted them and silenced the ringer. He let out a soft groan at how his day was already shaping before him. Roseding Point was the nearest beach to Fayette Bay, just a short drive down to miles of glistening sand and serene waves lapping over the shore.

Silas couldn't stand the beach. Sand in his shoes was his worst nightmare—one that'd inevitably keep replaying when he brought back half the beach, only to find sand everywhere he went for the next month.

The last time he went to the beach was when he was sixteen years old, and Ma had dragged him down there for the last day of summer. She loved lounging on a beach towel for hours with a good book in her younger years, but all Silas had done was glare at his watch, waiting for the parking ticket to run out on the car so that he could get away from the screaming children running too close to him and kicking sand into his stony face.

From that day, he vowed never to return to the beach. But now, he had to break that promise—otherwise

Damned Desmond would surely have something to say about it.

He threw on a pair of dark-coloured shorts and a white T-shirt. Raking his hair back into its looped ponytail, he tamed the shorter pieces around his face with a pair of black sunglasses. Black running shoes completed the look. It was about as close to a beach-ready outfit he'd ever be caught in.

Thirty minutes from his initial wake up call, Silas was out the door and on his way to Roseding Point.

☆☆☆

Despite the day still being young, the beach was already crawling with people. Kids screaming, dogs barking, and teenagers playing terrible music through their speakers. Silas forced himself out of the car. The beach stretched before him, salty air caressing his face instantly. The air smelled of seaweed and suncream, and the sun glistened delicately off the calm ocean.

A small dog appeared at his feet, sniffing his shoes. Silas shook the golden dog away, cursing under his breath. "Go away," he grumbled as the dog persisted in invading his personal space, nudging it away with the inside of his foot. "Get!"

"Come on, Ziva," the owner called from behind them. "This man clearly doesn't want to be bothered."

Shit.

Glancing over his shoulder to follow the voice, he spotted Jessica standing behind him, a gorgeous smirk accompanying her raised eyebrows.

"Funny seeing you here," Silas gasped, feigning shock and hoping she wouldn't notice how he was still trying to nudge her dog away. "Jennifer, right?"

Her smugness didn't fade as she rolled her eyes, not believing his act. "It's Jessica. Are you following me, Mr Knight?" She crossed her arms tightly.

"Now why would I be following a pretty girl like you?"

She let out a lyrical hum, but she walked past him towards the ocean, the dog eagerly following behind her. Silas followed too, stumbling over the uneven sand as they got closer to the shoreline.

"It's strange seeing you two days in a row," Jessica mused, waving Ziva into the sea. The dog wasted no time, racing into the wall of waves and trying to attack each one. Jessica and Silas walked along the damp sand slowly.

"One might say...a happy coincidence." Silas winked at her, and she smiled towards the sea.

"An explanation for everything," she agreed.

"Fate," he said with a definitive nod. She looked at him sidelong, quietly assessing.

He knew he toed a dangerous line, only knowing her for two days. But he needed a way into the manor, and he had no desire to drag this on for longer than it needed to be.

"Do you come here often, then?" Jessica asked, changing the subject.

"Only sometimes," Silas answered. "It's my Ma's favourite spot, so I like to come here to remind me of her. We made a lot of good memories here." It was a lie, but he did feel a tinge of sadness as he remembered all the times she'd brought him here.

Jessica's step faltered as she finally faced him, putting her hand on his arm. "I'm so sorry—is she gone?"

"Oh, no. No, she's still alive. But she's ill. She can't get out much these days. She lives with me now," Silas looked towards the horizon, suddenly feeling very exposed. "We're making the most of our time together."

Jessica gave his forearm a reassuring squeeze. They started walking again as Ziva bounced up ahead of them.

"Do *you* come here often?" Silas asked, wanting the conversation to return to a more surface level. He didn't talk about Ma to anyone—even her nurses had a tough time forcing a conversation from him.

"Only every morning," Jessica returned with a rich laugh, understanding the change in tone. "It's Ziva's favourite place to walk. If we're not here, we'll be at Emsterel Thicket—do you know of it?"

Emsterel Thicket was a full, overgrown forest on the outskirts of Bluetine Park. Silas walked past it every day as he waited for Barney to leave the betting shop. He would often look toward the forest and imagine a life beyond the treeline, away from everyone and anything he knew.

"I know of it."

Jessica's eyes lit up beneath her sunglasses. The tortoiseshell pattern paired perfectly with her caramel complexion and white floating dress. Her curly hair was wrapped in a high bun, accentuating her angular jaw and soft cheekbones. She was effortlessly cute and sophisticated all in one. Her beauty even managed to mellow the irritation swirling around his head from the damp, gritty sand seeping into the crevices of his shoes.

"The forest is my favourite," she said. "And the waterfalls. I go there whenever I can. There's something about nature that just brings me so much peace."

"I can't imagine you need much more peace when you live in a mansion with one hundred rooms," he said dryly. It was a joke, but her expression had him wishing he could suck the words back down his throat instantly. She turned away from him. "Shit, Jessica. I'm sorry, that was meant to be a joke. I didn't mean that."

"It's fine," Jessica said to the ocean, but the warmth in her voice had turned to ice. "You're not the first person to say something like that to me; you won't be the last. It's time we were leaving anyway. I must get back to my *one hundred rooms.*"

She ignored his attempts at more apologies, called a reluctant Ziva in from the ocean, and disappeared beyond the dune. Silas stood on the wet bank, water creeping around the soles of his shoes, as he cursed himself.

He wanted to scream, to shout, to release his anger to the ocean.

What was he thinking?

But that was just it—he hadn't been thinking. He'd been too busy considering how easy Jessica was to talk to, how quickly he'd opened up and told her about his ma. His mind hadn't been on the mission, it had been on her.

Grains of sand caressed his toes, turning his stomach and making him feel violently ill. The sea air whipped and knotted his hair, and the shrieks of children aggravated an emerging headache. He made to leave, stumbling over the sand looking much less gracious than Jessica had. He didn't see her on the way back to his car, but that might have had something to do with the red now clouding his vision at his completely careless mistake.

Silas *really* hated the beach.

CHAPTER SIX

✦

Silas spent the next few days away from his phone, and away from Desmond's daily updates of where Jessica would be, to focus on his time with Ma. His admission at the beach had shattered the veil he'd been using to mask how little time he might have left with her, and how much he wanted to embrace it.

That, and he was in no rush to see Jessica again. Not after the colossal mistake he'd made at the beach. He was embarrassed, and it had taken him four days to come up with a plan to salvage the mission. Silas knew he needed something stellar to win her trust back, as he highly doubted she ever wanted to see him again, either.

So, he turned off his phone and focused on his family for a change. When Ma was awake, they spent the entire time watching movies, playing board games, and flicking through the old photo albums.

It was the first time Silas had actually allowed himself time away from work in the long three years he'd known Desmond, focusing on his mother rather than money. He overcompensated by spending every second with her until the sun was long gone and she struggled to keep her eyes open.

He knew he was being selfish, but he couldn't help it. Ma had a way of making everything feel better, even on days when Silas thought that he could never feel okay again.

She seemed happy enough to keep him company.

On the fifth day of ignoring real life as much as possible, Silas plucked up the courage to turn his phone back on. He cringed as the vibrations started instantly—messages, calls, and even emails flashed onto the screen.

Headed to Roseding Point again today, Romeo?

Silas gritted his teeth until his jaw ached as he skimmed each new message, their timestamps ticking up to the present.

Rumour has it that your lady will be at Grand Athenaeum today—see you down there.

Don't make me send my boys to check in on you, Knight. Ignore me again, they'll be at your door.

The last message was sent only an hour ago. Silas knew he could take any of Desmond's *boys* in a second, but he had no desire to introduce them to his mother. So, he shot a quick reply back.

Where will she be tomorrow, boss?

According to Desmond's reliable source, Jessica was planning a trip to Crystal Shower Falls. Luckily Ma had an appointment with her doctor tomorrow, so her nurses would be at the apartment all day to keep an eye on her.

Silas spent most of his final day off relaxing, oddly intrigued—maybe even a little nervous—about the thought of seeing Jessica again.

☆☆☆

Silas woke to the buzzing of what was becoming his personal alarm clock—a message from Desmond. He pounded a fist into the pillow before dragging himself out of bed to get ready, leaving the message unread.

Dressed head-to-toe in black, Silas gave Ma a quick peck on the forehead before leaving. Bea, one of her specialist nurses, had already arrived and was busy setting everything up for the appointment. Silas gave her a wink as he swung the door closed behind him.

Crystal Shower Falls National Park was a few miles away from Fayette Bay, away from the bustling town and into the wilderness. He used the drive to perfect his redemption plan, rehearsing a few lines he hoped would get them back on track.

Tiny insects descended on him and hovered around his unshaven face as soon as he got out of the car. Swatting them away hopelessly, he started down the gravel path to the main waterfall. He passed the smaller attractions quickly, only sparing a glance at each to make sure Jessica wasn't there before moving onto the next.

Silas neared the main waterfall, spotting his target immediately. Jessica was the only person there, shoulder-deep in the turquoise water underneath a magnificently tall waterfall. Silas climbed down the stone steps to get to the pool quietly, carefully avoiding the shallow puddles and patches of slippery green algae.

Standing at the edge of the pool, he watched her glide underneath the tumbling water. She was a graceful swan, diving in and out of the wall of water, frolicking in its salty spray. Her laugh was melodic. The corners of his mouth dared to twitch.

She only noticed him when she began swimming to the shallow edge of the pool. He met her at the side, standing over her to help pull her out. Her hair was smooth and sodden, the black strands now shimmering silver. She wore a crimson bathing suit that complimented her beautifully, but Silas didn't have much time to admire the look as she wrapped a large towel around her body.

"Hi," he said.

"How did you find me this time?" was all she said in way of greeting, bristling at his casual tone. "Just tell me—are you working for my father?"

"What? Jessica, no. Why would I be working for your father?" Silas tried to catch her eye, and when she finally allowed it, her expression was full of hurt.

"Then how did you find me?" she asked again.

He huffed a sigh. "You mentioned the waterfalls at the beach. It sounds ridiculous, but I've been coming here every day since, hoping to run into you."

It was a lie, but she couldn't know that.

"And why would you do that?" Jessica asked, repositioning the towel with her arms tightly folded. Her voice had lost its icy edge, but it was still a long way from the playful pitch he'd been introduced to.

"I came to apologise," he said as earnestly as he could manage. "No, better yet—I came to start over." She didn't move, a perfect statue. He continued with his hand outstretched, "Hi, I'm Silas Knight. I like long walks on the beach and I make terrible jokes when I'm intimidated."

Jessica's expression didn't soften, but one eyebrow flicked up curiously.

"I tend to value my own company. I don't make a habit of letting my guard down—with anyone. So, when someone as gorgeous as you comes along and makes me feel the way you do, I tend to get a little off my game."

Her expression remained hard, but he could've sworn something flickered in her eyes. He dared to step closer, tentatively stroking her arm down to her fingertips, linking them together. He was so close to her now that he could smell her strawberry perfume mixed with minerals from the pool. He whispered his next words onto her slightly parted lips, "You don't know what you're doing to me."

It was another rehearsed line from the car journey, but the softening of her face told him he'd won. Before she could react or change her mind, he closed the small space between them and brushed his lips over hers.

She tasted like salt, honey and sunshine.

When they parted, she looked breathless and a little surprised. She hid it terribly, trying to remain coy. "Okay, Mr Knight. You get one more chance—but don't mess it up." He caught a wicked glint in her eye before she pulled him towards the muddy bank.

They sat and talked for a long while, Jessica kicking her feet in the water as Silas tried not to pay attention to the wetness seeping through his jeans. She wanted to know everything about him, asking questions in her sinfully sweet voice that he couldn't help but answer. He wanted to bend the truth, but the earnestness in her voice had him spilling any detail she asked about. He gave careful answers, but they were all truthful.

Once his interrogation was over, it was his turn to ask the questions.

"Tell me a little more about you," he said, nudging her shoulder with his lightly. "I want to know the real Jessica."

Her shoulders sagged slightly. After a long pause, she started, "I'm sure you know my father is a business mogul, owning two businesses himself—"

Silas placed a hand over Jessica's in silent interruption. She stopped talking, looking from their hands to his face with surprise. "The whole town knows the Mortons, Jessica. I want to learn about you. Not your father, not the family businesses—*you*."

Her cheeks flushed and she averted her eyes from him, looking back into the mesmerising turquoise portal before them. "I'm not used to people wanting to know about me," she mused, and even the water seemed to hush in intrigue.

"How so?"

A small scoff. "When you're the daughter of the wealthiest businessman in the county, you get used to people only spending time with you to get closer to the family. Once they're in with my father, I'm often nothing more than a forgotten memory." She shrugged, but her smile didn't reach her eyes.

"You don't seem to let it affect you," he said, delicately prying. "I was nothing more than a stranger at the market; how did you know I wasn't using you?" Silas knew he was walking that very dangerous line once again, but he needed her to open up.

Jessica hummed a long sigh. "I'm not sure I've made up my mind on you yet, Mr Knight. But I'd like to think I'd know if you were just here to meet my father. Most people aren't very subtle when it comes to talking about my family."

Silas leaned in closer to where she lounged, leaning onto her elbows to watch a group of small birds dance before the sun. "Can I let you into a little secret?" he whispered, and she nodded. "I don't give a damn about your father."

Jessica's face broke into a large grin at that, a gleeful laugh escaping her. "And isn't that just music to my ears."

Silas winked at her before repeating, "So, tell me about you."

And she did. Jessica told him everything, from her dreams and the plans for her future that she held near, to her paintings, her fear of clowns, and the reason why the waterfalls and forests and beaches were her favourite places to visit.

"I'm not to stray far from the manor," she said as they balanced across the rocky pathway behind the waterfall. "I come to places like this to disobey my parents without actually breaking the rules. They want me at home all day, in one of my *hundred rooms*—" A playful jab, and Silas returned a self-deprecating smile, "—but so long as I'm still in Fayette Bay, they can't reprimand me."

"But why do they not allow you to go wherever you please? You're a grown woman, Jessica. You should be in control of your own life."

"You don't know my parents. Everyone has a role to play in the perfect image they portray, and I'm not to disrupt that. Otherwise," she took a deep breath before continuing, "there will be consequences."

She talked in such a matter-of-fact way that he struggled to comprehend the amount of control her parents were lording over her. He was outraged for her. *Furious* for her. But she seemed to just…accept it.

"What kind of consequences?" he asked as casually as he could. But she just smirked at him.

"I thought you didn't want to know about my family?"

"Only if they're keeping you captive in plain sight," he said. It was a joke, but the playful glimmer dulled from her eyes.

"My father…is not a nice man, Silas. I don't know the ins and outs of it, but I'm not naïve enough to think that his business ventures are always above board. He'll stop at nothing to keep the family businesses running, even if that means paying people to do unspeakable things to his rivals—or his own family."

Silas listened quietly, storing all of this information away for when it might be best used. But the quietness of her voice told him she was done talking about it, and he was ready to move onto a happier subject. "You're very brave," was all he said to end the conversation.

But as she saw the fire in his eyes, she stopped in front of him and affirmed, "I'll get out of there one day."

He believed her. Her confident smile didn't leave any room for doubt. Then she kissed him so ferociously that the bouncing water couldn't cover the sound of thrumming blood through his veins. They stood behind the waterfall now, hidden behind the glistening curtain. Water sprayed onto them, turning their clothes sodden and clingy. But they didn't care, staring into each other's eyes.

"I'll help you," Silas whispered, barely audible over the water.

A feline smile. "How will you do that?"

"I'll kill them—anyone that dares hurt you."

She laughed as quietly as his confession. "You'd really do that for me, Mr Knight?"

"Yes—and stop calling me that," Silas purred.

"But I like your name," Jessica retorted, breaking their closeness and twirling on the slippery rocks. "It sounds like you're here to save me."

"Do you need saving?"

That made her stop instantly, though the smirk didn't leave her face. "That's quite a loaded question to ask a stranger, don't you think?"

He began to apologise, but she walked back to him and hooked her hands around his neck. She reached up to graze the shell of his ear with her bottom lip before humming, "Will you be my knight in shining armour, Silas?" Her tone was goofy, but with just a hint of a challenge.

She left no time for a response as she planted a light kiss on his cheek, then his lips. But before Silas could pull her back in to deepen their embrace, she was off again, prancing underneath the waterfall without a care in the world.

And if it wasn't the most beautiful thing he had ever seen.

CHAPTER SEVEN

✦

After spending the rest of the day together at Crystal Shower Falls, Jessica had asked Silas for his phone and added her number as a contact. Three days had passed since, and they had been messaging back and forth relentlessly. It was like he was back at school again, talking to his first crush. Even Ma noticed how much time he was spending on his phone, chortling at the smile that forced its way onto his face every time the screen illuminated with her name.

The only person to message him before was Desmond, and he sure as hell didn't elicit any type of positive reaction.

Smitten. That's what Ma had been calling him every time he grinned at the screen. But he pushed the remarks away—he was buying into his own con, nothing more. If he didn't believe his feelings, how would he expect Jessica to react? Silas was a master of his craft, and he prided himself on it. If that meant getting a little too deep into his web of deception to make the lies more believable, then that's what he'd have to do.

Desmond had called him into the office that morning, and Silas walked into the metal container late. Still, his boss didn't seem to mind. "Knight! I've been on the edge of my seat all morning waiting for your update. Come, tell me all about it."

"Not much to say, boss. I've got Jessica's number now, so I can live without your daily updates. I think she was starting to get suspicious of me just *happening* to show up everywhere she went for those few days."

"I'm sure you schmoozed your way out of it, my boy. No one gets past you!" Desmond snickered.

"I did," he confirmed dryly.

A dirty smile. "Good. So, any closer to a home visit yet?"

"Not yet, Des. Give me a few more days to scope her out. I need her to trust me before she brings me back to the manor."

Desmond grumbled but nodded reluctantly. "Well, just don't leave me waiting too long, Knight. I want to see the look on Morton's face when we take him for all he's worth."

Silas cleared his throat. "I've been thinking about that, boss. Why bother with Jessica at all? We should leave it at blackmailing Richard with the documents. If they're as scandalous as you claim, he'll surely pay enough for them on their own—without involving Jessica," he said as casually as he could. "She's innocent in all of this."

Desmond's eyes flashed with glee. "Oh, don't you go soft on me now, Knight. We know how this will go—Richard will hide the majority of his money, just like all the other men we've taken from in the past. They think they can best us, but we always see them coming!" he chortled, offering a drink to Silas. "That's what makes us a dream team, you and me. So Jessica will be used as the final bargaining chip, to make sure we clear that sucker out completely."

"I just think that—"

Desmond groaned. "I'm not changing the plan, Silas. Why do you care so much? Don't tell me you're *actually* falling for the girl," he said with a cackle.

Silas ignored the comment, standing up to leave. It was pointless arguing with his boss, anyway. "Fine. Will you at least back off with the updates?"

"But what will I do without our morning messages?" Desmond asked, eyes widening. *Provoking.*

"Don't you have someone else to be spying on? What about the new guys that haven't delivered a single penny all month?"

"I have many men; I can keep an eye on you all."

"Desmond."

Delight shone blindingly over his boss's smug face. "Oh, Knight. Why do you never allow yourself to have any *fun*? I'll ask my boys to back off your lady since you're doing such a fantastic job. Happy?"

Silas grunted, turning on his heel and leaving the tin office before his boss could change his mind.

☆☆☆

Silas stopped to pick up some snacks on the way home. It was movie night at the apartment, and Ma had requested toffee popcorn. The film was a cheesy romance. Not to his taste, but Ma loved it. And, although he wouldn't care to admit it, it also gave him an excuse to talk to Jessica.

That's my favourite film! The actors are so dreamy.

Silas paid a little more attention to the TV after that text. He could surely use his new knowledge to score some brownie points the next time he saw her. The leading man was in love with a woman, who was leaving for the other side of the world in just two days. The acting was awful, but Silas still found humour in understanding the time crunch of it all.

Yes, very dreamy indeed. I do have some questions about the plot, though. Might need to meet with an expert and discuss this.

A reply vibrated through after a few minutes.

Smooth. I'm sure I could squeeze you in. How's tomorrow, Roseding Point at 10?

He let out an audible groan as another sandy day materialised before him. Despite his better judgement, Silas agreed to the date, and Jessica ended the conversation.

Sleep well, Mr Knight.

Once the film had finished, Ma was surprisingly alert and had enough energy to suggest a quick look outside. Silas tore back the stiff doors to the balcony and turned her armchair towards the stars. He helped her up from the green sofa and into her old chair so she had the perfect view of the shimmering sky. Silas stepped out onto the thin balcony, hidden behind the wall so Ma could still see from inside. Stargazing had always been one of their favourite things to do together.

"Look, there's the Summer Triangle," Ma said in a soft voice, pointing vaguely to the lights above them. She always spoke in such a mellow tone when they stargazed—Silas was sure it was one of the reasons why he found it so comforting. "Deneb, Vega and Altair. You see them?"

Silas hummed in response. He had memories of his mother teaching him the different constellations as far back as he could remember. She took him out almost every night after the sun had set to talk him through the stars, their groupings, the planets, and everything magical in between.

In hindsight, Silas assumed this was probably just to get away from his father, who had a habit of smashing up their house after any minor inconvenience. Before long, Silas learned the map of the sky throughout every month and season.

He was now almost as good as Ma when it came to spotting the constellations—*almost*.

"And there's my favourite!" Ma acknowledged softly, her voice rich velvet. Silas drew his eyes to the left of the obsidian sky, knowing exactly which constellation he was looking for.

The Teapot.

Ma would always joke about the Teapot grouping—better known as an asterism from part of the Sagittarius constellation—being her favourite, with how much she loved tea.

Tonight was no different, and Silas grimaced at the overused joke but still gave her his obligatory laugh. "Did you want some tea, Ma?" he asked, smiling at her as he leaned around the balcony door.

"No thank you, Sy. I think it's time for me to turn in," she said, slowly lifting herself out of her chair. She gave him a kiss on the cheek before retiring to her bedroom. Silas remained out on the balcony for a while, leaning against the cool brick, as he whispered the constellation names to himself as he spotted them.

After exhausting his knowledge of the summer sky, he turned himself in for the night, the gentle stars keeping him company against his eyelids as he fell asleep.

☆☆☆

Silas awoke to the sun already blaring through the window and his bedroom unbearably humid. He immediately rolled out of bed to crack the window and open the door. But with the outside air painfully stagnant and no breeze to offer relief, he shoved on the first clothes he found and headed into the living room.

One of Ma's nurses was already in the kitchen, unpacking some groceries as he fixed himself a bowl of cereal. He ate it silently as the nurse busied herself around him.

He quietly got himself ready before slipping out the front door and slinking into his car. The drive to Roseding

Point was busier than he'd hoped for—it was a Saturday in late June, after all. It was prime sunbathing season, when everyone flocked to the beach to damage their skin for hours on end.

The car park was full of flustered drivers blocking each other in, the air full of horns blaring for attention. He took one look at the queue and turned around. This definitely wasn't the time to get worked up before a date—he needed to be on his best behaviour.

Parking a few streets away, Silas used the extra walking distance to clear his head. He hadn't been able to stop thinking about what Jessica had alluded to at the waterfall. That Richard would put his family—her—in harms way to protect his image.

He'd spent his free time since coming up with plans to destroy Richard Morton himself, then snapping himself out of it. Because this was a job—a means to an end. In less than two months, he'd never need to think about Jessica again.

But still, the fact that she was so scared to go against her own father didn't sit well with him.

As soon as he reached the top of the first sand dune, a long groan escaped him. Far too many people had gathered, packed like sardines in a can, unable to move without touching someone else's beach towel or windbreaker. He didn't have too long to judge them all though, as a thudding impact from behind almost made him lose his balance and fall right into the soft sand.

Then he heard her gasping through giggles at her practical joke. Looking down, he saw Jessica's delicate hands clasped around the waist of his dark brown hoodie, still gripping him from where she'd tackled him. Her laughter was so infectious that Silas actually joined in—*what was happening to him?*—and he turned within her arms to look down at her. Cupping her jaw in both hands, thumbs stroking her rosy cheekbones, he leant down to give her a quick kiss. "Hello, pretty girl."

Jessica cringed again at the nickname, scrunching her nose so the freckles littering it danced, but the secret smile that followed confirmed she really did love it. So much so that she pulled him in for another, deeper kiss.

Ziva jumped and twirled around them, blunt claws scratching at Silas's jeans and Jessica's summer dress. Jessica broke them apart to throw the ball for Ziva and the dog bounded through the crowds, kicking sand every which way into too many people's faces. Silas smirked as she gasped, covering her grimace as she watched the destruction she had just caused.

She was still staring through wide eyes as Silas stepped back a moment to take her in. She was wearing a sunshine yellow dress that cut off just above the knees. The colour brought out the golden strands in her dark curls, and her amber eyes sparkled with the reflection of the clear ocean. The tiny freckles that littered her nose extended to her cheeks, her lips stained cherry red.

She caught him staring as Ziva made her ungraceful way back through the crowd, eliciting a few angry reactions in her wake. "And what are you looking at, Mr Knight?"

"Just something gorgeous, Milady," Silas said as he dramatically bowed, extending his hand for hers. She smirked, playing along as he kissed her knuckles, lingering for a moment.

"You do flatter me," Jessica hummed with a smile as she removed her hand from his and busied it with an attempt to restrain the hyperactive puppy.

Silas squinted an eye at her. "Is everything alright?"

"Yes. It's just—" He had to work to earn her eye contact, but when she finally granted it, he could see a flicker of hurt. "It doesn't matter."

Before he could persist, Jessica was gone, running after Ziva, dress floating dreamily behind her. He walked after them, hands in pockets, not caring who he flicked sand on.

☆☆☆

They spent the full day together. Richard was out of town at some business convention, so Jessica's shackles had been loosened enough to give him the day with her.

Roseding Point occupied the first half, walking up and down the sandy shore while Ziva danced in the waves. But for the second half they drove aimlessly, talking about nothing and everything all at once.

Jessica directed him to a quaint little town, signposted Cirrane, that only housed a handful of shops—one of which claimed to sell the best ice cream in the county. Silas ordered one scoop of Rum and Raisin while Jessica tried a Knickerbocker Glory. Ziva was given a small tub of whipped cream as a treat from the owner.

As they strolled with their ice creams arm-in-arm, they continued their conversation. Jessica could talk for hours while Silas listened intently, only sharing intimate details when absolutely necessary. He told her about his mother's illness, and she told him about the authors and painters that inspired her. She listed the great films she'd seen recently, and he gave her the rundown of the classic books he'd collected so far.

The pair shared, laughed, and enjoyed each other's company until the sun began to set. Noting the fierce orange colour of the sky, Jessica said, "I guess we'd better be getting back."

"What's the rush?" he asked with a wink, sliding back into the driver's seat. Jessica climbed in beside him after ushering Ziva into the back.

"I really need to get back, Silas."

"Come on, pretty girl," he drawled, revving the engine. "Spend another hour with me." He waggled his eyebrows and gave her a lazy smile, and after a few moments, she gave in.

"Okay, but just one hour."

"Just one hour," Silas repeated before driving away from the tiny town.

Ten minutes later, the car pulled into one of Silas's favourite parking spots. It was a tall ridge looking over the town of Fayette Bay. They could see everything up here—the manor, Desmond's shop, Emsterel Thicket, his apartment block. The town looked so small, so insignificant. He felt pure peace whenever he could escape above it all.

Jessica got out of the car, Ziva jumping over the seats and following closely behind her. "It's so beautiful," she gasped, staring at the blazing red sky burning over their town. The sunset cast an amber glow over her skin, melting into her dress. Her hair was untamed and windswept, making her look gloriously free. Her eyes turned glassy as he watched a range of emotions overcome her. It was the face of someone who had never felt so liberated, unbound.

He guessed she had her father to blame for that.

"Sometimes I escape out here and just read for hours," Silas said, joining her in front of the car, slipping his hand around her waist. She rested her head against his shoulder. They remained there, admiring the sunset, leaning against one another. Silas didn't know how much time had passed when Jessica lifted her head to look up at him, but he knew that it hadn't been long enough.

"Silas, would you hurt me?" she asked in a small voice. Her eyes pleaded for the truth, and the vulnerability in the words told him it wasn't a joke. Without leaving much time for him to answer, she continued, "I've never been in a relationship—my father wouldn't allow it—so I don't know how this goes. But I know how I feel, and I don't want to be hurt later if you decide you don't feel the same."

He turned to look deeply into her warm eyes. They looked back at him, begging for an answer. Something told him that she wouldn't mind either way—she just needed the truth.

"No," he said, not fully knowing whether it was a lie or not. "I couldn't."

Jessica smiled, shoulders relaxing, before she turned back towards the sunset. Silas felt a strange pang of something in his chest as he allowed his eyes to linger on her side profile for a couple moments longer.

What was he doing?

Desmond had mentioned her being a wildcard—not that she'd be so *innocent*. So blindly trusting. His chest tightened as he took in what she'd just asked of him.

This was a *job*. He had no time for feelings, and certainly no time to stop her from getting caught in the crossfire. Desmond had made it clear that the plan regarding her wouldn't change—Silas wasn't even sure why he'd bothered asking.

It wasn't the first time he'd used someone as collateral damage for a paycheck, so why did he feel so guilty when it came to her?

Stepping away from the crook of his arm that she'd nestled herself in, Jessica's silhouette flashed against the fiery sky. She was an image of beauty. A goddess against the painted sunset.

Shaking his doubts about the mission away, Silas silently crept around the side of his car and found his old polaroid camera. Returning to his original place behind her, he captured the moment with a clicking flash. Her eyes lit up as she saw what was in his hands and posed dramatically for another picture. The final shot was of that sweet smile Silas was growing so fond of, with her hands clasped behind her back. Her unruly curls tore at the sky, flecks of fire burning into the film and creating an amazing pattern over the pictures.

"Let's take one together!" Jessica grabbed the camera from his hands and leaned into him. Silas tried to block the lens with his palm, but she was too quick in darting out of the way. She flung her arm around his neck, pulling him so close he could smell her jasmine-infused perfume and pressed their cheeks together. "Say cheese!"

The printed picture was nice—despite his usual hatred for photos of himself. Still, he let her keep it.

"Okay, I *really* need to get home now." Jessica pulled the arm of his hoodie playfully. He rolled his eyes but didn't make it difficult for her to pull him towards the car. Before he could slide back into the driver's seat, she hooked her arms around his hips. "Thank you for bringing me here," she said quietly, sealing her gratitude with a kiss. He smiled onto her lips, wishing they could stay there all night.

With the three of them back in the car, they set back along the winding roads. No words were shared between them as they neared Morton Manor. Jessica rested on her forearm as she gazed out the open window, Ziva snoozed on the back seat, and Silas drove with a ghost of a smile etched onto his face.

"You can drop me off here please," Jessica said, breaking the silence. They were still a few minutes away from her house, and the streetlamps were just starting to turn on. Silas gave her a questioning look, but her face remained firm.

"Your father is out of town," he started.

"There are cameras everywhere."

Silas put a hand on her knee, squeezing in silent reassurance. "It's dark out. I'd rather drive you home."

"I'm a big girl, Silas. I can walk the rest of the way." Her tone made it clear that she wasn't going to change her mind, so he pulled up on the side of the street.

"Thank you. Meet me tomorrow at the entrance to the Emsterel Thicket?" she asked, her tone softening as the car rolled to a stop. Silas nodded. "Ten thirty?" He nodded again, but before she could escape, he grabbed her wrist and pulled her back towards him.

"I had the best day with you," he said, and he meant it. Just the three of them, exploring without a true care in the world. The mission had been a distant memory.

Silas didn't want to consider what the deeper meaning of that realisation was. Not yet.

"It was perfect," she agreed, her eyes dancing before she brushed a light kiss over his lips. "I'll see you tomorrow, Mr Knight."

And then she slipped out of his grasp, Ziva loyally following her out of the car.

"At least text me when you're home safely, please?" he called out of the open window as he watched her walk away.

"So overprotective," she said over her shoulder, yellow sundress swishing as she walked. The smile in her voice made him laugh.

Silas waited until she was no longer in sight to begin driving again. He drove in a circle ending at the top of Ruby Boulevard, just catching a glimpse of her climbing the tall stairs outside the manor.

Satisfied she was safe, Silas drove himself home, playing the events of the long day over and over again.

He *was* being protective. Maybe too much, for a woman he barely knew. The only people he'd treat similarly would be Bea and Maria, and he'd known them both for years. Perhaps it was the sinister impending threat that his boss posed to Jessica that had him acting in such a way.

Impulsive. Invested. Far too dedicated.

But was he dedicated to the mission, or something else entirely?

With Jessica out of the car, Silas was able to turn his attention back to the mission. He was getting closer to the house; he could feel it. He just needed one invite in, and he'd be able to find those files and put this whole mess behind him.

He was still detailing possible routes into the manor when his phone vibrated with a text from Jessica.

> *I'm home, safe and sound. Although a suspicious car was driving super slowly by the house as I was walking in. Probably just some obsessive fan who's hopelessly in love with me.*

Silas snorted as he read it at a stop light. Obsessive fan, indeed.

CHAPTER EIGHT

✦

After a relaxing morning at home, Silas descended the stairwell to head to Emsterel Thicket. He'd been so content with his own company that he hadn't checked his phone until he'd locked the door behind him. Three missed calls from Desmond—one last night and two that morning.

Strange, but not enough for Silas to care.

He made a mental note to call his boss back later, shoving the phone back into his pocket and pushing his way out into the sickly sticky morning air. Stopping at his car only to pick up his sunglasses, he began the walk to Emsterel Thicket.

He arrived early, positioning himself on a sharp rock to read a few more chapters of his back-pocket book.

A few minutes later, her shadow eclipsed the sun across his page. Squinting as he looked up at Jessica, he gave her a small lopsided smile. She wore a long blue dress with buttons down the front. Her hair was free, flowing down her back in cascading waves. She'd tried to tuck it behind her ears with a headband, but the curls were too large to obey such constraint.

"What are you reading today?" Jessica asked as he stood up, brushing himself off.

He angled the worn cover towards her to read. "It's the only book that'll fit in my back pocket. I just reread it over and over again." Silas winked. Her amber eyes twinkled in the sunshine, golden rings encasing her pupils as she laughed.

Silas nodded at the entrance to the forest. "So, why this place?"

She simply shrugged and looked longingly into the tall trees. "Why not?" She started towards the entranceway, which was no more than a break in the thorny bushes. He only noticed her open-toed sandals as she pranced over the first overgrown bramble.

Silas followed, stepping across the threshold and immediately feeling the thorns dig into his jeans. He stifled a growl.

The path offered only enough room for one person at a time, so he loomed sheepishly behind her like a puppy following its owner. He watched her dance around the sharp twigs reaching out from every angle across the path. The angry shrubs seemed to allow her to pass while taking pleasure in clawing at his clothes and jolting him back as he tried to keep up with her.

"Come on, slowpoke!" Jessica called back, beckoning him before spinning on her heel to continue.

They walked for a long while in silence, nothing but the sound of wasps and other insects buzzing around them. The bushes grew taller, nipping at his arms. It'd be a miracle if he got home with any clothes still on his back at all.

"So, about that film—" Silas started, but Jessica came to an abrupt stop before him. He narrowly avoided crashing into her, grabbing onto both of her shoulders for balance. His hands lingered for a second before pulling back.

He peered over the top of her head to see why she had stopped and almost fell back in surprise.

A small deer blocked the path ahead, grazing on the leaves of a fallen branch. It had fiery red fur and white blotches trailing down its back. Snapping twigs underfoot alerted the deer to their presence, but it didn't run. Instead, it simply looked up at them with wide black eyes and pointed ears, before returning to its lunch.

"Maybe we should go back," Silas whispered, but Jessica was already cautiously creeping up to the animal. Her hand floated up in front of her and stroked the deer—a true fairytale princess.

She turned towards him slightly. She was smiling, her entire face glowing with excitement. Her curls fell from behind her ear and acted as a curtain, blocking the sight of her pure happiness. He frowned, stepping closer as quietly as he could to scrape the hair away from her face, tucking it back behind her ear. Her eyes flickered to his, sharing her infectious joy.

Silas was infatuated in that moment, completely under her spell. He even considered petting the wild animal himself for a second—before coming to his senses and taking a large step back again.

Instead, he took his phone out of his pocket and snapped a sweet picture of the pair. She didn't notice.

The animal eventually got bored and disappeared off into the backdrop of thick trees and shrubs. Once it was out of sight, Jessica broke out of her trance, wonder-filled laughter bursting from her in shallow gasps. He could listen to that sound all day. He grinned back at her, shaking his head, as she took a few moments to compose herself.

As he followed her deeper into the forest, their resuming silence gave him plenty of time to overthink how his entire being changed when he was with her. He didn't know how or why, but he liked himself better when she was with him. It was more peaceful, somehow.

He was happier with her.

"We're here!" Jessica exclaimed as she jumped off the trail and into a clearing, extravagantly waving her arms around to show it off. Silas was more than happy to be torn away from *those* thoughts.

Before them stood a turquoise lake, surrounded by thick shrubs and marshy grass. He turned to look at her, but she was busy slipping her straps off her shoulders. As the periwinkle fabric fell to the floor, a white swimsuit was all that was left in its place.

"What are you—" he began, but Jessica stepped out of her discarded dress and cannonballed into the water before he could finish.

And then a large splash erupted from underneath the water, Jessica bursting up towards the sky looking as radiant as ever, skin glistening, laughing hysterically.

She scraped her sodden hair from her face. "Get in here!" she called, beckoning him as she began to float on her back, gazing up at the bright blue sky between the high shimmering trees.

"Yeah, I'll pass on that," he said with a smirk, picking up her dress from the boggy floor and slinging it over his shoulder, watery soil squelching beneath his feet.

Jessica lazily turned her head to look at him and rolled her big eyes dramatically, cloudy water lapping over her features. She turned onto her front and paddled to the side of the lake nearest him, giving him a cunningly beautiful smile and summoning him with her eyes.

He thought he might just give her anything she wanted from that look alone.

Sure enough, Silas found himself walking slowly towards her, his shoes sinking deeper into the marshy grass. She held out a hand and he bent down to accept it. "Too cold?" he gloated, taking her hand in his to pull her out. But she suddenly tugged his arm towards her sharply. Silas barely kept himself out of the water, falling back onto the muddy floor.

"Woah now, pretty girl," Silas smirked grimly. Every impulse in his body was telling him to snap, but her mischievous expression stopped him. "You really thought you could outsmart me?" he asked in mock disbelief, flexing his muscles theatrically.

"Whatever." Jessica kicked up to float on her back again. But her playful smile gave her true feelings away as she refused to look at him.

Silas sat down on a broad stone at the edge of the water, leaning back to admire the same view as her. The trees towered high above them, every branch compact and entwining with one another. But over the lake was a parting in the thick greenery, a portion of perfect sky managing to peek through. They stared up through the opening for what felt like hours.

Every now and then a white cloud floated through the parting, and Jessica shouted what she saw.

"A dog with an incredibly fluffy tail!"

"A cloud."

"What? No! That's a butterfly—see, look!"

"Oh, yeah. I see that now."

"You are such a grump."

He smirked at the truth in that statement, but as he squinted to find the bird wearing a top hat in the clouds, it dawned on him—he didn't want to be his usual self around her.

Just a job, his inner voice reminded him. *There's too much riding on this to mess it up.*

But how could he ignore the fact that he was searching the sky for fancy birds, and *enjoying* himself? She wasn't forcing him to play along, Desmond wasn't watching him to make sure he kept her sweet…Silas was playing along willingly.

"Silas?" Jessica asked as she swam over to him, breaking him out of his thoughts. "Can I ask you something?"

"A pretty girl like you can ask away."

She rolled her eyes theatrically, but her face was clouded with nerves. "Promise me you won't laugh?"

Silas dipped his head in agreement. "Shoot."

She paused, chewing on the inside of her lip. He reached out to take her chin, guiding her eyes to his, giving her a reassuring smile. She returned it and shook her head. "Okay, here goes. Am I coming on too strong? I don't know how these things go, and I don't want to scare you off…" She tore her eyes away from him as a bright fuchsia blush bloomed across her neck.

He couldn't help but smirk. "Where's this come from?"

"I don't know," she said with a helpless laugh. "I've just been freaking out that what I said yesterday was too much. I know you're definitely more experienced than me in the whole relationship field, and I'd rather know now if I've been coming on too strong—so I can take a step back."

"I'm not easily spooked, Jessica," he replied, taking her wet hand in his. "You're going to have to do a lot more than that to get rid of me. And I don't want you to take a step back."

"I'm sorry—"

"No," he cut her off. "You're not going to apologise for being you. I'm enjoying our time together, Jessica. Don't overthink it."

She looked surprised yet a little relieved, a small smile dipping beneath the water. "Okay," she replied before floating away again.

Silas looked back up to the clouds, but his mind was far away from silly shapes and chirping birds. Because she *should* be scaring him off. She *was* coming on too strong. But somehow, for whatever reason, he didn't mind it.

He really was enjoying her company…and he didn't want her to take a step back at all.

And he was in deep, *deep* shit.

They compared cloud shapes for another good while before Jessica climbed out of the lake, shivering. She thanked him sweetly as he handed her back her mostly dry dress and slipped it over her head. Dark patches blossomed over the fabric as it gripped onto the wet swimsuit, but she didn't seem to notice. She twisted her dripping curls up into a low bun as she asked, "Wouldn't this be a lovely place for a picnic?"

He hummed in agreement, wrapping a hand around her waist and pulling her closer. "I'll make us one for next time," he said onto her lips. He felt her smile as she closed the gap between them, her warmth radiating through him like liquid sunshine.

Then she broke them apart, taking his hand and leading him back onto the uneven path.

Silas usually couldn't care less about the life cycle of a leaf. Today, however, the large summer fronds were his nemesis. They hung far above him, taunting him with their unique height and ability to keep the air around him still and humid. He longed for a breeze, but it was hopeless until they could get out from underneath the wooded canopies snickering above them.

"Isn't this place just wonderful?" Jessica asked him, but she didn't receive a response. "Look—butterflies!" A spotted brown butterfly skimmed across the path right on cue. Silas agreed quietly.

"And those beautiful flowers!"

Jessica picked a white daisy as she walked past a budding shrub. Silas pondered his life choices as he felt the familiar prick of a bramble slice into his ankle.

"And the lake!"

She stopped and turned around to face him so quickly that he stumbled, trying to halt on the spot. But his right ankle rolled underneath him, crunching on impact. His vision thrummed red. Jessica grabbed onto him as he ducked down into the slip.

"Whoops, steady," she laughed before repeating herself. "Wasn't the lake beautiful?"

He nodded, shuddering a breath as his jaw clamped shut. Flashing him a toothy grin before running off again, she left him still cowering on the ground. He gave himself the grace of a few frustrated growls before hauling himself up and taking a tentative step to follow her, immediately stumbling into a limp. Searing pain shot up his calf with every step, the uneven floor certainly not helping.

Suddenly the treeline opened, exposing them from beneath the dim forest and onto a bright plane. A golf course.

"Shoot, we're not supposed to be here!" Jessica turned and threw her hands up in front of his face like it was somehow his fault that they'd ended up in the wrong place. "We have to go, come on!"

She pulled so hard on his arm that he lost his balance and had to slam back onto his injured foot to stay upright.

Pain-fuelled ire boiled over. He let out a low-pitched roar and yanked his hand back from hers. "Just…stop," he breathed, hopping to a large stone on the outskirts of the forest and collapsing onto it, face buried in his hands.

Jessica hurried over to him, glancing around worriedly as she did so. She knelt next to his leg and tentatively placed her palm on his shin. "I'm sorry, I didn't think you'd hurt yourself badly." There was genuine regret in her voice and eyes, and his rage melted away.

This was new territory to him. It was in his nature to want to retaliate—to shout or curse until she left him alone—but instead, he found himself closing his eyes and nodding in acceptance of her apology.

She gave leg a small squeeze. "Do you think you can walk?"

The thought alone made him want to retch, but he also just wanted to get home. "Sure, let's go."

Jessica helped him stand and guided his arm around her shoulders, her fingers wrapping around his waist for stability. He appreciated the support, even if their height difference meant he was uncomfortably towering over her. They half walked; half hopped back towards the forest opening when a small figure of a man standing across the green caught the corner of his eye.

The mysterious golfer was staring at them. Silas might not have thought anything of it if it weren't for his human crutch. Her body tensed instantly, and she began walking much faster than was comfortable for his throbbing leg. He followed her, being pulled along like a lazy dog on a tight leash, but kept his eyes fixed on the man over his shoulder.

Silas was missing something.

Once the golf course was firmly hidden behind them, Jessica finally allowed them to slow down. She refused to leave his side, so they awkwardly walked too close together down the same path, past the lake, and finally to the entrance to the forest.

Silas clumsily collapsed onto the same rock he'd been reading his book on earlier in the day, and Jessica knelt on the ground next to him. The sky had turned into a blazing orange, illuminating the crease between her brows. She looked up at him with weary eyes. He knew something was wrong, but he'd experienced the same feeling too many times to know not to ask about it. If she wanted to talk, she would tell him.

He scanned her whole body—the now blue and brown dress almost dry, an expensive-looking bracelet that had no place being submerged in the cloudy lake water, and her bloodied ankles from countless bramble scratches. It appeared that she'd stopped skipping over them on the walk back.

"I'm sorry," Jessica whispered, breaking the silence. Her chin was perched on her palms as her doe eyes looked up at him. "That man back there. It was—"

"You don't have to tell me," Silas interrupted her quickly. He wasn't sure why he'd stopped her. Perhaps because he didn't want to know, or didn't care enough to know—or maybe it was because he *already* knew. Desmond had been his boss long enough to recognise an underling when he saw one. Someone who kept tabs on a certain person for another, usually in exchange for money or acceptance.

Someone to do their dirty work for them.

Jessica gave him a tight smile, shoulders falling slightly, but straightened her back. "No, I think you should know." She paused to take a shuddering breath. "My father likes to have me *watched* when I'm away from the manor. He says he can't have me doing anything that might upset the investors. The golf course is where lots of them spend their time, so that man was warning me to get you out of sight before we were spotted."

"Why would the investors care if you were on the golf course?"

A humourless laugh. "They like to think of me as their *eye candy* at their investor functions my father throws. If they saw me with another man, it might jeopardise how much money they give him."

Silas blew out a low whistle. "And your father allows that?"

Another sharp laugh. "He noticed that one of his top investors couldn't stop looking at me during one of his parties. From then on, he decided that he needed to oversee my outfits for each function. Before every event, he'll give me a new dress to wear." Her voice quietened into a whisper as she continued, "The more money they give him, the smaller the dresses become."

Richard Morton cared more about his business ventures than his only daughter's autonomy. Silas held back a snarl.

"Jessica, say the word and I *will* kill them," Silas vowed quietly. "I'll hunt them all down." Her only reply was a weak smile, so Silas continued, "Thank you for telling me. I'm sorry your piece-of-shit dad does this to you."

That earned him a small snicker, but it didn't reach her eyes. He leaned down and hooked her chin with his finger, making her meet his gaze. "You'll get out of there one day," he reminded her.

Her eyes turned glassy. "I'll get out of there one day," she repeated, barely louder than a whisper on the wind.

They remained there, connected, for a long moment. Pain and embarrassment swam in her eyes, but also a flicker of hope. Silas pulled her closer and pressed a kiss to her forehead, stroking her hair. When they both finally braved standing back up, the sky had faded to smoky charcoal.

They made their way back to Jessica's mansion—or a couple of streets away from it, at least—hand in hand. They didn't speak. Nothing more needed to be said. Jessica leaned in to give him a soft peck on the cheek before leaving him, walking away without the skip in her step that Silas had been unknowingly growing so fond of.

As she disappeared around the corner, Silas made a silent vow to avenge Jessica's light, targeting anyone who had dared to dull it.

CHAPTER NINE

✦

The walk back home was agonising. Jessica's mansion was further away from Emsterel Thicket than his apartment, so Silas had a long journey ahead of him—with or without a busted ankle. Jessica was all he could think of while he tried to make sense of the day. His heart was still thundering, brain reeling from what she'd told him before he walked her home. Richard Morton had an underling follow his daughter to make sure she maintained her *perfectly pure princess* appearance.

So his businessmen would still deem her worthy of their filthy gazes and roving hands.

He snarled under his breath. He'd kill them all.

Red flashes skimmed his vision at the thought, but the flames licking up his ankle with every step fought for his attention. He still hadn't made it halfway yet.

As if a glorious beacon, the Twinkling Bliss neon lights shimmered like a mirage against the dark night before him. Maria would help him out, get him a coffee to refuel for the rest of the way home. A grim smile tugged at his lips as Silas stumbled towards the door.

The lights were dimmed, no one to be seen through the large windows. Maria often kept the doors unlocked while she closed up, so he continued walking towards the entrance anyway.

As he reached for the door, his phone vibrated through his jean pocket. He abandoned the handle and loosened the phone quickly, hoping for another chance to talk to Jessica before the day was done.

Wishful thinking.

Desmond's name and number flashed across the screen, and Silas stifled another snarl. He'd forgotten to call his boss back this morning, but far too much pain and anger was coursing through his veins right now—any conversation with his boss would lead to them coming to blows.

Desmond could wait a little longer.

A crash sounded from within the café, tearing Silas's eyes back through the window. Nothing. Maria must've dropped something in the back. He pushed through the door, the bell ringing twice as he entered. Using the tables for balance as he walked, he plopped down on the cool leather bench of his usual booth, head spinning.

Another tingle of vibrations from his pocket came, and Silas pulled the phone out to confirm that it was still his boss. If there was one thing he knew about Desmond Rose, it was that he wouldn't stop calling until Silas picked up the damned phone.

"What do you want?" he asked in way of greeting.

"Brr. Someone's frosty today!" Desmond's raspy voice boomed through the phone, winding its way through all the inner workings of his head until it found its sweet spot. The voice ploughed as hard as it could into the raging flame, radiating a sharp numbness throughout his whole body. "Where've you been, son?"

"Working," he spat through clenched teeth.

"Oh, I know that. But tell me more!" Desmond crooned, words bubbling through his damaged lungs. Silas rolled his eyes, pulling the phone away from his ear to get away from its cackle, throwing a vulgar gesture to the screen as he did so. "Come on, Knight. Indulge me! Tell me all about her—you must be dying to tell someone."

Actually…he did want to tell someone about her. But it certainly wasn't his sleazy boss who knew nothing of real companionship. Desmond would use anything he said about Jessica against him, and he was not about to allow him a slither of that satisfaction. A small part of him wanted to keep her all to himself.

"Not right now, boss. Use your imagination, I'm busy."

"Wait, wait, wait! Don't hang up on me," Desmond commanded—almost begging. "I do need to speak with you. If you won't tell me about her, tell me about the mission."

"I'm on top of it, boss. All on schedule, lots to do."

And that was that. Silas pulled the phone away from his ear, about to end the call, when he heard the three questions that sent a shiver down his spine.

"Why, whatcha doin'? What's so special about that café, anyway?" Desmond's voice darkened for the final question, "And where *is* your waitress?"

A static sound followed, and the phone screen faded to black. Silas leered out the large bay window next to him, scanning for any sign of the worker Desmond was using to tail him.

But the final line replayed in Silas's head over again—where was Maria? She'd greeted him at the door without fail for all the years he'd known her, no matter the time, date, weather.

He glanced around the café. Something wasn't right.

The main lights were shut off—only the battery-powered candles on each table were casting a cheap glow over the room. The coffee pot was still on the warmer—empty—old coffee grounds smouldering on the bottom of the glass pitcher.

Maria never left her coffee pot empty.

Silas rose slowly. His ankle sang in response to the weight as he shifted across to the counter.

"Mar?" he called towards the back room. "Maria, it's me. Can you come out please?"

The only reply was a loud thudding sound and scraping shoes. Silas didn't take the time to second guess himself as he stormed around the counter and through the beaded curtain covering the kitchen entrance. His eyes widened and locked onto the two targets hovering over

Maria's unconscious body. Blood dripped onto the freshly mopped tiles from a thick gash on her forehead.

Silas stood silently, glancing from one man to the other, surveying the situation.

They had no visible weapons. Their faces were smothered in thick balaclavas and they wore all black, but there were no hidden surprises. Shame. Silas would've enjoyed using their own weapons against them.

The three men stared at each other, Silas blocking the only exit as he drank in the horror before him. One of the strangers—brazen and stupid—cleared his throat and sneered, "We were just getting to the good part. Want to join in, mate?"

Silas smirked grimly and cracked his knuckles. That was all he needed to hear to get to work.

☆☆☆

After the two miscreants had been dealt with, Silas left them in a pile on the tiled floor and carried Maria straight out of the café to his apartment, before driving her to the hospital. His ankle was a numb afterthought, barely catching his attention as adrenaline took over and his actions seized his mind, replaying over and over and over.

He spent the rest of the night and early morning in the hospital with her, waiting for test results while Maria recounted her story to the police.

She'd woken up not long into the drive, screaming and convulsing as Silas tried to calm her down from the driver's seat.

"Silas," she gasped as the sky cleared enough for the moonlight to unveil his stony face. "What—what happened?"

He told her. He told her every sordid detail, what he'd done to her attackers, and what she'd need to tell the police. She'd sobbed for the rest of the drive, half from the crushing terror and half from her gratitude that he'd been there at the right time.

Silas left out the part about him being almost completely certain that his boss was to blame for the intruders.

"I was conscious the entire time, officers," Maria whispered their rehearsed story to the two policewomen who'd come to interview her. Silas sat by the window of the private room, watching the stars twinkle out against the dusky blue sky. He hadn't missed the stern look one of the officers kept throwing his way, though. "One of them hit me over the head with something hard—I think it must've been metal. I fell to the ground, and that's when Silas found us. They bolted straight past him and out of the door. They wore these big black masks; I didn't see any faces."

"And what about you?" The first officer lifted her chin to Silas.

He shook his head. "No, I didn't see them either."

"What were you doing at the café?"

He glanced between the three women all staring at him. "I was getting a coffee…I twisted my ankle last night and was hoping Maria could fix me an ice pack. Turns out it's lucky I was there."

The policewomen looked at each other, then back to Maria. Silas shook his head slightly but bit his tongue. He was in no position to demand the higher ground right now. Not after—not after what he'd done to the attackers.

"Do you have security cameras at the café?" one of the officers asked Maria. She nodded. "Good, then we'll swing by in a couple of days, when you're feeling better, and take a look. The men might have been foolish enough to put their masks on only after they'd been caught on camera."

Maria breathed out a little laugh, and the officer squeezed her hand. After a few farewells—none directed to Silas—they were gone, leaving him alone with Maria. He walked over to the bed and perched on the edge, pushing her matted hair back from her freshly stitched forehead. The blood had dyed patches of it pink.

"I'm so sorry, Mar."

She gave him a tight smile that didn't meet her eyes. "Thank you, for *everything* you did."

He curled an arm around her shoulders and offered a gentle squeeze. She relaxed into him. Still he held her, moving them both in a gentle sway, until the doctors came to confirm she could go home.

They drove back to the café in silence—Maria wanted to drive her own car home—an unspoken truth settling between them. Silas led the way into the café through the still unlocked front door, hand in hand with the brave owner. He looked back at her and asked, "You ready?"

Her pursed lips quivered, but she nodded anyway. Good, because Silas wasn't sure if *he* was ready to face what was waiting for them behind that beaded curtain.

It never got easier, seeing what Desmond made him capable of.

But he pushed on, weaving around the counter and into the kitchen to see…nothing.

No bodies. No blood. No trace of what had happened six hours ago in this spotless kitchen.

Maria gasped, "What…happened?"

But Silas knew. Even before he spotted the folded note on the side counter, he knew it reeked of Desmond Rose. To be the hero by forcing Silas into the role of villain.

The note read,

> *You're welcome. I'll see you in the office Monday morning. Otherwise, the footage I've borrowed might end up in the wrong hands. - D*

Silas ripped the paper into ribbons before screwing it all up into a tiny ball, shoving it into his pocket. He rubbed a hand down his face and turned to Maria, who was slowly making her way around the edge of the room, clutching the counter as she did so. "Ready to go, Mar?"

She looked back at him, as if just remembering he was still there, and nodded. Her face was gaunt, lifeless. "Yes," she stammered.

They walked out of the Twinkling Bliss together, still holding each other's hand. The milky sunrise softened everything it touched, washing away the darkness of the night. He didn't let go until she was safely locked in her car, driving home to get some much-needed sleep and see her sister at their shared apartment.

It wasn't until Silas slid back into his own car that he allowed himself to take some of his own raw emotions out on the steering wheel. A slam for Desmond forcing him into such a position. A punch for the disgusting men hired by his boss. Another blow for the raging pain flaring in his ankle. And a blare of the horn, because he was exhausted and in an extra crappy mood.

He stared at his mottled knuckles for a moment, each bloom a reminder of the faces he'd never forget, before driving home.

Exhaustion hit Silas like a punch in the gut as soon as he reached his apartment, the emerging sun chasing him up the stairs and into the comforting confines of his bedroom. He was powerless to do anything but crash into bed and sleep, sleep, sleep.

CHAPTER TEN

✦

After waking up to the sun long gone and a nightmare-fuelled haze clouding his thoughts, Silas stumbled into the living room to look for clues as to which day he'd woken up in.

Jessica had messaged him a few times throughout the day, completely unaware of what had happened since their departure last night. What he'd *done*.

Bea stood in the kitchen, tapping her fingers on the counter as she waited for the kettle to boil. A tiny smile spread across her face in a way of greeting, but Silas was in no mood to return the sentiment.

"You're working late," he said as he limped over to the raggedy chair and tentatively fell into the cushion. Allowing his head to fall back onto the backrest, the pain in his leg reawakened, begging for attention.

No response came from the nurse in the kitchen. He dropped his head to look at her. His eyes flickered to the wall clock—past midnight. She *was* working late. *Really* late.

"Everything okay?" he asked, noncommittal.

Again, only silence followed.

Strange. Bea was one of the friendlier nurses that visited his ma. The first time he'd met her, they'd had a twenty-minute conversation about rare books. From then on, he might've even considered them friendly.

Perhaps on any other day, he'd ask her what was wrong. But today he was perfectly content with her quietness, fresh memories taunting him silently.

That was, until a nagging thought appeared—she'd never stayed past 12 am before. *So why tonight?*

His pondering of her work hours was only interrupted by the pounding pain spearing through his entire body. Vibrant colours danced along the darkness of his eyelids, spinning and colliding together to make a muddy rainbow mess. The whorls expanded and contracted with every throb.

"Hey, Bea?" he gasped, and she turned slowly. "Would you be able to bring me some aspirin? I've sprained my damned ankle."

Within half an hour Silas was starting to feel the faint effects of the painkiller. It was merely touching the sides of the swirling kaleidoscope of agony, but the stool and ice pack Bea had made him were soothing the ache much better.

He thanked the nurse before she moved silently into Ma's bedroom with a pot of tea and a plate of biscuits.

While he attempted to gather any trace of energy he had left to drag his useless body back to his bedroom, another thought dawned on him. Bea was a specialist nurse that only came to the apartment under specific orders from Dr York and the hospital. Ma hadn't needed Bea's attention in months—and yet this was her second visit this week.

How had Silas not pieced this together earlier?

Suddenly fuelled with all the energy in the world, Silas limped towards Ma's door and knocked lightly. Bea slipped out a moment later, closing it silently behind her.

"Bea."

"Silas."

Bea's voice was dainty and small, laced with a slight accent from her Italian roots. Her sandy blonde hair—almost identical to his—was tucked up in its neat ponytail. Her eyes were so blue and clear that they looked as though they could reach for miles. They were kind, gentle, patient. On other occasions, Silas had found peace within them. But today, his patience was beyond the point of wearing thin.

He stared at her, waiting.

She nodded at the silent command, dipping her head as she took a steadying breath. When she looked back up at him, he noted her expression. She looked tired, but not physically. Mentally and emotionally drained. As a quiet woman, her eyes often spoke enough for her. But today they were louder than ever.

"Silas—"

"Why are you here, Bea?" he interrupted, unable to take another second of waiting. His voice had been reduced to a pleading whisper. "What's wrong?"

Bea's gaze flitted around him, landing on anything but his own eyes. He'd been around enough doctors to know that they all had the same body language when something as sinister as death was on the cards. He was just about to repeat the question when the nurse squared her shoulders. "The tests came back this morning. I'm sorry Silas, but they're not good."

It took him a moment to remember what tests she was talking about. Just the other week Dr York had told him the sarcoma removal was still looking successful and that there was no sign of its return. But—the angiosarcoma was only a symptom of the inoperable brain tumour that had landed Ma in the hospital initially.

Silas felt his face fall, a high wall slamming shut to hide any feeling he felt from the outside world. "Please. I need to hear you say it," he said with a ferocious quiet. Emotion boiled beneath his skin.

"The tumour in your mother's brain has stopped responding to treatment—it looks like it's been resisting for quite some time now—and it's making its way through your mother's blood vessels. It's spread all over her body, Silas. There is nothing more we can do."

Bea continued to spit out medical jargon about cancers and growths, and how rare this type of cancer was, but his eyes had glazed over, hardly hearing anything she was saying.

"So how long do we have left? Before it gets her?" he interrupted.

Bea stumbled on her words and shifted from one foot to the other. "Dr York will have more information for you, Silas. I've already said too much." She didn't look up from her shoes.

On any other day, Silas would have argued back for answers. But today, he only nodded. With the splintering pain of his ankle only spurring him on, he turned on the spot, grabbed his keys, and set off into the dark night.

☆☆☆

Silas swung his car into the nearest space outside of the Heartstone Clinic Hospital, not bothering to stop for a ticket. He barely even waited for the sliding doors to part before barrelling through them. His mind wasn't with him—it was far too busy reeling off questions and arguments he'd prepared on the drive over. His head only managed to snap back into reality once he'd reached the office door he'd become so familiar with.

He didn't bother to rethink what he was doing and where he was before loudly crashing his fist into the solid wood.

Silas waited, pacing back and forth with his fists and jaw clenched. There was no answer, so Silas knocked again—louder this time, the door reverberating the bangs back to him.

The golden plaque screwed onto the door read *Dr Marlow York* in proud lettering, and all Silas could think of was ripping it right off its mount and jamming the sharp metal corner into the side of Marlow's neck. The vivid image was still playing out in his head when the door opened a crack and the doctor's tired eyes appeared in the opening.

"I'm sorry, it's after office hours—" Dr York started, before realising who was behind the knocking. His shoulders straightened as he stepped back, opening it further. "Mr Knight, come in."

Silas pushed his way past the doctor into the lavish office. There were frames lining the walls of all his accomplishments, tall plants in the corners, and an expensive computer sitting on a carved oak desk. It smelled like disinfectant and pine forests. The chair behind the desk was brown leather, probably selling for more than a month's rent on Silas's apartment.

Dr York walked tentatively around the desk, noticeably giving Silas a wide berth, and pulled his white coat around him as he sat. His top buttons were undone on his shirt, but a stethoscope still hung around his neck limply.

"Please sit."

Silas looked towards the armchair the doctor gestured at. Two options flashed before him—he could smash up his entire office and snap the bifocal frames right off the doctor's nose, or he could sit down and talk through the situation amicably.

Silas certainly knew which choice he'd prefer.

But Ma's love of Dr York kept him from doing anything he'd regret. He took a deep breath before sitting in the plush armchair, wringing his hands.

"I think I can guess why you're here," Dr York said as he pulled a thick file from the top drawer of his desk. Silas didn't say anything as the doctor opened it to display numerous images of black and white scans. There were pages of scribbles between each image, like York had been studying Ma's illness for quite some time now. "I was actually just working late to finish off these new notes."

"You got quite a stack there," Silas nudged his chin towards the open file. "How long have you known?" His voice was rough and assertive, yet there was a distinct whisper of desperation entwined within the syllables.

Dr York remained silent, not taking the bait as he laid the scans on the desk. Silas didn't look—he couldn't read the damned things anyway.

"I don't understand these pictures and drawings, Doc. I'm not in the mood for a game. You're supposed to tell me what's happening. You're *supposed* to be saving my ma—that's what I pay you for, isn't it?"

Again, the doctor didn't bite. Instead, he held up one of the images. "This scan was done a couple of weeks ago, when Dianne was last in. We checked her with a full-body scan and found the cancerous cells almost straight away."

York pointed a long finger onto the scan, circling groups of small white dots littered over the arms and chest. The dots became more concentrated in certain places—bunches on one shoulder, across the left of the chest, and just below the ribcage.

"We saw that the cancer had spread throughout the cells right across her chest." Another image was held up, this time of a brain. The same white dots infested the page, like someone had taken a paintbrush and flicked the bristles toward the paper recklessly. "That was when we discovered that the tumour had stopped responding to treatment."

Silas chewed the skin of his thumb. He didn't stop when a coppery tang invaded his tongue.

The doctor continued, but he couldn't keep up. Silas gripped his head in his hands, trying to hold all of the questions whirring within steady enough so that he could focus on which to ask first.

He finally landed on, "What happens now, then?" The silence was answer enough, but his desperation pushed on. "Doc, what's the plan?"

Dr York cleared his throat and sat straighter in his chair, straightening his spine and running a hand through his dishevelled grey hair. "Mr Knight, I'm deeply sorry for this news. I'm afraid that there is nothing more that we can do for your mother." Silas clenched his jaw. "I've already called around to the rest of the hospitals in the area and they have all agreed with my consensus. Metastatic cancer is incurable, your mothers' is too widespread, any efforts at removal would prove futile and painful for Dianne."

"What about therapies?"

Another too-long pause lingered between them.

"We could begin the therapy plan that Dianne was on before, yes. But," Dr York looked down and pushed the metal frames back up his nose. "Please understand that this was your mother's decision, and she declined the treatment."

Silas let out a quick sneer before he could stop himself. The doctor rose from his expensive chair and started towards the door, not-so-subtly hinting that he was no longer welcome.

"Doc, she isn't in her right mind!" Silas made no effort to leave. "Why did no one tell me about this?" he demanded desperately.

"I'm sorry, Mr Knight. Dianne has made her decision, and I'm not at liberty to tell you any more. She chose to keep it from you for a reason."

"I'm her *son*."

Silas had to clench his hands together to avoid punching every single framed certification right off of the wall, one by one.

Dr York said no more before opening the door, half-angling his body behind it.

Silas still didn't move, trying to calm his thoughts, biting the inside of his cheek and looking around the office wildly. Oh, the havoc he could wreak in this stuck-up place.

But he wouldn't.

Silas wasn't his boss, he wasn't a violent man at heart, and he knew that the cowering doctor wasn't to blame—even if he did look like a spineless fool hiding behind the door.

"Fine. Just answer me this. How long do we have left?" He winced at the bitter taste of the words.

The silence was agonising.

"Weeks; a few months." The doctor cleared his throat. "Six months at most, Silas. I am truly sorry."

He nodded, but he'd heard enough.

Back out in the poorly air-conditioned hospital hallway, Silas felt the whoosh of the door firmly close behind him. It took everything left in him not to fall to the ground and weep.

☆☆☆

A tight pain in the lower side of his face pulsed as Silas finally walked towards his car. Trying to relax his jaw and unclench his teeth away from each other felt like trying to pry open a clam to unveil a shining pearl within. But when his face did begin to relax, there was no reward waiting. Just shooting pains whizzing down his teeth into his skull.

He reached his car, snatched the half-written ticket right out of the traffic officer's hand, and slid behind the steering wheel.

Silas started the engine and unlocked the handbrake. After backing out of his precarious parking position, he pressed his foot onto the acceleration pedal. But before he could speed off back home, his damaged ankle gave way. The car responded by rolling one foot forward in a mighty lurch. The motion slammed the back of his head onto the headrest, sending snakes of pain slithering down his neck and spine.

The traffic officer backed away slowly, desperately looking for another driver to punish.

In an almighty moment of weakness, Silas roared loudly, releasing a beast of pure rage. He didn't stop, even when his voice cracked and sputtered. His throat was dry and irritated at the break, but he wailed again without a care in the world to who heard him.

The calm that came after the screaming was accompanied by an almost deafening silence. Silas sat in the quiet for mere seconds before he couldn't take it anymore.

And before he knew it, he'd jumped the car back into action and was running away from the hospital as fast as he could.

CHAPTER ELEVEN

✦

I'm outside. Do you have a moment to talk?

Silas sent the text without giving himself time to rethink his questionable decision to drive to Jessica's house at two in the morning. She'd made it clear she didn't want him seen near the manor, and yet here he was. Sitting in his car right outside her home, with all the lights turned off and his seat reclined back as far as he could get it in a bid to remain hidden. He'd even turned down the brightness on his phone.

The morning was still starry, but the manor was alight with frenzy. Every room was awake, and a subtle hum of classical music drifted on the wind around him.

He waited, waited, waited.

As the long minutes ticked by, desperate for something to take his mind off what Dr York had declared, Silas unlocked his phone and called the only person who'd give him that at such an early hour.

"Silas Knight, what a nice surprise," the voice crooned through the phone, full of vigour despite the time.

"Artie," Silas sighed. "I need you to tell me what you know about the Mortons." Arthur Avila was Desmond's personal hacker, and one of the best in the country. He could find information on people within seconds.

"Nope, not a fan of that nickname. And are you talking about Richard Morton?"

"The one and only," Silas confirmed with a flat voice.

"I'm glad you called me in such a good mood," Artie drawled and Silas rolled his eyes. Artie made being a sarcastic piece of shit his entire personality. "But you're in luck. Dirty D has had me in Morton's business more times than I can count now. Something shady's going on in that manor of theirs, but I can't find it. Rich likes to keep his correspondence offline, it seems." The faint sound of clicking came from Arthur's end of the call. "Which, obviously, is a huge problem for me."

"Were you the one who tipped Desmond off about the offshore accounts?" Silas asked.

"Finally, I'm recognised for my brilliance. Yes, that was me," Artie confirmed. Silas wanted to laugh for not piecing it together sooner.

"What do you know about his investors? He seems to throw these big functions for them every week—why?"

"Not much more than they seem to be for networking purposes. Richard Morton is worshipped at them, like some sort of cult meeting. But I do know that the parties go on for hours, and from what I've seen through the cameras, the investors certainly enjoy using Richard's daughter as entertainment."

Silas's blood ran cold at that. "What do you mean?" he pushed. If Artie knew something that Jessica hadn't told him, he needed to know.

"Well, from what I can tell, Richard and his wife schmooze the investors, and the daughter follows them around in tight dresses to give the guests something to look at. Some even dare to cop a feel, too."

"What does Richard do about it?" Silas asked, in case there was something Jessica didn't know. If her father had even a single scrap of humanity left.

"Some say Richard endorses it," Artie said, still typing away. "Yep—a quick look here at the email chains between investors confirm that the daughter is some sort of enticement; a reason why a lot of the older men show up. It'd be impossible for Rich not to know what was happening at his own parties, I'd say."

Silas's blood boiled beneath his skin. "Thanks, Artie."

"Don't call me that," the hacker repeated. "Why are you so interested, any—"

Silas ended the call. Arthur hadn't told him anything Jessica hadn't already, but hearing it from a third party made his temper flare.

The party continued in front of him, and Silas tried not to consider what Jessica was having to endure as he sat there, useless.

With his mind now reeling between his ma's condition and Jessica's treatment from her family, Silas fixed his chair position to drive home. What a stupid idea coming here had been. Jessica wanted him nowhere near her house, and who could blame her?

He was a horrible excuse of a human, forcing his mother to go through a fight she could never win, then beating and cheating people out of their money to pay for the pleasure.

And to sit here, right in front of Jessica's house, unable to save her from what might've been going on inside. Because barging into an investor's function to kill the host might attract some negative attention, possibly leading to Desmond. And that was like signing his own death sentence.

Silas was powerless—to his mother's illness, to Jessica's exploitation. He was failing both of them.

In that moment, Silas had never loathed anyone more than himself. He was no better than his boss or Richard Morton.

He was about to kick the engine into life when the door flew open, Jessica sliding into the passenger seat next to him.

She wore a tight silver silk dress that glimmered in the starlight and an exhilarated grin on her face. Her eyes were wide and she was breathless, but her joy faded as soon as she looked into his eyes.

"Silas, are you okay?"

And then it hit him—why he'd driven here in the first place. The news about this mother, the cancer, the weeks or months she had left.

Despite himself, he took a moment of silence to appreciate her—a flicker of happiness in his darkened world. How her dress flowed across her curves perfectly. How her hair was tamed with golden pins, flashing against the pure darkness of her hair. How her face was effortlessly beautiful, charming, and empathetic all at once—albeit now tainted with worry.

How she was dressed for a party, and yet she was sitting outside with him, choosing him.

He grazed his fingers over the thin silver strap of her dress before leaning down to press a kiss against her warm shoulder. He remained there, bowing to her, as a tear slipped free. She must have felt it, as she wrapped her free arm around him in a gentle embrace. And in her arms, the scent of brown sugar and flowers surrounding him, he allowed every single bottled-up emotion within him to come spilling out.

The tears wouldn't stop. She gripped him tighter, keeping him close as he convulsed with thick sobs. He didn't know how long he stayed there, but when his eyes finally dried and he found enough courage to lift his head, her shoulder was glistening. He pulled away gently, feeling utterly empty.

And only when he was sure he wouldn't collapse into his emotions again, did he tell her everything.

"That's how I ended up here. I'm sorry, I know you can't have me anywhere near the manor. I just needed to see a friendly face," he said. She stroked his damp hair away from his face idly, never looking away from him for a moment. "I won't keep you, though. Thank you for this, but you should get back to your party or whatever's happening inside. I'll be fine, truly."

Her eyebrows knitted together. "And where will you go now?"

Silas let out a humourless laugh. "No idea. Not home, but around. Driving helps clear my head, so…" He nodded, lips a thin line. He didn't know where he would go, but he couldn't face Ma or Bea yet, and he was already becoming embarrassed about pulling Jessica away from her function to blubber on her shoulder.

"Honey, will you stay with me tonight? The party is almost finished, and the investors are far too drunk. Honestly, I'm glad to be away from it. Let me take you inside. There's a back entrance we can sneak into."

The investors. A primal instinct reared its head then, readying him to rip into anyone he saw inside.

Silas didn't particularly feel like sleeping, or talking, or anything. But the thought of sending Jessica back into the manor alone, to those *guests*—it wasn't an option. Not when she'd bravely invited him in. He nodded, and she squeezed his hand.

She directed him to a parking spot down the next street and they walked hand in hand around to the back of the manor. She must've sensed the tension rippling off him as they got closer to the door, as she said quietly, "Don't *kill* any of them, they're not worth it."

Her smile told him she was joking, but he wouldn't make any promises.

The white panelling shone brightly against the dark dusk of the night, and the illuminated windows we proud spotlights displaying the pristine garden. High-pruned hedges and water fountains shot up towards the sky. The chimneys pumped out silver smoke and musical notes swept around them.

As they neared the back door, Jessica became rigid and slow, silencing her steps as they crept up the stairs. Silas copied her every move, wondering what it must be like to be trapped and alone here, living this life with such joy and compassion left in her heart.

He wouldn't be strong enough to do it, that's for sure.

But she kept on, firmly in the belief that she would escape this prison one day to live the life she truly wanted. And deserved. Silas couldn't help but marvel at her.

Jessica led him through the tall glass doors, entering a lavish kitchen made of solid stone and marble. The diamond chandelier twinkled above them, but he didn't have much time to admire it as she yanked his arm across the tiled floor.

"Just a moment, Edmund. I'll see where she has got to!" A low voice chuckled down one of the hallways, getting closer.

Silas didn't have time to match a face to the voice, though, as Jessica had already pulled him through another hallway in the opposite direction. His ankle splintered with every step, but she held him up as they wound deeper into the manor. The walls caressed the sky, covered in deep magenta wallpaper with gothic whorls curling over it. Golden carved frames lined them, each housing a unique piece of artwork. Sconces filled the empty space between the frames, casting a sombre glow across everything.

When they finally reached the right door, Jessica let him go to unlock it. So much light flooded into the dim hallway from her room that he had to squint to allow his eyes time to adjust.

She locked the door again behind them. "A small mercy," she smirked, holding the key up to him before placing it on a hook beside the door. "Please, make yourself comfortable."

The bedroom was more like a suite, with two adjoining rooms and floor-to-ceiling windows along one wall. In the centre of the room stood a king-size bed, stacked high with pillows and crisp linens.

Suddenly, his body felt annihilated. His ankle hurt. His head pounded. His heart lay shattered at his feet.

So he limped over to the bed, perching carefully on the edge. The fluffy duvet swallowed him whole, billowing around him as he sank deeper into it. Jessica snickered before disappearing into one of her other rooms.

He took the time to take in the bedroom around him. A vanity and pink plush chair sat on the far side, with stacks of books covering the desk. Vases of flowers littered any free surface, with blooms of all colours shining against the cream walls. Artwork of paint, charcoal, and pen filled the empty space, stuck up messily with tape. And in the corner lay an easel with a large canvas on it. The piece wasn't finished, but he could make out what it was.

A painting of him, holding a bunch of sunflowers and roses. Just like he had done at the market, the day they'd met.

Even from the bed, Silas could see the effort that had been poured onto the canvas. His hair grazed his shoulders, moving slightly on a phantom wind. The tip of his nose was flushed pink, and the green in his eyes was freshly cut grass. An idyllic version of himself—a hoax.

"Oh god. You weren't supposed to see that!" Jessica squealed, following his gaze from the doorway. She hurriedly dropped the tray she was now holding onto the chest of drawers and turned the canvas around. He smirked at her rose-stained cheeks.

"Why? It's brilliant. You really captured my beauty," he said dryly. She shot him a glare that made him zip his lip.

"No one ever sees my art. I make it for me—it's one of the only things I'm allowed to do for myself within these walls. So, when the subject of one of my paintings sees it *unfinished*, it's more than a little embarrassing," she said as she retrieved the tray and placed it on the fluffy rug beneath his feet, kneeling beside him. "To say the least."

"Okay, I'm sorry." He hooked her chin with his finger and lifted it to meet her eyes. "But I wasn't joking. It is brilliant."

An appreciative smile graced her lips before she looked down again, taking his ankle in her palms. She tentatively guided him so his leg now lay on the bed, placing a towel beneath it. Then, an icepack on top of the thrumming joint. Silas fought this urge to moan at the stinging relief.

"Do you want anything? Food, a drink?" Jessica asked, lightly stroking up and down his shin. He shook his head. "Then sleep it is. I won't be a minute," she added, turning back towards the archway she's just come from.

When she returned, she wore a silky, shimmering nightgown. Her hair lay free and all makeup had been wiped from her face. She looked radiant. Asteria herself.

"You're killing me," Silas groaned. She snickered, turning off the lights before sliding into the bed next to him. She rearranged the covers so they were both ensconced in feathers, only his iced ankle left out. She turned towards him, nestling into the crook of his arm as he planted a kiss on top of her curls.

"Won't they be expecting you back at the party?" he asked into the darkness, the faint hint of music and chatter still reaching every corner of the house.

"Please, they're all too drunk to notice. My mother is probably the only one looking," she whispered, tone full of resentment. "Besides, they've had me all night. Now I only want you."

He felt her smile stretch across his skin, and despite himself, he smiled too. Her hand dragged across his unshaven cheek as she turned him to face her, leaning up into a firm kiss.

Silas had shown more emotion that night than ever before in his life, and his entire being felt empty. Lost. What was left? What would *be* left once his mother lost the war?

Nothing made sense.

And why was he *here*?

In that moment, outside the hospital, Jessica was the only person Silas wanted to see. But their relationship—it wasn't real. At least, not to Silas. This was his mission. He'd been tasked with making her fall in love with him. No feelings from his side were required. So why, in his darkest moment, had Jessica's face been the only one he could bear to see?

Nothing made sense.

All he knew was that he was lying with Jessica, surrounded by her light and warmth, his heart daring to glimmer with an emotion other than despair. So they fell asleep in a tight embrace, neither willing to let the other go, as the party down the hall continued until dawn.

CHAPTER TWELVE

✦

Flecks of sunlight floated across Silas's face, shimmering in through the tall windows next to Jessica's side of the bed. She had the perfect view of an outdoor pool, which was reflecting broken shards of the morning light through the thin linen curtains.

He groaned, wincing as he dared move his injured ankle. The ice pack from last night slouched onto the mattress with a grim squelch. A tentative circle was all he could manage until the pain burst like a beast awakening from hibernation. No miraculous healing, then.

Rouge curls tickled his nose. He stroked them away, eliciting a tiny murmur from the still-asleep woman beside him. He considered sneaking away, checking out her room a little more or stealing another glance at his portrait.

But Jessica looked so peaceful curled up into his bicep, mouth parted, eyelids flitting ever so slightly. His face relaxed into a smile as he traced a line down the side of her cheek with his thumb. She looked so gentle, so serene—and dammit, he wanted to share some of those feelings before being thrown back out into the real world.

She didn't stir at his touch, so Silas snuggled deeper into the feathers beside her, content with the safe warmth of their shared body heat.

☆☆☆

Impudent knocking on the solid wood door had both Silas and Jessica startling right out of bed. Blinking himself back into reality, Silas barely had time to process what was happening before he was shooed into Jessica's ensuite.

"I'm sorry!" was all she whispered before the door clicked shut and he was plunged into darkness. His ankle throbbed, so he perched on the edge of a large, cool tub. The room smelled like roses, strawberries, and humidity. Still, there were worse places to hide out. He leaned closer to the door to hear what was happening in the main bedroom.

"We missed you last night, where did you sneak off to?" A woman's voice, nasal and wicked, asked. Footsteps sounded on the hardwood floor, moving closer and further away, over and over.

"I had a headache, so I came up here to rest," Jessica answered, her voice rough from their lazy slumber. "I'm sure I didn't miss that much, mother."

"The investors were asking after you." It sounded like Jessica's mother was rustling something. "Your father isn't happy."

Silas bit back a snarl.

"What are you doing?" Jessica asked, a touch frantic.

"Nigel reported that he saw you enter through the back door last night with a young man. Is that true?" Doors banged open and shut.

"Nigel ought to mind his own business," Jessica retorted, defiance kicking in. Silas wondered whether now would be a good time to introduce himself.

"Where is he, Jessica?" her mother huffed.

"He left early. I'm surprised Nigel didn't tell you himself. I snuck him back out the same way we came in."

Not a good time to introduce himself, then. Silas readjusted on his slippery porcelain perch. His eyes were thankfully beginning to adjust to the darkness.

"Right. I'll let your father know, and he can decide what to do with you." Threatening her with discipline like a child. He fought the urge to burst through the door and defend her. But a small slam of the bedroom door told him he'd missed his chance.

A slither of light widened before him, exposing a grimacing Jessica still in her delicate lacy pyjamas. He returned an exaggerated awkward expression, and she burst out laughing.

"Remind me to punch Nigel the next time I see him," Silas sighed, limping over to her and hooking an arm around her neck, pulling her in for a quick squeeze. "It can't be that bad, right?"

"Oh yeah, totally fine," Jessica nodded into his chest. "Absolutely nothing could go wrong from my father finding out about you."

"What's the worst he could do?" They both looked at each other, eyebrows raised.

Her tone grew a fraction darker as she said, "He's not a nice man, Silas."

"Neither am I."

She hummed a soft laugh at that, pushing away from his chest and picking his shoes up from beside the bed. "I don't believe that. Come on, we'd better get you out of here before he starts trying to break my lock."

Luckily, one of Jessica's windows doubled as a door to the gardens. She told him which direction to head in to find a dip in the iron gates that he could slip through back onto the street. A much dirtier way of getting into the manor, and one that would've certainly ripped her thin dress last night, but one perfect for his quick escape this morning.

He whispered, "Thank you for last night," onto her lips as he grazed them, and she gave his hand one last reassuring squeeze before he left.

☆☆☆

Silas drove home slowly, silently dreading what he would find when he opened the door. Ma wouldn't be surprised that he'd spent the night away from his own bed, but she might have something to say about his outburst at Dr York's office. Someone would've surely told her by now. She was friends with everyone who'd ever stepped foot in that hospital.

Last night had been a welcomed distraction to the mess awaiting him at home, but he'd run out of time to escape it.

He had a mission to complete for his boss, and his mother's health was about to flatline. Silas needed to get his head in the game before it was too late.

Parked in his usual spot, he checked his phone desperately for any reason not to go inside. Just one text from Jessica graced the home screen.

Anytime you need me, I'm here. And thank you for last night, too.

A flutter danced within his chest. He didn't even recognise himself anymore.

Climbing the stairs, Silas stopped again briefly before his front door. He exhaled a deep breath and pushed through it, ripping off the band-aid. His eyes fell on Bea first, pouring a stream of tea into Ma's ceramic teacup. She smiled at him, but her face was full of unwanted pity. He ignored them both as he walked straight into his bedroom and closed the door—firmly but carefully, so as not to startle Ma.

Silas didn't know exactly why he'd walked straight past them and locked himself away, but he regretted it instantly. It felt childish. He paced his room in three short strides, back and forth, gearing himself up. But as he opened the door, he was greeted by Bea's hung head that jumped a little as the door swung away from her.

"Silas…" Her tone was poison to his ears. "Come and see your mother."

Anger laced with resentment bubbled in his stomach and threateningly crept up the walls of his insides. He forced it back down violently. Bea had betrayed him by keeping his mother's condition secret. The small, sane part of his brain knew it wasn't her fault, and urged him to apologise to her.

But at that moment, it certainly *felt* like betrayal.

So he pushed straight past the nurse blocking his doorway and walked up to his mother, kneeling in front of her. She still had her teacup and saucer on her lap, but her hands were shaking so much that the delicate porcelain clattered together. He took the cup from her fingers and placed it on the table behind him. Replacing the teacup with his hands, he looked into her eyes and forced himself to smile at her.

Silas hadn't realised it until he was right in front of her, but he hadn't truly looked at his mother in a long while. Now that he was, he wished he could wipe the memory from his brain as it was being created.

She looked sad, defeated. Like she was more than ready to leave behind the pain she'd been pushing through for so long.

How had he been so blind, missing what was right in front of him these past weeks—months? His ma had been keeping this secret from him for so long. Why couldn't she have just *told* him?

Silas had been so busy trying to help her live that he'd done the complete opposite. He'd helped the cancer speed up its process.

He couldn't bear the guilt. He closed his eyes tightly, wanting—*needing*—to see anything else but her pain-etched face. It was no use. What he'd done had taken root in his brain and would never let him forget this moment.

What he had forced upon her.

He had been fooling himself this entire time, only seeing what he wanted to see—the young woman who had raised him and played with him for hours, even when she had a million things to do and not one ounce of help. Now, as Silas opened his eyes once more, he could see what the years and disease had really done to his sweet mother.

"I'm sorry, Ma," he whispered as a tear escaped him. She wiped it away and pulled him towards her with stiff hands, kissing his forehead. She slipped his head down onto her chest and held it there until he lost control. Thick, stifling sobs threatened to choke all the air from his lungs.

"It was my decision, Silas. You have nothing to be sorry for." Her raspy voice was still warm, still so soothing.

"I forced you into all of those treatments—"

"No, you didn't," she said with absolute certainty. "I would've tried anything the doctors offered me to spare you from this pain, from this grief. You might've pushed the doctors too hard, Silas, but I was always right there behind you, agreeing with you. It wasn't until Dr York told me that any future treatments would be futile that I finally accepted it."

"Why didn't you tell me?"

A small stroke down the side of his face. "I didn't want you feeling this way. I wanted to give you as much time as I could to stay believing in the treatments. And don't be mad at Bea—she only found out yesterday."

Silas glanced up at Bea, who was waiting across the room, and she gave him a little nod in confirmation.

"Then I'm sorry to you, too."

She nodded again, wiping her own eyes on a hankie pulled from her nurse's tunic.

Silas remained lying on his ma's chest as she patted and stroked his hair, weeping into her clothes that smelled so strongly of his forgotten childhood.

A long while passed before he took back control of his head and met her gaze once more. Looking deep into her eyes, Silas could see her unwavering, resolute acceptance to her fate. And in that moment, he knew. He knew he would have to accept her death, just as she already had.

He finally understood that, while he was busy desperately searching for any cure imaginable, she was quietly coming to terms with the end.

A strange feeling swirled around in his chest, but it took him a minute to recognise it as…peace.

"I'm still sorry, Ma," Silas repeated as he willed the burning tears to stop flowing.

Ma stroked the side of his face again. "Hush now," she said. "No one needs to be sorry for the cards we've been dealt. I won't hear another word about apologies."

And that was that. Ma nodded to the television and Silas choked out a laugh before rising from his knees and sitting down next to her. He turned it on to a channel showing a low-budget Christmas film. Before he could change the channel to something more seasonally appropriate, Ma grasped at his hand and lowered the buttons. Silas smiled as she winked at him and sunk deeper into the chair.

"Did you need anything else from me?" Bea interrupted, walking back into the room now that the crying had mainly dissipated. Her own eyes were puffy and moist, but she bore a quiet grin.

"No thank you, Bea," Ma said with a shake of her head before fixing her attention back on the television.

Silas offered to get up and show her out, but she noticed his wince as he put weight onto his ankle and forced him to sit back down, refusing to leave until she'd made him another ice pack. She made a stool out of a pile of old books and propped his foot up, the ice already melting against his flushed skin. She left the apartment with strong advice not to put any weight on it for the next few days, and that it was likely a torn ligament sprain.

Silas wasn't usually one to follow advice, but he made an exception that day. Any excuse to spend the rest of it watching old, cringe-worthy films with his ma.

And that's exactly what they did, her hand carefully tucked under his the entire time.

CHAPTER THIRTEEN

✦

Monday rolled around far too quickly for Silas's liking, and he'd been ignoring Desmond's calls all weekend. Entirely focused on spending time with his ma rather than entertaining his boss's impatient personality, he silenced his phone and went radio silent. Desmond's note had summoned him on Monday, and that's when he'd see his wretched boss again.

So when he woke up to a threatening text from Mr Rose himself, Silas did nothing but roll his eyes.

I swear to god, Silas. If I don't see you in my office by 5 pm today I will kill you—and your precious girl.

Desmond had always been one for dramatic flair, and Silas often ignored it. But the end of that threat…Silas would not ignore the deadline.

He found Bea and Ma already in the living room, so made them two steaming cups of tea and himself a coffee.

Bea had been visiting every day since she'd told Silas the news, but not on orders from the hospital. She came over on her lunch breaks to sit and chat with Ma, sharing stories and giggling like schoolgirls.

Silas put his headphones on when she came around, but he was secretly glad. Glad that Ma had another person to talk to, glad of Bea's unwavering compassion. Glad that he had a few moments to himself where he didn't have to pretend like he had it all together.

They both thanked him for the drink and went back to nattering. He planted a quick kiss on Ma's forehead and winked at Bea before grabbing his keys and heading out the door.

Jessica had called him last night and asked him to meet her at Temisstone Port, a small harbour northward of town.

He arrived early, giving himself enough time to rake his hair back into its usual ponytail and straighten his beige shirt. The linen material swayed across his chest in the wind, allowing the delightful breeze to cool him down as he waited.

Jessica joined him on his weathered bench a few minutes later, bouncing up to him and kissing his cheek before sitting down. She was always full of so much energy, so much positivity. Silas swore he felt lighter whenever she came around.

Jessica was wearing a short white T-shirt and a long, flowing floral skirt. Her hair was twisted up into a clip, silver sunglasses pushing the shorter pieces out of her face.

"Don't you look smart?" she said in way of greeting. "Very handsome indeed."

"I had to make an effort for my favourite lady," he replied, leaning in to steal a proper kiss. "You look gorgeous as ever."

"Why thank you." She pinched the fabric of her thin skirt and threw it into the air, letting it catch on the wind.

She took his hand and pulled it around her, nestling into the crook of his shoulder. They sat there for a while, watching the docked boats gently dip and flow over the quiet water. A group of children sat on the edge with buckets, laughing and shrieking about the crabs they were catching on their reel of fishing line.

The briny air pricked at his nose, but he took a deeper breath anyway. He *craved* stillness like this.

Jessica finally glanced up at him, looking not as relaxed as he felt. "So, I bet you're wondering why I asked you here last night."

"It wasn't just to look at my handsome face?" His tone had turned lazy as he listened to the swaying boats gently knock together, the chirping seagulls flying far above them.

"Well, of course, that too—but I did have something I needed to talk to you about…"

"Spit it out, pretty girl."

She sighed and sat up straighter, turning her entire body towards him. He opened an eye to look at her, the high sun forcing it into a squint immediately. "You know my mother told my father about you spending the night." A statement, not a question. He hummed in agreement, drawing small circles up and down her stiff back. "Unsurprisingly, he was angry—shouting about how I'd embarrassed him, how we could have been caught—blah, blah, blah."

She was flailing, desperately trying to find the right words to tell him whatever she wanted to say. He remained silent, letting her skip, twirl, and jump over the point, until she lost her amazingly intricate train of thought and blurted out, "He wants to meet you. Wants you to come to the function he's hosting Saturday night. I tried to tell him you wouldn't come, but—"

Silas pressed the pad of his thumb to her lips, allowing her a moment to catch her breath. She looked at him thankfully, shoulders slumping slightly.

The chance to attend a famous Richard Morton party. His first reaction was to laugh, to decline straight away. He wanted to, but a small voice stopped him. Desmond's shrill tone saying, "*Infiltrate the manor.*"

He had to admit, it was the perfect way in. No breaking or entering required.

He could keep Jessica happy and appease his boss in one go. How he'd stop Desmond from following through with the second part of the plan, he didn't know yet. But one thing was certain—not a hair on Jessica's perfect head would be violated by Desmond Rose.

"Yes," he replied. "I'll come to your little party."

"You will?" she asked, her breath tickling his thumb. "Really? Because these events, Silas, they're a big deal to him. It's black tie, all the investors are invited, classical music. *Really* boring. Are you sure?"

"How important is it that I meet your father?" he said, cool reassurance lacing each word.

A few moments passed before her voice cracked and she whispered, "Very."

"Then I'm sure." He took her hand and pressed it to his lips. She looked like she might cry as she flung her arms around his neck, squeezing too hard. He groaned, but she didn't loosen her grip. Instead, she squeezed tighter, planting kisses all over his face and neck while murmuring, "Thank you, thank you, thank you."

They spent the rest of their hour together in their private soft serenity. The only time either of them spoke was when Jessica thought of something else to remind him about the party. But she spoke in hushed tones, and he reassured her with idle drawings on her shoulder, only half listening to her advice.

☆☆☆

Jessica's parents had tightened their leash on how much free time they allowed her, so Silas dropped her off too soon, right outside the towering gates, and made his way over to Desmond's shop. As much as he'd have loved nothing more than to go home and collapse on the sofa for the rest of the day, the threat from earlier rang loudly in his ears.

Rule number one—Desmond never delivered empty threats.

His boss was unhinged and unreliable, perfectly proven by what he'd done to Maria. It was almost a certainty that there were at least three hitmen on standby to *deal* with Jessica if he didn't follow the rules.

The shop looked exactly as it did the day he'd first been given his current mission—old, worn, tired. Silas walked confidently through the front entrance and down to the office, rapping his knuckles firmly on the metal door. A hoarse invitation hollered from inside, and thick, bitter smoke billowed from behind the door as he entered.

"Mr Knight!" Desmond crooned. "I'd assumed you were dead! Look here," he continued, gesturing to a pile of crinkled newspapers, "I've been scanning the obituaries and everything."

Desmond looked just as he always did, with his hair slicked back into a greasy ponytail to highlight his receding hairline, and a stained white vest covering his protruding stomach. A bottle of whiskey sat proudly on his desk, along with three empty packets of cigarettes.

Silas sat down in the seat opposite his slimy boss and waited for the reprimands to begin.

"So, Knight," Desmond drawled, stubbing his current smoke out into an overflowing ashtray. "Where've you been, buddy? We've been sinkin' without ya here!"

"I sprained my ankle pretty bad last weekend and had to rest it."

Desmond looked Silas up and down, eyebrows raised, before asking, "And how is it now?"

"Better, Des." Silas nodded. "Still a bit tender, but we're getting there."

"Hmph. And how's the lovely Jessica?"

"How should I know? Just thinking about her makes me want to put a fist through a wall," he sneered, but the words felt sour on his tongue, and he wished he could take them back as soon as they were spoken.

Desmond sat up straighter and hit his whiskey tumbler on the steel desk with so much force the metal cried out with a deep pang of pain. He leaned over the table as much as his belly would allow and looked Silas right in the eyes. "Is that right? Because a little birdy told me that you two had a little sleepover the other night."

The twinkle in his eye made Silas feel physically sick, but he swallowed his retch. He had to look away from Desmond's hungry eyes. "I thought we agreed you'd have your boys stop following me," he said with a lethal quiet.

"And I thought we agreed you'd get me my files."

"I'm working on it, Des."

"I'll take your avoidance as a yes to the sleepover, then!" His boss cackled as he lit up another smoke and blew a large cloud of soot into the air above them. "But Sy, I'm not seeing any progress with the mission—at all. I mean, you were in the house all night, so where are my documents? You were too busy playing happy families to bring me the goods?"

"I have another month."

"So, what? You're going to keep fucking her until the deadline? Take all you can get before she finds out what a piece of shit you are? I mean, have you even considered what she'll think when she finds out that one of her captors is the man she's been screwing for the past two months?"

Desmond's eyes were dancing with glee, but Silas remained stoic. No, he hadn't considered what would happen when they were to move on to the second part of Desmond's plan. Because no one working for this damned fool would be getting near enough to breathe the same air as his Jessica.

"Look, I know I fumbled the bag the other night, but I had some personal shit going on. She's invited me to one of Morton's investor events this weekend, and you'll have your precious proof then."

Desmond leaned over the desk even more, eyes wide. "You sneaky son of a bitch. How the fuck have you managed that? Those parties are some of the most exclusive events in the game, Knight." He stopped blowing smoke rings enough to muse, "Maybe I should start sleeping with that pretty young thing, too."

Anger roiled in Silas's stomach as he snarled, but Desmond just winked. They were both now too aware that his boss had something to hold over him. The smarmy man could get him to do anything he wanted with a simple mention of Jessica's name.

"Well, don't let me down. I'd hate to see Jessica end up in the same position as your pretty waitress friend," Desmond said innocently. Silas paled at the threat. "You don't want to add another two to your hit list, do you Knight?"

Silas wanted to punch the light right out of his boss's eyes at that, splintering his jaw so he could never blow those stupid smoke rings again. "How *dare* you—" he began, leaning over the table to grab his boss. But Desmond pushed his chair back to the far wall, tutting.

"Ah, ah, ah Knight. I wouldn't do that if I were you. Do you have any idea how many men I have waiting for my order right now? How many of our boys would just *love* to take you down?" Desmond's snarl ripped through the small room, attacking him from all angles. "I don't want to lose you, son. That's why I wiped those tapes—"

"After *you* set me up."

"—So I could teach you a lesson. Sy, you may be my best worker, but you're mine. You belong to *me*. If I see you straying, or thinking about abandoning a mission, you're gonna feel the consequences."

"When did I look like I was going to *abandon the mission*? You sent those men to the café in cold blood. To swing your dick around and show me who the boss was. Maria could've been seriously hurt—killed!"

Desmond swatted the words away with a dismissive hand gesture. "Collateral damage. And she's fine, so calm down. It's me who lost two good men that day."

Silas scoffed, feeling lightheaded all of a sudden. He stood up and strode towards the door. He'd heard enough.

"Pristine on the streets, a freak in the sheets—eh, Knight?" Desmond called, followed by a shrill cackle. Silas didn't turn back, but he heard his boss's tone turn sinister for his parting threat, "I'll be seein' ya."

Silas reached his car and slammed the door behind him, crashing his hands into the steering wheel, over and over, until his palms smarted. He scrubbed his face with his hands, whistling a long exhale out between his clenched teeth.

That was it. Desmond now had more than one thing to lord over him and keep him from abandoning ship. Silas couldn't be everywhere all at once, and he had no doubt that there were people keeping tabs on not only Jessica, but Maria and his ma, too. Probably even Bea. He needed to get those files, keep Desmond sweet, and figure out a way to cut all ties with the damned con game.

Another stinging slap ricocheted off the leather before he drove home, silently swearing an oath to himself.

One way or another, he would get Desmond Rose out of their lives—forever.

CHAPTER FOURTEEN

Silas knew there was only one person for the job when it came to styling him for a formal introduction with Richard Morton—Maria.

He enlisted her help on Friday, waiting in his booth until her morning shift had finished. He then drove them to the fanciest part of town, where only the richest residents dared to visit.

They looked incredibly out of place—Maria in a waitress pinny and short black skirt, and Silas in black jeans and a faded T-shirt. They'd headed into the tailor's, dodging the glares of snooty shoppers waiting for their drivers to pack their shopping bags away.

Maria gasped as she saw the prices, but Silas dismissed her outrage with a flick of his hand. She gave him an incredulous glare, but quickly forgot all about the price tags as she delved into her element, spending far too long picking out contenders for the perfect suit.

If she'd had her way, Maria would have spent the rest of the day perusing the racks. But after already wasting two hours of his life, Silas was far beyond his shopping limit. He needed out, so they purchased the best of what Maria had approved and got the hell out of there.

As a thank you before dropping her back off at the café, Silas treated Maria to lunch at a local bistro. She looked happier, finally gaining back some of her confidence as the scar on her forehead began to fade.

"My sister is spending all day with me at the café at the moment," she sighed, picking at her food. "She made me put your number on speed dial, I hope you don't mind."

"Not at all."

"It makes me feel better that they're…dealt with. I don't think I'd ever be able to leave the house again if I knew they were still out there."

He gave her a tight smile and she returned it, and that's the last they spoke about what happened. Maria changed the topic and Silas listened.

She didn't dare ask him how he was able to pay for his suit with cash, but he could still see her trying to figure it out as he watched her walk into the café and into her sister's embrace.

Before he could drive away, a text vibrated through his pocket. It was from Arthur.

I have something that Desmond wants you to see.

Silas grumbled to himself, but turned the car around and drove straight to Bluetine Park. Artie's lair remained in anonymity above the betting shop in the square, owned by the hacker's father.

Arthur had helped Silas with Desmond's schemes many times before. With all the necessary equipment to be the best underground hacker for con men everywhere, Desmond couldn't find anyone better. Artie charged enough for the pleasure, but no one could outdo him. Silas had built up a love-hate relationship with his associate.

As Silas let himself in through the unlocked door, he was greeted by Artie sat behind his desk, already grinning at him. "Hello, sunshine."

"Artie," Silas growled back. "What do you want?"

"Don't call me that. It's not what I want, but what your boss wants." Arthur turned back to the three monitors facing him on his desk, pulling up various tabs of camera footage and blueprints. "I've been tracking movements at the Morton Manor for the past week, collecting anything that might be of use to you tomorrow night."

"Desmond told you of the plans," Silas said, looking over the detailed floorplans of the manor.

"Only that you were to infiltrate the building and steal something from Richard's office," Artie said innocently, pointing at a white outline on the centre screen. "Which is here, by the way."

On the third floor, just past the second stairwell.

"You two really are so secretive about all these missions. It hurts my feelings to be left out of whatever fun you're having with Richard Morton!" Artie sighed dramatically, drawing a line down his cheek to mimic a tear.

"How did you get all of this?" Silas asked, sitting in the chair next to him, ignoring Artie's attempts to bait him.

Instead, he marvelled at the screens. He worked with Artie for years—known he was the best in the business. But still, this was another level. He'd mapped the entire building by himself.

"They don't pay me the big bucks for nothing, Sy." Artie grinned. "I see everything. All it took was a few minutes to hack into Richard's camera system and match the movements on each camera to a new room. They employ so many staff, it didn't take long for all of the hallways to be mapped."

"Wait," Silas drawled, his face paling. "They have cameras in the manor?"

Artie's smile grew into that of a Cheshire cat. "They certainly do, lover boy. That," he pointed at another white room on the floorplan, "is where I caught you being snuck into in the middle of the night." He waggled his eyebrows.

"Does Desmond know about the cameras?" Silas asked, not taking the bait. Artie was a master at pissing him off, having spent the past three years learning all the ways to trigger his temper.

"I told him about them," Artie confirmed. "He had me wipe any trace of you from the playback footage. And I'll be watching tomorrow night, deleting you from the stream as you go. The cameras are only in the hallways, so no one will even notice you're gone from the main hall."

"You're sure about that?" Silas asked dryly.

Artie clutched his chest with an exaggerated gasp. "Your scepticism pains me, Knight. Yes, I'm sure that I can cover your ass while you're on whatever fool's mission Desmond has you on now."

"I was planning on using tomorrow's party as recon work only," Silas mused. "Scope out the building. Don't you think it'd be less conspicuous to break into the office when there's not one hundred guests already there?" Silas didn't bother voicing his true concern—that the next stage of the plan would be set in motion once Desmond had those documents.

Artie held his hands up. "Take that up with the big man. He wants you to get them tomorrow, I'm just the shmuck in charge of making sure you have everything you need to get to the office."

Silas sighed, but nodded his acceptance.

They spent the rest of the afternoon and evening going over the plans Artie had drawn up. He'd thought of everything, and by the time Silas stepped out into the cooling summer twilight, he was ready to set the plan in motion.

☆☆☆

Silas arrived at the manor at 7 pm Saturday evening, straightening out his crisp suit and holding a bouquet of red roses and sunflowers. The florist had made a remark about such a combination symbolising *loyal love*, and even Silas's poker face couldn't hold his balk. He smirked as he looked down at them now, the idea of Jessica's favourite flowers representing such a thing.

His tux was made of blue wool, so rich it was almost black. But when the golden sunlight hit it, indigo waves glittered across the fabric. The lapels were cut from lustrous satin, and the silhouette fit his form perfectly.

He looked good.

As he stood at the edge of the gated gardens, Silas watched the suits and ball gowns littering the trimmed grass, steadily streaming up the stairs and into the manor's grand entrance.

Suddenly, he felt very exposed. What was he thinking, trying to steal from the host of such a great event?

Why was he still bothering with the mission at all?

He smoothed his hair, trying to block out the nagging voice that had been telling him to give up on the mission for the past week. He didn't want to consider where the voice was coming from, or why he suddenly had such a powerful conscious.

Silas was still trying to convince the doubtful voice that it was *just a job* when he locked eyes with the most beautiful woman he'd ever had the pleasure of knowing. Jessica stood at the entryway, wearing a golden satin dress that hugged every curve precisely. Diamonds glittered around her neck as she walked down the stairs toward him, curls bouncing, skin gleaming.

She was eternal sunshine.

And then it hit him. All at once, like a mountain of bricks collapsing onto him from far above, that it was real.

All of it.

His feelings for this woman…he was tired of hiding them. Pretending like they were all a ruse, a part of his con. They were *real*.

How long had he been lying to himself?

By the time they reached each other on the stone pathway, Silas was speechless. And not only because she looked unbelievable. He handed her the bouquet silently.

"Oh, you remembered?" she cooed, pressing her nose to the petals. The brown paper crinkled as he leaned closer, wrapping his hand across the small of her back. He was close enough to feel her warmth, smell her honeysuckle perfume.

He gave her a secret smile. "Hello, you," he breathed.

"Hello, Mr Knight," she replied, just as quietly. The hundreds of guests around them dared to fade into oblivion as they took each other in.

"You look gorgeous," he purred, looking her up and down. The sunset bounced off the golden fabric, casting a radiant glow from her entire body.

"Get a room," she drawled at his longing stare.

"Is that an option?"

Her laugh was a breath of fresh air as she playfully pushed him away. "Silas," she gasped, face breaking into a wide grin.

He grabbed her hand before she could remove it from his chest and leant down to kiss her knuckles. "I am, of course, joking," he said with a smirk. But as he leaned closer to steal a kiss, Jessica turned her head. He settled his lips on her cheek smoothly, lingering for a second too long.

When he stepped back, the bustling crowd had returned around them. He lifted his eyebrows in a silent question, but she simply glanced at him apologetically before taking his hand and leading him up the stairs.

He couldn't blame her. They were both far too aware of who could be watching them. Richard certainly wouldn't approve if his investors started pulling their money from his ventures because their *pretty little plaything* was suddenly getting closer to another man.

Still, Silas couldn't help but feel a tinge of disappointment mingling in his chest.

"I won't be able to spend all night with you," Jessica said quietly, as if reading his thoughts. "My father has made it very clear that I still have a role to play here." Something like anger flashed across her face, if only for a second. "But I'll come and find you when they're free to introduce you."

He nodded, skirting around a circle of greying men with boisterous laughs.

Jessica had led them through the foyer and into a large banquet hall. The ceilings towered above them, lined with solid gold carved beams. The floor-to-ceiling windows were loosely covered in gossamer curtains, lifting in a lazy wave on the evening breeze. An orchestra was setting up on the far side of the hall, their stage towering over a square dance floor. The rest of the room was taken up by round dining tables, dressed with white linens and crimson chargers. Behind them, mercifully, was a bar, lining the entire back wall with its finest liquor bottles.

"Okay, I should go. But you'll be okay. Right?" Jessica was spiralling, skin turning slightly flushed and dewy. "You *will* be okay?"

He dared to take her face in his hands, forcing her eyes to his. "Jess, calm down. I'll be fine. See over there?" He pointed behind him to the empty bar. "That's where I'll be. If you need me, just find my eyes." He took a step closer, pressing his body gently to hers. The brief connection made his breath hitch. Leaning down, he caressed the shell of her ear with his lips. "And if any of these fuckers dare to touch you, there's no telling what I'll do."

He could feel her heart racing through their elegant clothes. Reluctantly, he backed away, running his fingers down her exposed arm before breaking their contact.

Jessica smirked. "Oh, Mr Knight. So territorial," she mused, but her eyes shone with something like gratitude. She drifted away through the hall then, and he blew a deep breath through his nose.

Damn, he hated watching her leave.

☆☆☆

Silas wanted to waste no time. The sooner he could slip out and find Richard's office, the more time he'd have to get back to the bar and wait this wretched night out. He wanted to be free to oversee the hall by the time the investors started putting away too many dirty martinis. When Jessica would be their prime target.

He knew she could handle herself—Silas didn't want to think about how many functions she'd been forced to attend before—but he didn't want her to. If she looked over to the bar, he needed to be looking right back at her.

So, he took his position at the mahogany bar and ordered himself a Macallan 52 on the rocks. The young barman placed his crystal tumbler on a black napkin before going back to polishing glasses. Open bar.

Silas drank his whiskey silently, surveying the room that was now beginning to fill up with guests. Women took their seats at the large tables and men stood around talking between them. No one dared approach the grave-faced stranger at the bar, shooting daggers at anyone who dared meet his eye.

Jessica floated between tables, a wide smile painted across her face that didn't quite meet her eyes. She seemed to know these guests well, nodding along with their booming jokes, slipping away before they had a chance to get too close. He couldn't take his eyes off her.

He drained his glass as a microphone hummed into action. Richard Morton swaggered across the stage, looking every bit as illustrious as his résumé indicated. He wore an emerald velvet suit with a black shirt and bowtie, his dark grey hair gelled back into a sophisticated quiff. As he reached the microphone stand, a wave of applause rumbled across the tables.

"Oh, hush now," he said, laughing as the clapping burst louder. "You honour me. But let's get the festivities started!"

The crowds listened then, silence overcoming the hall. There wasn't a single person looking away from the stage, every set of eyes seemingly transfixed on the host.

"Thank you," Richard said, his voice smooth like warm honey. "Tonight, in the company of esteemed guests like yourselves, we bask in the vibrancy of opportunity, where ideas flourish and partnerships thrive. Let us seize this moment to explore new ventures, share our knowledge, and kindle the flames of possibility. For it is in this synergy of minds and ambitions that we create a legacy that transcends time. I want to quickly take a moment to thank my respected colleagues who have made it out tonight—"

That was Silas's cue to leave. He'd been dragged to one of these events before during business school, and he knew how long these speeches took. It would take Richard an hour, at least, to get through his dedications for his most prized investors.

With one last glance at Jessica, who sat at the front table, attention fixated on her father like everyone else, Silas weaved his way out of the hall seamlessly. No one seemed to notice—even the staff had their eyes trained on the host. He lingered by the door for a moment, pretending to listen to the speech while making sure no one's eyes had followed him to his new position, before slipping out into the cool, dark foyer.

It didn't take him long to find the door to Richard's office thanks to the plan Artie had laid out for him the night before. There was no one around to stop him and ask where he was going. It was almost *too* easy. He loosened a pin from his scraped-back hair and picked the lock. The click came quickly, door swinging open silently.

Silas huffed a laugh to himself, almost a little disappointed.

The office was dark, the setting sun supplying the only light source through the bay window. The walls were littered with certificates and framed newspaper clippings. There were no family pictures to be seen.

In the centre of the room stood a magnificent, hand-carved desk piled high with neatly stacked papers. It looked like an office out of an entrepreneurial magazine, showcasing what the reader should aspire to achieve. He dared run a finger over the whorls in the wood, caressing the waxy dips and ridges. It was a gorgeous piece of craftsmanship, probably tailored for Mr Morton himself.

Silas shook the wonderment away. He got to work, rifling through papers with such efficiency without skewing a single one out of place. It took him seconds to find the first document Desmond requested—a form confirming an offshore account with a gross sum of money deposited. He took his phone out to snap a photo.

"And who, may I ask, are you?"

Shit. Silas didn't dare move to look at the source of the female voice behind him. The overhead light flicked on as he put his phone away, lining the papers back up in their neat stack.

"Let me guess, you got lost on your way to the bathroom?" Her voice was a deep melody, dripping with tight agitation. "Turn and look at me, coward."

He obliged. The woman standing before him, arms tightly folded, wore a magenta gown that brushed the tops of her toes. Her face was granite, a single eyebrow raised as she waited.

"My name is Silas Knight," he said, forcing his voice to remain steady. "I am a friend of Jessica's, and I was just taking a look around."

"Looking around, in my husband's locked office?"

Jessica's mother, then. She looked every bit as terrifying as Jessica had made her out to be. Her bleached white hair was scraped back into a high bun, forcing the corners of her eyes upward. Her neck was tall and thin, wearing a necklace of dainty pearls.

"The door wasn't locked when I got here, ma'am. To tell you the truth, I was hoping to learn something here that I could use to impress you and Mr Morton later. I know this introduction is a big thing for Jess, and I just wanted you both to like me. I'm sorry if I overstepped here." He laughed sheepishly, stealing a glance at her hard face through his eyebrows.

She wasn't buying it for a second.

Richard's wife took a step towards him, forcing him to look into her eyes. "Did you take any pictures?" she asked, pointing to the pocket he'd slipped his phone into.

"No, ma'am."

She sighed through her nose. "I don't like you. You're nowhere near good enough for my daughter, and the sooner she realises that the better. But for some reason, she's willing to piss her father off for your *relationship*," she spat the word like she couldn't bear the taste of it on her tongue for a second, "so I'm going to forget about this little mishap, and let you break her heart all by yourself." Her face twisted in a grim smirk as she looked him up and down. "Let's go, Silas Knight."

She led him all the way back to the ballroom, slipping through another door as he slunk back to his seat at the bar. The speeches were just coming to an end and another bout of clapping accompanied Richard off the stage, the orchestra behind him kicking into a beat instantly. People were out of their seats and mingling again as soon as Richard was back on the floor. They approached him eagerly, patting him on the back and shaking his hand like he was a messiah. Silas barely contained his snarl.

Another hour dragged by. He didn't dare move from his barstool, not trusting Jessica's mother wasn't watching him from somewhere hidden in the crowds. Instead, he sipped another drink and watched his girl weave in and out of the tables like a fairy floating on a breeze.

Every now and then she would glance up at him, her siren eyes burning deeply into his soul. She'd smirk like she knew exactly what he was thinking, and that she might even be thinking the same thing, before turning her attention back to her guests. But that wicked glimmer always returned when she looked at him.

Trouble.

It was nearing 10 pm by the time Jessica rested her chin on his shoulder and whispered in his ear, "Mr Knight."

Her voice tickled his neck, a welcome cooling sensation across his heated skin. He had wasted his opportunity, failed his mission, and been caught by Richard Morton's wife. If it weren't for the promise he'd made Jessica at the start of the night, he'd already be grovelling at Desmond's office.

"Pretty lady," he replied, savouring the grounding weight of her head before she straightened and he twisted to face her. "Having fun?"

"I'd rather be having fun with you," she mused quietly, straightening his suit jacket. The implication hung in the thick air between them. He huffed a chuckle, eyes widening, as she grinned and she squeezed his hand. "Ready to meet them?"

No, never. But he nodded definitively, following her as she took his hand and led him to the front of the hall.

CHAPTER FIFTEEN

✦

Richard Morton sat at a full table, dominating the crowd with his enchantingly deep voice as they approached. But as soon as he saw Jessica weaving her way through the crowd with Silas on her arm, he rose. The entire table hushed. Standing just an inch or two lower than Silas, it wasn't difficult to see how this man had built such a name for himself. His millionaire's smile almost had even Silas bowing beneath his charm.

Richard gave his daughter a quick kiss on the hand before turning his attention to Silas, extending an arm in a gracious handshake.

"Let's go somewhere quieter, shall we?" Richard said, not waiting for a response before leading them out of the hall. Jessica's mother fell into line behind Silas, not bothering to acknowledge him. They stopped in a large living room decorated with rich red wallpaper, a marble fireplace and two ornate loveseats positioned towards each other.

"So," Richard began, his unnaturally white teeth beaming. "You must be Silas! I've heard so much about you," he chuckled, briefly tipping his head towards Jessica. "This one won't stop going on about you."

"Daddy!" Jessica scoffed. Her mother clicked her tongue.

"What? I'm just messing. It's great to meet you, son," he crooned, turning back to the room and slapping Silas on the shoulder. "I'm Richard, as I'm sure you know. This is my wife, Scarlette."

A member of staff came out of the shadows and busied himself around the drinks cart. The women were given martinis, the men whiskey poured over a single ice cube. The smoky aroma told Silas it was the same whiskey he'd been ordering from the bar all night.

"I hope you don't mind, Silas, but I can't stay long. Lots of guests to look after out there," Richard said between sips. "Isn't that right, Jessie?"

Jessica paled but nodded quickly. Richard bared his teeth and threw her a wink. Silas chewed the inside of his lip to keep a straight face, resisting the terrible urge to snarl or guide Jessica far away from the house there and then.

They drank their drinks quickly while Richard asked a flurry of personal questions, Silas answering all of them as best he could without giving too much away. He could see where Jessica got her stellar personality. Richard seemed kind, proper, and genuinely interested in everything he had to say. Honestly, it was a little unnerving—the stark difference between this interaction and what he'd heard from Desmond and Jessica.

Scarlette, on the other hand, was exactly how he'd envisioned her, sitting absently next to Richard, eyes frozen in a bitter glare. If looks could kill, he'd be six feet under by now.

Once Richard had exhausted all his grilling questions, he drained the amber liquid in his tumbler and gave his daughter a dazzling grin. "Jessica, Scar, why don't you ladies leave us men to have a quick chat, eh?"

Jessica's face fell. "Daddy, is that really necessary? What about your guests?"

"You can keep them company while I'm away, sweetheart."

Silas began silently counting to ten at that.

"Come on, it will only take a moment. Shoo." Richard waved his hands towards his wife and daughter, and Scarlette led Jessica out swiftly. "I promise I'll leave him in one piece!"

Once the women had left and the door was firmly closed, Richard swivelled back to Silas. "Another drink, son?"

Silas shook his head. "No, thank you. I'm driving and want to have a clear head." That, and he needed to be sober as the rest of the guests got drunker.

Richard smirked but put his own glass down. He leaned back in his seat, squinting his eyes at Silas. "Son, let me be honest with you. I have the very best private investigators looking into your past as we speak. But I'm not in the mood for waiting for an answer. So, tell me," he said, standing to tower over Silas, "who do you work for?"

"Excuse me?" Silas asked in the most casual tone he could manage. He glanced around the room, trying to spot anything that would help him should this go south.

Richard smirked again, standing to brace his hands on either side of Silas's chair. Their faces were so close, but Silas didn't balk. It was a common intimidation tactic; one that he'd used many times before himself.

"I assume someone has given you the order to snoop around my office, unless you're incredibly stupid and doing it for fun," Richard said quietly.

Scarlette had told him, then.

Silas's mind was clear water as Richard spoke again in a lethal calm, "See, Silas, I could kill you right now. I have a dozen men on standby to cover any trace of you ever being here. No one would ever know what truly happened to the insignificant Silas Knight, and we would all happily get on with our lives." A vicious smile. "But something tells me my daughter wouldn't be happy with that, and she's an important part of my empire. So I'm giving you one chance. One chance to tell me who you work for, and why they've sent you here."

Silas fought a shudder, never looking away from Richard's glare. But he'd been around enough of these crooks to know that Richard wasn't lying; that he'd end up dead if he didn't play this right.

So, Silas told Richard everything.

Fuck Desmond Rose. Fuck his shitty business. Fuck anything his boss thought he could hold over him. Silas was done—let the two crime lords battle it out between themselves. He was *done*.

By the time Silas had finished, Richard was pinching the bridge of his nose. "Desmond Rose believes he can blackmail me, and then get *more* money out of me by kidnapping my daughter for a ransom?"

Silas nodded. "Yes. I never said he was smart."

Richard scoffed. "And you're working for him to pay for your mother's medical bills."

"Yes sir."

Richard sat on the information Silas had just dumped on him for a long moment. He'd backed away was now pacing before the fireplace, but he never took his eyes off Silas, attempting to gauge whether he was lying or not.

"Look, Silas. Let's not pretend we like each other. We both have our reasons for doing the things we've done, that the other might not understand. But my daughter seems to tolerate you, although I'm not sure how she'll react when she figures out you've been lying to her—"

"My feelings for your daughter are real—"

"Let me finish, son." Richard held up a firm hand. "My point is, I don't care enough about you or Desmond Rose to do a damn thing. He wants my money; he can come get it like a real man. But my advice to you would be to get as far away from him as you can. Trust me, he'll be stabbing you in the back before you know it."

Richard slapped Silas on the back to emphasise the point. Silas bowed his head in agreement as he was ushered out of the room and into the foyer. But before he could walk into the main hall again, Richard stepped around him and squared up, face shadowed in a menacing grin.

"One last thing. If you hurt my reputation, or if I find out you're conspiring with Desmond behind our backs,

I will kill every single person in your life." The words were laced with poison, oozing with grim suggestion. "Are we on the same page?"

Silas nodded again, but Richard didn't wait around as he swaggered back through the crowds in the ballroom, who were noticeably rowdier than when they'd left.

Now Silas had two people threatening to kill anyone he held close.

He pushed his way through to the bar, ordering another drink as soon as he sat down, trying to push away the realisation that Richard had just alluded them to being comparable.

Silas Knight, who'd lied to earn the money for his mother's life-saving treatments.

And Richard Morton, the con man willingly turning a blind eye to the harassment his associates threw at his daughter every chance they got.

They weren't the same. Not even close.

Were they?

Jessica was still mingling with the guests, her smile a tad tighter than it had been earlier in the night. Perhaps she'd be better off without both of them in her life.

The curtains still swayed on the summer's breeze, but they were now tangled with moonlight rather than the blazing sunset. The guests showed no signs of slowing down, dancing and chatting and schmoozing. Noise swirled around him from all angles, and Silas clenched his fists to keep from collapsing into himself.

What had he just done?

Desmond Rose had spies everywhere. And Silas had just sold him out to his enemy to save his own skin. He had single-handedly ruined his mission. If he were being truthful, Silas didn't care about Desmond's plan—hadn't in a long while. Perhaps he'd secretly been sabotaging it all along. He wasn't even sure why he was still going along with it.

But the fact remained that he'd sold out his boss, and Silas knew he'd be dead once news reached Desmond's ears.

So he tipped another finger of whiskey to the back of his throat, savouring its warmth, and scanned the room again, spotting Scarlette sitting at a full table of exquisitely dressed women with a positively wicked smile on her face. She lifted her martini glass to him knowingly.

He clenched his jaw. But before he had a chance to wipe that smugness from Scarlette's tight face, his eyes flicked to Jessica, who was now shooting quick glances back at him.

Quicker than a lightning flash, Silas was up and weaving his way through drunken investors. He didn't care what they thought of him as he reached her, sliding a strong arm around her waist and pressing a kiss to her temple.

"Sorry I'm late, honey," he purred, loud enough for the white-haired man sitting before them to hear. The man looked at the others around the table, all visibly dumbfounded by his presence. "Did I miss much?"

"No, not at all." Jessica leaned into his touch, a silent thank you. Her tone remained warm, but her body language was anything but. He squeezed her hand and laced their fingers together.

"Sorry, I don't think we've been introduced," Mr Handsy said, deep voice rumbling. He wore bifocals and his wrinkled skin was far too orange to be natural. He extended a hand to Silas, whose eyebrow twitched at the sight of a wedding band. "Harrison Woods, chief investment officer for Rich—and you are?"

Silas glanced around the rest of the table before taking the old man's papery hand. They were all staring intently at him, desperate for the gossip. He smirked. "Silas Knight, devoted companion to this gorgeous lady here."

Screw it, he thought, and kissed her passionately. He'd already fucked up enough already tonight—what was once more?

She rested her fingers on his cheek as he angled her back, and he could feel a smile shuddering through her. It might have been the most precious feeling in the world.

Once they came up for air, Harrison was plum red and wide-eyed. "Sorry, are you sure? I'll have to have a word with Richard. I wasn't aware Jessica was *available* for companionship."

Amusement at Jessica's flushed cheeks drained from his face as Silas turned back to Harrison, eyes shooting pure flame. "I don't see why you would need to talk to Richard, Harry. We've just told you all you need to know. Jessica is her own woman, free to date whoever she chooses." His voice was low, acrimonious. "Just because she chose someone her own age, handsome, *available*—" Silas flicked his eyes to the wedding band and Harrison quickly slid it underneath his other hand, "—doesn't warrant a telling off from Daddy, does it?"

Harrison choked on his words, veins pulsating at his receding hairline. "No, no. I suppose not."

"Good. Oh, and I'd thank you to keep your hands to yourself from now on. And tell your friends to do the same. Because next time," Silas leaned in closer, still holding onto Jessica's waist, "I might not be so civil." He gave the stuttering buffoon a wink before leading Jessica off across the dance floor.

She softened in his arms as he spun her gently to face him, taking her waist and inviting her to clasp her hands around his neck.

"Thank you," she breathed. "He's one of the worst for it. Seems to think *I'm* the bonus he's owed for working for my father. I can usually handle him on my own, but having you here—you're the first person I've ever known to be in my corner. To willingly go against my father's contacts like that."

"I will always be in your corner, Jessica," Silas said as her eyes turned glassy.

"I believe you," she whispered before resting her head on his chest.

They swayed in time to the emotional melody being played from the stage, and Silas smiled into her hair. He felt…proud.

Proud to be the one person backing Jessica in this room full of hunters. Proud to be her confidant, her lifeline.

Silas was *nothing* like Richard. He made a silent vow to prove that every single day of the rest of his life. For her, he would prove it.

As they danced slowly, Silas was painfully aware of how many eyes were fixated on them. It felt as though the entire room was watching. "Everyone seems to think they have a right to own the mesmerising Jessica Morton, don't they," he mused quietly.

She huffed a bitter laugh but met his gaze, something like wonderment in her eyes. "And then there's you."

"And then there's me."

Jessica truly smiled then, eyes glinting and cheeks beaming. She rested her head on his chest once more, the weight of it releasing the tension from his stiff muscles and stilling his rapid heartbeat. He hoped she wouldn't hear the terrified thumping thrumming beneath his ribcage.

He held her tighter, memorising every part of her—her touch, her smell, her taste.

They danced and danced, round and round, until it felt like no one else was in the room with them. Until it was only him, the girl who had turned his life upside down, and the glittering moonlight.

CHAPTER SIXTEEN

✦

It was nearing 2 am by the time the last of the guests were shooed out of the grand hall, singing vulgar limericks at the top of their lungs. Perched on the barstool he'd been warming all night, Silas rested his forehead on Jessica's shoulder. Facing outward, she leaned into him, grazing the back of his head with her cheek.

Richard and Scarlette had been missing from the festivities for hours, their absence forcing the hosting duties onto Jessica. After they'd finished dancing, she'd pulled Silas around the room with her, introducing him to far too many guests, obviously no longer caring about what her father thought.

Silas stood behind her like a bodyguard, glaring at any investor that even thought about getting too close to her. She called him her *courtier*, with a wicked wink back at him every time, knowing how much it would annoy him.

She was right, but the playful glint in her eye reduced his response to a meagre grunt. She could call him anything she damn liked.

But the long evening had taken its toll on both of them, and as the orchestra packed away and the staff tidied around them, neither could summon enough energy to call it a night.

So, at the bar, they rested.

An unknown number of minutes later, Jessica pushed off his chest and turned to face him. "Thank you," she said as he forced his neck to straighten. "For tonight."

He hummed a lazy response, to which she leaned into him further and took his hand in hers. "I fear you're too tired to drive home?"

The suggestion laced between each syllable was like a bucket of ice water over his head. All feelings of exhaustion were swept away, being replaced with another feeling entirely.

"It would be reckless," Silas drawled, stroking the pad of his thumb over the base of her own.

"We wouldn't want that," she mused, pulling him gently from his seat. His muscles grumbled at the movement. The remnants of his old ankle injury sang.

Silas hardly noticed.

Not when Jessica was pulling him through the foyer, up the corridor, towards her bedroom. Her eyes never left his, enchanting him like a siren at sea. He was captivated, willing to follow her anywhere.

The only time she looked away was when she turned to unlock her bedroom door. Following her closely, they entered the dim room together. The only light came from the large moon outside her window and the lit candles spread across the furniture. Jessica's golden dress illuminated in the firelight as she turned, expression now expectant, waiting for his reaction.

"It would appear," he said quietly, hooking one of her fingers with his, "that someone had an ulterior motive for tonight."

She blushed for a second, but then her siren eyes returned. He would allow himself to be lured, mesmerised, charmed—as long as she kept looking at him like *that*.

With a quick tug at her arm, the space between them closed and her breath hitched. He smirked, looking over her features hungrily. Everything outside Jessica's bedroom fell away, and he dared to be completely present.

Tension between them crackled as they remained still, devouring each other with only their eyes. But as their gazes linked, something close to impatience shone over her face.

Very well, then.

Silas lowered his lips to her neck, and she tilted her head to grant him better access. He dragged his bottom lip over her exposed skin, devastatingly slowly, until he reached the dip of her collarbone. He kissed her warm skin, blood thrumming against his lips. But her tiny moan told him he wasn't moving fast enough for her liking.

He traced a line up her neck to her ear, using a low breath to leave a trail of goosebumps. He nibbled the lobe, tugging lightly, and asked, "You don't like it slow, Jessica?"

He wasn't sure she was breathing. If it weren't for her hands getting tangled in the ends of his hair, he might have stopped to check. But he couldn't stop teasing, even if it was becoming more and more difficult to keep his own breath from rasping.

After what felt like an eternity of him paying too much attention to her neck, Jessica dipped her head and guided their mouths together. Their bodies pressed against each other so tightly they might've joined permanently, thick kisses turning to sweet molasses as they stumbled towards the bed, neither bothering to check for burning candles in their path.

As the back of his thigh hit the mattress, Jessica pulled them apart briefly. Her swollen lips shone in the flickering light and her eyes twinkled dangerously. Silas placed a large hand on either side of her jaw to pull her back in, but she abruptly pushed him back.

He fell onto the feathery bedding before she climbed on top of him.

Time stood still as fire ignited between them, burning ferociously throughout the early hours of the morning. Their flame never wavered, even as the stars burned out and milky sunlight washed over them.

☆☆☆

Silas woke up underneath the thick duvet, head vibrating and lips still tingling. A stupid smile wouldn't budge from his face. He granted himself the grace to find it amusing rather than ridiculing it. Letting his head fall to the side, he admired the sleeping beauty beside him.

Just like the first time he'd awoken next to her, Jessica's face was a picture of peace. Her eyelids flickered in a dreamworld. Her skin was slightly puffy, pink lines pressed into it from the sheets. The duvet was pulled up right underneath her arms, only a lacy strap peeking out from underneath it.

Memories of their night together flashed through his mind as he watched the rising sun shimmer on the pool outside her window. His entire body ached with exhaustion, but it sang with happiness.

Silas rested his eyes, trying to hold onto their moment for a little while longer. Less pleasant thoughts of Desmond and Richard threatened to invade his mind, but Jessica began to stir before they could win.

She immediately flung her forearm over her eyes, shielding herself from the fragmented light beaming in. She let out a long groan. Not a morning person, then.

He watched her carefully, stretching and writhing under the covers as a way to ward off sleepiness. When she finally turned her attention to him, a hint of a smile peeked through her tired eyes.

"Mr Knight."

He brushed a light kiss over her shoulder. "Pretty girl."

Her black hair was frizzy, lazily lying next to her on her pillow. Her skin was glowing, and he couldn't stop himself from planting kisses all over its shine. She purred gently, running her hands through his hair and lightly tugging him up to face her. He leant on an elbow to tower over her, dipping to meet her in a deep kiss.

She hummed happily against him before they broke apart. She carefully tucked a lock of his tangled hair behind his ear.

"There are no boys allowed in this room, you know," Jessica said, a challenging grin spreading across her face. "My father would kill you if he caught you."

"Good thing I'm no boy, then." Silas matched her cunning tone. "Or do I have to prove that to you—again?"

He grazed his teeth along her jaw as she giggled. "Oh, I think I might need reminding…"

Silas let out a slight snarl at the contest, brushing the tip of her nose with his own. The air between them was stifling, almost unbearable.

They spent the rest of the morning together, not bothering to break apart for a moment. They were the only two people on earth that mattered. And when Desmond's name flashed across his phone every few minutes, Silas ignored the calls without a single care in the world.

☆☆☆

Silas finally snuck out of Jessica's bedroom in the mid-afternoon, climbing through the bushes and gap in the iron gate as he did the last time. He'd parked his car in the same place, so it was easy to find. That damned smile still hadn't fallen from his lips, and he felt lighter than he had in months.

No, *years*.

The feeling was short-lived, though. As soon as he reached his car, he was overcome with a dizzying feeling of paranoia.

He was being watched.

Glancing through the car mirrors quickly so as not to grab attention, he immediately spotted a shifty guy in a forest green sedan. As if cast in some comical black-and-white undercover police drama, the man sat engrossed in his crossword book, pencil balancing on his upper lip. He wore thick sunglasses, presumably to hide the fact that he was watching Silas from afar, and his chin twitched every now and then as he spoke into a hidden recorder.

Richard or Desmond, Richard or Desmond. Which fool was having him followed this time?

If he'd been sure it was his boss, Silas would have headed straight to the car and beat the living hell out of the person foolish enough to trail him. But the possibility of it being one of Richard's men, especially after last night, loomed over him. He had no interest in getting on Richard's bad side, nor did he want to piss off his lackeys.

Pushing away all his instincts to confront the stalker, Silas got in his car and drove straight home. The roads were unusually busy for the time of day, but Silas could still see the sedan weaving its way through the traffic behind him. He was too tired to try and lose them—let him report back to whoever he worked for that Silas Knight was returning home. *Killer* story.

The journey took double the amount of time it should have done, and Silas finally pulled up outside of his apartment block in a foul mood. He was met by a man bearing a black hat and all-black clothing standing on the kerb, in perfect alignment with his usual parking spot.

Silas didn't miss a beat as he slid out of the car, staring at the man in black, and walked slowly past him towards the front entrance. Within a flash, the stranger turned towards Silas, crashing into his shoulder as he walked straight past him.

Silas looked down at the brown paper envelope now resting in his hands.

The stranger was almost out of sight already, so he tucked the package beneath his arm and walked as quickly as his tired limbs would let him.

A swift glance behind him as he entered the foyer confirmed his suspicions—the sedan was parked half a mile or so up the road. He didn't know what was in the envelope, but he sure as hell knew that he didn't want Desmond or Richard knowing, either. He paid it no attention until he was safely up the stairs with his bedroom door closed firmly behind him.

Ripping open the envelope, he emptied the contents onto his bed. £5,000 in cash, and a note in Desmond's spidery handwriting.

Dearest Knight,

Shingles is pissing me off. He owes me too much and I'm bored—teach him a lesson for me. The 5k in here is for you, go buy yourself something pretty.

Des.

P.S. Morton has his guys following you, so be careful. Can't have them sniffing around me or my business.

The back of the note bore an address not too far from his own. Silas screwed up the paper and threw it into the plastic bin by his wardrobe. He picked up the wad of cash—it was thick enough to fill his entire palm. He twisted his wrist back and forth so that the light caught it from different angles.

He toyed with his moral compass. Richard's threat from last night still rang in his ears. But so much money for a single job? That was an offer only a fool would refuse. And he needed all the help he could get to fund his and Jessica's eventual escape from Fayette Bay.

A grim snarl escaped him as he realised that this would be a test, designed by Desmond to make sure he was still on the right team. Not following through would be turning his back on his boss, and there was no telling what the unhinged Desmond Rose would do then.

Silas didn't know how truthful Richard was with his threats, but he knew Desmond. He had no choice but to fulfil this task, unless he wanted Jessica thrown into immediate danger. Vivid images of Maria lying helpless on tiled flooring flashed through his mind.

You have no choice, his inner voice warned.

Silas silently stacked the money with the rest in the bottom of the wardrobe before getting changed into a dark-coloured outfit and combing his hair back into a band.

Kissing Ma on his way out again, he slipped into the evening breeze. No sign of Mr Sedan or the man in black. Silas took a deep breath, savouring the cooling dusk before getting back in his car and setting off to the address Desmond had supplied.

CHAPTER SEVENTEEN

✦

Silas knew Shingles to be a young man, a newbie in the business. His real name was Ethan Bennett—hell only knew why he'd gone for such a crude alias. Desmond's underlings barely made it past a few months working for the master crook—Silas was the most experienced by far.

He saw each new guy come and go and had developed an eye for figuring out the kind of men they were. Some were similar to him, getting roped into the business out of sheer desperation. They had nowhere else to turn, and Desmond had found them at the perfect time to help pick up the pieces.

Others were lazy, searching for the biggest payday for the least work possible.

And then there were the select few, Shingles among them, who joined Desmond's force because they *enjoyed* the work—got a thrill out of each scam, beating, and death overseen by them.

These guys were Desmond's favourites, and Silas's least. Every time he saw Shingles, the cocky lad was swaggering into Desmond's office, ready and raring to jump straight into anything the boss would trust him with.

Shingles, who took pride in missing almost as many teeth as the years he had lived, squatted on the outskirts of town in an apartment block that hadn't seen maintenance in years. As Silas stood outside it, leaning against his car and waiting for his spine to steel, he wondered how the building was still standing. Every window was black with thick layers of grime and pollution, kicked up from the busy motorway running directly behind it. The foul dust had also spread onto the walls, infesting every cinder block.

Some balcony doors sat boarded up, while others were covered in graffiti. The paint was peeling from the front door and it looked as though the bottom had been kicked in a few too many times, judging by the way the wood warped and splintered.

With a lasting breath, Silas squared his shoulders and pushed off the car. He ignored the rancid smell getting more pungent the closer he got to the building, the kids shouting at him from one of the windows. He zoned everything out, tunnelling his vision on the mission at hand.

Desmond wanted Shingles to be taught a lesson. That's all he needed to focus on.

But what would Jessica think if she knew what he was about to do? How much blood money he'd accepted for such a task?

He paused in the dirty foyer, considering the risk of turning on his heel and heading straight home. He didn't like this shit. He didn't want to *teach lessons*. He wanted to lead a normal, quiet life enjoying Ma's final days with her. Maybe even with Jessica.

But with Desmond encroaching on him from one side, and Richard threatening him from the other, Silas knew he had no choice.

Not when they were threatening Jessica's safety.

So instead of walking back to his car and driving away as fast as the old engine would take him, he blew out a heavy sigh and rolled his neck from left to right, sounding an orchestra of cracking noises as he did so. He shrugged his shoulders back to make himself appear larger and began the ascent to the top floor.

Damn, he was tired. By the time he'd reached the correct floor, Silas's legs were leaden. He'd need to make this quick.

Silas pounded the back of his wrist on the correct door three times. The sickening smell from outside had only become fouler the higher he'd climbed, the stifling air trapping it.

The door opened a crack—just enough for Silas to see a wide eye and the large black bag that cushioned it peering out at him. The pupil dilated unnaturally fast, the red rim turning brighter as Shingles recognised the visitor.

"Silas Knight? What are you doing here, hoss?" His voice was high—warped.

"You gonna let me in, Shingles? Or leave me waiting out here like an idiot."

Shingles warbled something unintelligible before slowly opening the door for Silas to enter. Another stench of beer and urine mingled with the one from the stairway, and it took great effort for him not to gag.

The lights were turned off and the moth-eaten sheets draped across the windows cast a gloomy essence over the space. Silas could only make out illusive shadows of furniture—a bed, a mini fridge, a TV stood on the floor. Shiny tin foil balls littered the dirty rug, twinkling as they reflected the dusky light peeking through the sheets.

"So, to what do I owe the pleasure?" Shingles asked, failing terribly at acting nonchalant. They both knew who had sent him.

As his vision adjusted to the darkness, Silas inspected the small kitchen slowly, buying time. The paint was peeling off the walls and mould crept into every crevice. He turned slowly to face Shingles.

"Look, Shin—"

A deafening thud cracked the words right from his mouth. Immense pain radiated through his stomach and twined around his ribs.

Silas doubled over just before another blow came, this time a knee to his nose. A warming sensation instantly coated his mouth and a metallic taste seeped in through his teeth.

Silas swung a fist towards the scrawny man, but his arm was intercepted by a stomping boot. Bone snapped into the floor, vision bursting with bright light.

He surged up, thrusting his good arm upwards, his elbow connecting with Shingles' abdomen. His attacker doubled over, and Silas shot a fist into his nose. A crack filled the darkened room.

But as Silas stood tall over a bowing Shingles, suddenly not so bothered about delivering Desmond's message after all, the front door swung open beside them. Two silhouettes stood in the doorframe, the light from the hallway forcing Silas into a squint.

Before he knew what was happening, Silas's legs were swept from beneath him. Shingles was back up, directing the two new voices through bloody gasps. Kicks and stomps and rouge punches flew, connecting with any part of his body they could find.

They cackled and barked orders at each other while taking turns branding his skin with the rubber markings on their shoes.

Silas was powerless. He tried to fight back, but every time he grabbed one of the attackers, another would step in. He tried again, swiping an ankle away, but all it earned him was a foot to the cheek, slamming his skull into the filthy carpet.

After what felt like hours and seconds all at once, Silas began drifting back and forth from reality. Still lying helplessly, he was completely paralysed.

Broken.

He swam in and out of consciousness, welcoming the fleeting relief of nothingness. Every time he came back to shore, though, the agony only flamed brighter.

☆☆☆

Silence surrounded Silas.

Shapes and whorls swirled before his eyes, the bright colours too loud in his broken head.

His hands were still up by his face, but they had dropped to the floor in his battle with consciousness. One of his eyelids fluttered open. The other remained glued shut. His vision was blurry, creeping to and from focus in waves. The thin spears of sunlight that had been beaming into the room earlier were now replaced by artificial orange light from the streetlamps below.

How long had he been down?

Silas dared to lift his head slowly. The muscles in his neck were stiff and pain surged through his bloodstream with every movement.

The only sound was coming from the motorway outside. There was no one left in the apartment but him.

Shingles and his two accomplices had left him there. Reduced him to a feeble child and abandoned his remains to dissolve into the tar-crusted floor.

Did they think he was *dead*?

It took a few long moments to convince himself that he could, and should, move. Rolling himself onto his side, agony bloomed in his chest and stomach. He hissed through gritted teeth as he pushed up to kneeling, then to his feet.

Something was wrong with his chest. It felt deflated and crushed and splintered with every single staggered breath he took.

Judging by the pulling sensation around his nose, his face was covered in dried blood. But looking down at his hands—where Shingles blood had been—they had been wiped clean. All traces of DNA vanished.

A strained grunt escaped him as he heaved his right leg in front of him, his left scraping along slowly after. An involuntary grimace stretched his face at the jutting step, making whatever injury he'd acquired there tingle.

Each step was slower than the last, and he had to clutch his ribs as they threatened to split apart with every movement.

Silas didn't know how long it took him to get to the stairwell. But he didn't give himself time to process the pain as he grasped the rickety handrail for balance and tentatively dropped one foot to the first step. He pulled the second to meet it with a resounding thump.

There must have been eight flights of stairs for him to climb down, and sweat had already begun beading at his temples. But he kept going. Desmond had double-crossed him, and that could only mean one thing. Someone had sold him out, knowing what he'd told Richard. And there would be no uncertainty about Desmond going after Jessica himself now.

Or, if his boss knew that he couldn't go after Richard's money anymore, Desmond might've turned his attention wholly to Silas. He'd need to be punished, and would a single beatdown be enough to appease the scorned crime lord? It wouldn't surprise him if Desmond used Jessica to punish Silas, throwing the reason for his betrayal back in his face.

So, he continued, pulling himself down each step, *needing* to stay conscious. For Jessica. For Ma. For anyone in his life that Desmond and Richard might go after next.

But obsidian glitter fizzed along the outside of his vision, threatening to consume him whole.

He'd lost count of which floor he'd reached by the time he slipped on a puddle of his own blood and went crashing down towards the unforgiving earth.

☆☆☆

Spinning lights flitted above him, much too bright to be comfortable. They bore their way into his one working pupil, like a spear to the brain, sending forks of lightning searing through his head in all directions.

The bulbs raced past his head too quickly for him to focus. All Silas knew was that they were a lot different to the buzzing lights that occupied the stairwell he had been in just a few moments ago.

He lay on a bed of hard plastic. People surrounded him, dressed in bottle blue scrubs underneath white coats, bobbing in and out of his line of sight.

How had he got to the hospital?

Why couldn't he move?

Ringing, louder than a foghorn blaring in the dead of night, sounded too close to his ears. It drowned out anything the doctors around him were saying, but their faces looked far from pleasant.

His bed was wheeled into a dark room. More people joined them, fussing around him with wires and outdated machines with pixelated screens. He was poked, twisted, picked up, put down, stroked, and examined for what felt like hours.

Powerless. Useless. *Weak.*

A needle was forced into the back of his hand and liquid quickly filled the plastic tube. The concoction offered almost instant relief, those delicious painkillers flowing through his body and numbing the throbbing pain felt through his entire body.

Floating on his little cloud of morphine, all coherent thoughts drifted away from him.

So Silas continued watching the frantic doctors around him, humming a little tune in his head. The concerned eyes watching him were his fans, admiring his song in awe of such beauty. The flickering screens around him were spotlights, dancing slowly to the rhythm of his tune, creating quite a show for the crowded theatre.

And there stood Jessica, in the middle of the dance floor, swaying with him just as they had done in the ballroom the night before. A spotlight beamed from above her, everyone else fading into the shadows. She grinned at him, and he smiled back.

His Jessica.

The classical performance played on as his working eye fell shut and Silas's blissful cloud floated off into absolute nothingness.

CHAPTER EIGHTEEN

✦

Beep. Beep. Beep. Beep.

Turn that shit off.

Beep. Beep. Beep. Beep. Beep.

Silas peeled his eyelids open one at a time. His eyelashes were stuck together, creating his own personal jail cell before him. Beyond the bars was the white smudge of hospital ceiling tiles.

His vision was still blurry from sleep, but at least both eyes were working again.

He cleared his throat weakly, taking mental stock of what he could feel.

Toes—wiggling.

Legs—heavy, but movable.

Arms—fine.

Hands—left, working, right, numb.

Face—very painful.

Chest—laboured. He was breathing, at least.

He took a tour around his body through his mind, focusing on how every area felt. His face was tingling and felt fuller than normal, dry eyelids pressing into his eyes.

Why was his face so swollen?

His chest felt heavy and like it was being punctured with a butcher's knife every single time he breathed. But breathing meant that he was still alive, so he savoured the stabbing sensation for a moment.

He was still *alive*.

Silas still couldn't move his head left or right, but the high afternoon sun cast a warm glow across the plain wall before him. He'd awoken in Shingles' apartment while it was dark out, so it had to have been at least half a day since the attack.

But had it only been one day, or had they done more damage than that? He could've been out for days—weeks, even.

Silas needed to get someone's attention.

His attempts at shouting were futile. Each time his voice croaked its way up his throat, something blocked it and forcefully shoved it back down deeper. Try as he might, no noise was able to escape past the blockage in his throat, leaving nothing but a burning pain in its wake.

Giving up, he shuffled his hands around where they lay, searching for a call button. The sheets were crisp underneath his fingers, his uncut nails snagging on the cotton. After a few moments his left hand hit something, but it wasn't the block of cold plastic he was hoping for. It was soft and warm, and twitched as he explored it more.

Suddenly, a face jolted beside him.

He could just make her features out in the corner of his eye—Jessica. *His Jessica.*

Half of her face was flushed pink, lines of his fresh sheets imprinted in her soft skin from her slumber. A happy memory overcame him of when he'd last seen her looking like that. She pushed up to get a better look at him, locking his eyes with hers.

"Silas, oh my god—Silas?" Jessica's tone started excited and full of relief, but quickly became unsure. "Hang on, let me get a nurse…" She bounced up from her chair and scurried towards the door, looking back at him before she left in a fit of energetic panic.

A moment or two passed before she came barrelling back in with two nurses. Neither of them uttered a word to him before shining an intrusive light over his eyes and glaring at the dozens of monitors filling the room. Jessica pushed past the older nurse to grasp his hand again, holding it close to her chest.

The silence was finally broken by the senior nurse, who simply muttered, "Oh my." She examined the screens around him again and again, eyes flicking from the monitors to his medical notes, and back again.

She didn't look happy, but rather confused. Like no one had been expecting him to wake up.

The younger nurse—a student, maybe—was sent off to get the doctor. Jessica was silently sobbing into their clasped hands. Silas's tired eyes tried to ask her for any insight into what was happening, but she didn't look up from their interlaced fingers.

When the student nurse finally came back with a man dressed in a chequered shirt and grey trousers underneath his white coat, they burst into the room with urgency.

The doctor confirmed that Silas's eyes were indeed open, and he seemed as surprised as the rest of them.

Something wasn't right—how long could he possibly have been out for?

"Silas Knight?" The doctor finally addressed him, leaning over him so that their faces were square with one another. "Please blink twice if you can hear and understand me."

He obliged, blinking twice slowly. Loose crust from his lashes scratched at his eyes.

"Very good. I am Doctor Ayotunde Takara. I've been your primary care physician during your stay here at Heartstone Clinic Hospital."

During your stay here—it sounded like he had been here much longer than one day. Fizzing panic began to dance within his head.

"When you were first brought in, you had significant injuries to the head and chest. We needed to operate to stop the internal bleeding."

When you were brought in—but when was that?

"Unfortunately, there were complications during the procedure. We managed to fit a stent in your lung to keep it working, but visibility was too poor to stem the bleeding in your brain. It appeared you had been bleeding internally for quite some time before you were found."

Silas thought back to the repeated blows his head had suffered from Shingles and his playmates. The stairway slipping out from under him also came to mind.

"We had to stop the surgery and put you in a medically induced coma. A few days later we tried the operation again and were successful at stopping the bleed."

The doctors had patched him up then—so why was Jessica still unable to control the tears cascading down her cheeks?

"Our attempts to wake you up after the surgery failed," Dr Takara continued in his professional voice, but the next part of his sentence came out with a slight tinge of shame. "Multiple times."

The room turned colder somehow. The grave faces on the four people standing over him confirmed his fear—he had been here a heck of a lot longer than a couple of days. He tried to tell them to hurry up and just tell him the truth, but all that came out was a low squeak.

How long was I gone?

Skipping over this very important detail, his doctor continued, "But the good news is that you are awake now and seem to be responding well. I am going to have my lovely nurses remove the tube from your throat—I can't imagine that's very comfortable."

Silas hissed back at him in confirmation.

"Alright then. We'll need to book you in for some tests to make sure everything looks good, and I'll be back to check on you later." Dr Takara looked at his pager while backing towards the door. "We'll keep an eye on you, but you know where we are if you need us. Excuse me."

With a quick passing smile and a light touch on Jessica's arm, the doctor was gone.

The nurses took out his breathing tube, propped his bed up, and made sure that his call button was within reach.

As soon as they left the room, Jessica sat back on her visitor's chair, never breaking their connected hands. They both remained still and together for several minutes before a tiny voice sounded. "I thought I'd lost you."

Thick, hot tears slid down his hand as she hid her face behind it again. He tried to claim his hand back to soothe her somehow, but to no avail. He was too weak. She was too distraught.

Silas cleared his throat again, wincing at the relentless flames licking within it. "Jess?" he croaked, and her head shot up to face him. Her large eyes were bloodshot and exhausted, her skin looking like she hadn't seen the sun in weeks. Her cheeks were sunken, hair unwashed.

"Don't waste your voice, Sy. The doctors said it might take a while for you to get all functionality back to how you were before the accident."

He fought the urge to argue, his shredded throat filling with unanswered questions. But Jessica was one step ahead—she answered them all, reading them from his pleading face.

How long have I been here?

"It's the 24th of November. You were brought in mid-July. You've been out for four months, Silas. The doctors have been telling us to prepare ourselves for weeks.

We—we've been waiting on your mother to make a decision."

Who found me?

"I don't know where exactly you were, but the paramedic told me that you were found in some stairway at around 4 am by an unknown woman. She called the ambulance before leaving you to bleed out all on your own. They still haven't tracked her down."

What about Ma?

"Your mother—she's in a bad way, Silas. Bea has been visiting you both in her free time. Apparently, she's not been coping without you. Or with the pressure of making such important decisions about…your care. But I just texted Bea, she was so excited. She's telling your mother the good news right now, then she'll be over later."

Have they caught the bastards who put me here?

"They still haven't got any suspects. When you first came in, the police sent someone every day to see if you were awake yet. As time went on, their visits became less and less. I think they'll want to see you when they hear you're awake. Don't worry, though—we'll catch whoever did this to you."

The grim determination on her face was terrifying.

Jessica stayed next to his bedside for a few more hours, catching him up on the latest events and world news. She didn't notice Silas's eyes fluttering in a bid to ward off sleep, and he willed himself to stay awake. He never wanted to be away from her again.

As the sun began to set in the early evening, the nurse returned to tell them visiting hours were over for the third time. Jessica rolled her eyes dramatically at him, but stroked his hair away from his face and gently kissed him on the cheek. "I'll be back tomorrow morning, okay?" she promised.

He wanted to ask her to stay, to beg the nurses to let her. But his voice was barely more than a whisper and his energy was depleted.

Silas was asleep before the heavy door fully closed behind her.

☆☆☆

Silas awoke to the morning sky casting a mauve tone over his sterile room. The large clock hanging above the door read 6 am, and yet there were already two policemen waiting patiently beside him. One sat on the same chair Jessica had claimed, the other standing nearer the closed door.

Silas hated cops. And going by his encounters with them in the past, they weren't too fond of him either.

"Mr Knight, welcome back. My name is Sergeant Erwin Wegner, and this is my associate, Officer Harry Mills. How are you feeling?" Wegner's voice was a low rumble, a thick accent lacing each word.

Silas tried to respond, but sleep had seemingly claimed the last of his voice. He choked on the words, the officers simply watching him, before giving up and extending a shaky thumbs up towards them.

The sergeant smirked. "Alrighty then. We'll keep this short, Mr Knight, as we know you still have a lot of recovering to do. When you were first brought in, we scoured the building block for any signs of your attackers.

We think there were four of them, based on the bruises and shoe prints."

Almost, Silas thought to himself as he stared directly into the sergeant's grey eyes.

"We traced your blood all the way up to the top floor, but the apartment had been scrubbed clean and bleached to the nines of any DNA. If it weren't for the bloodstained carpet, we wouldn't even have a sure location of the attack. Seems like it wasn't their first rodeo, whoever it was."

No, not if Desmond had anything to do with it.

"We checked the records. The apartment hasn't belonged to anyone in years. If someone was living in it, they weren't doing so legally. So, here's where you come in. Any information you can give us about your attackers— features, weapons, voices—could help us find them and bring you some justice." The sergeant's eyes flared. "You certainly have some...*persistent* friends. They've been calling the station every day for an update."

Jessica. The sergeant turned to shoot a look at Officer Mills, who returned an exacerbated look. The first time Silas had seen him move.

When both sets of eyes rested on him again, Silas had already made up his mind of what to tell them.

Absolutely nothing.

Desmond was a snake, slithering his way out of even the worst situations. He had friends in the police force—associates that would *lose* any evidence Silas put up against him.

And to incriminate Desmond was to do the exact same to himself.

Shingles was an idiot, and Silas knew all too well about the venomous claws his boss had sunken into each of his workers. Some went so deep he knew they'd turn on him if he took their beloved boss down.

So Silas shook his head, training his face to look as disappointed as possible. The officers glanced at each other again. "Nothing?" Sergeant Wegner asked, not bothering to hide his disbelief. "You can't remember a single thing about that night?"

"Sorry, no," Silas whispered.

The sergeant gave him a final look before pushing off his knees and standing. "Thank you for your time, Mr Knight. If you do remember anything, please call us down at the station. We'd be happy to talk to you again when you're feeling better."

With a parting tight smile, both officers were gone, and he was alone again. Only the faint beeping of machines around him interrupted his broken thoughts.

He was tired.

No, he was *exhausted*.

Orange hues tinted the lilac sky through the large window on his left. A small robin chirped on the outside ledge, bouncing around a few times before flying away as misty droplets of rain began to caress the glass.

Four months. He'd been gone for a third of the year.

And yet Jessica had stayed by his side for those long dark months. Something unfamiliar warmed in his chest. She'd mentioned that both Bea and Maria had visited often, too. Despite the possibility of him never waking up again.

Just the thought of Jessica's warm whiskey eyes made him feel safer, allowing him to relax a little despite the harsh scent of ammonia and hand gel surrounding him.

Silas fell asleep again to the pitter-patter of rain on his window, visions of his pretty girl brightening his dreams with her melodic radiance.

CHAPTER NINETEEN

✦

The next few days were a flurry of tests, medical professionals, and physical therapy. Silas had been out for a third of a year, and his muscle mass had depleted. It was nothing short of a miracle that he was able to shuffle, slowly and with a cane, around his square room—the doctors had told him as much. But they trusted him enough to take the catheter out and let him walk freely to and from the adjoining bathroom.

It was small, just barely fitting a toilet, sink, and walk-in shower. The fluorescent light cast an amber glow on the white plastic, making the shadows even darker.

There was a mirror above the scratched sink, barely large enough to fit his entire face. As Silas stared at himself through the glass, he wished it would have been even smaller.

The bags under his eyes pressed out like swollen bruises—strange considering he had been asleep for four months—and the hollows of his cheeks were painfully prominent. There were deep lines on his forehead, and his skin was a sickly white. His hair was too long, his stubble was uneven from where Jessica had tried her hand at grooming. At least his facial hair softened the line of his too-sharp jaw.

Over his eyebrow sat a large, mutilated scar from one of his attacker's boots. Silas could still feel the phantom pain of that first stomp when he dared to look at it. The involuntary flashbacks surged into his mind whenever they felt like it, knocking him unsteady and forcing him to remind himself how to breathe.

Looking in that pathetic mirror, Silas didn't recognise himself. The man staring back at him was disgusting, embarrassing. *Useless.*

It had been seven days since Silas first woke up, and he was just starting to find his voice again. The words were still croaky and difficult for others to decipher, but the people around him did their best to make him feel heard.

Silas didn't mind being confined to his private room too much, with chocolate pudding every night and a gorgeous woman for company. The food wasn't the best, but he was eating anything they would give him to earn back some of his energy.

He had unfinished business to tend to when he got released, and he needed his strength back.

Jessica had been visiting every day since he awoke, and Bea and Maria often stopped by when they could get away from their busy lives. They always came with an assortment of snacks—grapes, chocolate, cakes—and they would share them as they watched whatever was on the tiny television in the corner of his room. None of them could find the remote, so they were often stuck watching the news or a daytime soap about doctors.

Silas had never had time to keep friends, so their company was strangely welcomed.

Bea would often video call Jessica's phone whenever she was visiting his ma, so he could talk to her. Ma looked as exhausted as he felt, slowly withering before him. Four months…four months apart meant that the timeline Dr York had given him during his late-night hospital visit was almost up. But Silas didn't let himself think about that too much. He wanted to enjoy his moments with Ma, even if they were spent through a screen.

"Hey, Bea?" he said as she sat in the chair next to Jessica, ankles perched on the edge of his bed as she enjoyed the snacks she brought in for him.

Bea looked at him, grape still in front of her face as she inspected it for any imperfections. "Yeah?"

"I really appreciate everything you're doing for me," Silas sighed, the words too heartfelt for his liking. Still, he continued, "Truly, thank you."

She gave him a cringing grin, but her weary eyes glinted ever so slightly. "What are friends for, Sy?"

He didn't know when it had happened, but Bea and Maria *had* become his friends. He would have been happier about the fact, if it hadn't been for the nagging feeling at the back of his head telling him it was only a matter of time before Desmond would use them to his advantage.

No matter how hard he tried to bat them away, thoughts of Desmond were frequent visitors, too.

Not only had the deadline of his original mission come and gone, but he also suspected that the attack had come after someone had sold him out to his boss.

So why had no one heard from Desmond Rose? Why was Jessica still next to him; why were Bea and Maria walking free?

Silas couldn't bear the overthinking. So when his visitors had to leave at the end of each day, he would press the call button and ask the nurses for more morphine. He'd feign pain in his healed injuries, claiming the physiotherapy must be to blame for the flare-up. Or, if his favourite nurse, Deena, was working, he'd play up to her soft side and beg for a dose to send him into a dreamless sleep.

Where the nightmares couldn't find him.

The strongest drugs were the best. Sometimes the nurses would only allow him a higher dose of something weaker, but this couldn't keep his dreams quiet. He'd dream of Ma, of Desmond and Richard, of Shingles and his friends ambushing him all over again.

And Jessica. Visiting the market in her sundresses and reading books by the lake without a care in the world. A life so carefree without him in it. It was probably what she deserved, and Silas knew a better man would've let her go by now.

But his thoughts of her were often the only thing that anchored him to reality, reeling him in when he was convinced he'd sunk too deep into the darkness and would never be able to reach the surface again.

So he pushed the feeling of guilt away, holding her extra tightly during her visits, silently vowing to himself that he would earn his place in her life. Because Silas wouldn't accept giving her anything less than she deserved, and Jessica deserved the world.

"What do you want?" Silas asked her one day, as she drew light lines up and down his forearm while reading her book on the bed next to him. "If you could have anything—one wish, what would you choose?"

Jessica looked up at him with a quizzical smile, but then pondered the question for a minute. "I'd wish to leave Fayette Bay, with you. I'd wish that anything keeping us here would disappear, so we could run off into the wilderness together and be happy."

She said it with a whimsical grin, but he knew she was only half joking.

"I'll make that happen," Silas promised.

She hummed, resting her head on his shoulder. "One day," she affirmed, and he sealed it with a kiss on top of her sweet-smelling curls.

With each day that passed after that, his desire to get out of the hospital grew. He needed to say goodbye to Ma, and get Jessica as far away from Fayette Bay as possible. Away from Desmond, her father, and anything tied to his shameful past. Then they could start their true, honest life together.

And Silas could hardly wait.

Doctor Takara had come to visit him several times since their first official meeting. He often beamed and marvelled at how impressed he was with Silas's progress.

For a coma patient, he seemed to be bouncing back *remarkably* well.

Silas didn't feel particularly remarkable—in fact, he felt downright worthless. And if the man staring back at him through the mirror was anything to go by, he *was* downright worthless.

They were planning on keeping him in hospital for a few more weeks to work on his physical therapy and regain his strength.

Good.

Silas had no way of knowing whether Desmond was satisfied with his punishment, and whether he'd need to fight to keep from landing back in this damned hospital again.

Even if his boss was satisfied with the sentence—four months of his life and the entirety of his manhood—Silas had some lessons to teach of his own.

On the way back to his room after each physio appointment, Silas felt strong. His muscles were blazing back up again, and with all the excess food he'd been eating, they were being fuelled just enough to stay warm.

☆☆☆

It had been four weeks since he had first woken behind the bars of his sleep-ridden lashes, and Silas was feeling better than ever. He had finished another successful day of physio training and was back to walking normally again. He could even jog for short bursts on the treadmill.

The eyes looking back at him in his bathroom mirror were much brighter than the ones he had seen a few weeks ago, and his cheeks were fuller. He was allowed to trim his stubble, and had even managed to tackle his hair, cutting it so that it just brushed his shoulder blades. Slightly uneven, but good enough. His hospital gown had been traded for some light grey joggers and a dark T-shirt Bea had brought in from the apartment.

He threw himself a quick smirk as he washed his hands. *Handsome once more.*

As Silas swaggered into the bedroom, quietly laughing to himself, he saw Jessica closing the door behind her. She raised an impressed eyebrow to him.

"Someone's happy," she said with an amused smile.

He took her hand and brushed a kiss along the knuckles. "I have you—how could I be anything but?"

But her smile didn't reach her eyes as she looked at him and said, "Silas…I spoke to Desmond. He—he has a message for you."

CHAPTER TWENTY

✦

"What?" was all Silas could think to ask as her words repeated over and over in his mind. *I spoke to Desmond.*

Silas would have remained frozen to the spot for longer had his body not started to give out on him, forcing him to take a wooden step towards the bed and fall onto the edge of it. "Why would you speak to him?"

"Don't be mad, but—"

"I'm not mad," he interrupted, the words sounding too far away from his body.

"—when you were first injured, I overheard my parents talking about it. They'd asked about you, and I told them that you'd been hurt. I didn't think much of it, really. They asked me why I was so upset, and I just told them. Then I heard them in my father's office, saying that you *deserved* it. Something about being careless. My father said it would've been Desmond Rose's doing, and I wanted—needed—to know why someone would do such a thing."

Pain flashed across her eyes. "His number was in my father's directory in the office…The first time I called him and told him who I was, he just cackled. For five full minutes. So I hung up and tried to forget about him. That was when you were first brought into hospital." She paused briefly. "But then you told the police that you didn't know anything, and I wanted to bring you some kind of justice. I tried to forget his number, but it just kept nagging me—the feeling that I might be able to get you some answers. So, I called him again this morning."

"What did he say?" Silas's voice was nothing more than a whisper.

"Nothing about the attack. But…he told me about you." Jessica's eyes flitted back and forth, like she was recounting the conversation over and over.

"What about me?" Silas pushed. He needed to know if she knew about the mission. If Desmond had taken her away from him too…

Her eyes softened as she looked at him, but something like betrayal gleamed within them. "I know what you are, Silas. I know…you're just like my father."

"Jessica, no," he started, but she turned away. "I promise I'm nothing like him."

A humourless laugh. "Oh really? You're not a con man, working for one of my father's biggest rivals?"

"Not by choice, no."

"What does that mean?" she asked, pushing her curls away from her face. She looked flustered, skin turning clammy as she paced around the bed.

So he told her about Ma and the two years of hell they'd endured, and how he needed the money to pay for her treatments, because he couldn't bear to live without her. That he'd been dealt a bad hand, and he hadn't known how to get out of it.

She sat with that information for a moment before saying, "You told me you didn't care who my father was."

At the waterfall. "I didn't—still don't."

"Am I supposed to believe that it's nothing more than coincidence that my first relationship is with one of my father's rivals?"

Desmond hadn't told her about the mission, then.

"Yes. Jessica, please know my feelings for you are real. There has never been any question," he pleaded. Not quite the truth, but knowing his true motive behind their meeting would only hurt her more. He pushed away the niggling feeling of why his boss hadn't shared that nugget of information with her. "I've been trying to get away from Desmond, to redeem myself."

Jessica eyed him sidelong. "Redeem yourself for what?"

He gasped a small laugh, although he was finding none of this amusing. "For you! To convince myself that I'm even a little worthy of having you in my life."

And that was the truth. He'd sold Desmond out to Richard, all but admitted to himself that he was done with the mission and Desmond's dealings for good. He'd decided to make an honest man out of himself for her while in hospital, but perhaps he'd been subconsciously ruining the mission for much longer than he realised, because he knew—he knew that she was all he wanted. Without her, nothing mattered.

"I don't want any part of Desmond's business or the con game anymore, Jessica. You're all that matters to me—you and our new life away from Fayette Bay."

Had Desmond tried to kill him because *he* knew—he'd figured it out before even Silas had? That Silas was turning his back on the con game…for Jessica.

She chewed her top lip, considering. "What did you think when you realised my father was Desmond's enemy?"

"I don't care about Desmond or your father. Let them fight it out themselves. I'm done with all that, Jess. *You* are all that matters to me—your safety. Since I met you, I've been doing everything I can to keep you safe from the both of them."

The internal conflict was written all over her face. He felt it too, that conflict. But in that moment, he realised his words were the truth. That the mission was over as soon as he met her.

She picked up her bag and cradled it tightly in front of her stomach. "I have to think about everything, Silas. I need some time."

Before she took another step to the door, Silas sprung off the bed and grabbed her wrist gently. His head spun from the sudden movement. "Jessica, wait. I am so, so sorry; I'll give you all the time you need. But please," his voice cracked on the last question, "tell me you'll come back?"

She looked at him in the eye then, the betrayal she clearly felt shining across her face. Despite it, she whispered, "I will come back."

Tears pricked at his eyes at that, and he let her wrist drop to her side. He nodded, and she turned to leave. But before she disappeared, she looked back for a final time. "Silas," she whimpered quietly. "Desmond's message. He said to tell you, 'Game over'."

Then the door snicked shut, and she was gone.

Silas took a second to compose himself, considering those two words from his boss. *Game over.* He sneered grimly. Desmond had taken his pride, confidence, and looks. He'd told Jessica his secret, and she'd left. *Of course* she'd left—he looked no better than her father, than his investors.

All because of one man. Silas stilled himself, focusing his lethal energy on one target. His final target. Desmond Rose.

☆☆☆

Excellent job at butchering the plan, Silas. Really sublime work. Glad I was involved in the planning process.

Bea had brought him a new phone at his request, and Silas instantly regretted asking. He'd used her existing contacts list to program everyone's numbers into it that mattered to him, just in case Jessica wanted to reach out. He'd sent her a message so she had his number, but she hadn't acknowledged it.

Of course, he hadn't asked Bea to program Artie's number into the phone. And yet, Silas knew exactly who the anonymous message had come from.

Was it you?

A response to his text came through within seconds.

> *No. I deleted all footage of you with Richard before anyone else could get their hands on it, but I don't know who sold you out to Desmond. I'm just a messenger, Knight.*

Silas didn't really believe Artie would have anything to do with Desmond's retaliation, but he needed a release. It'd been three days since Jessica left this room, and the silence was driving him wild. He was sure he'd been annoying Ma with how many times he'd been calling her.

> *Do you know anything about Desmond's plans after I get out? He delivered a message to me—game over. Any information on that?*

The minutes drew long as Silas waited for the reply. The implication in Artie's next words settled heavily around him, and he knew the hacker would've been going through his own internal conflict.

> *Are you asking me to look?*

Silas considered the backlash of using Desmond's own freelancer against him. What his boss could potentially do to both of them if he found out. Then he decided he didn't care.

> *Yes.*

Before he could dwell too much on what he'd just done—what Artie had just offered him, despite the potential danger of helping Desmond's new target—Dr Takara knocked on the doorframe and strode into the room.

"Hey, Doc. How's it going?" he asked as lightly as he could.

"Very good, Mr Knight," the doctor said from over the top of his chart as he skimmed the nurse's notes. "In fact, I came to tell you that I'm happy to let you go home today."

A shock rippled through his body as he tried to digest what had just been said. "Home? Today?"

"Yes." Dr Takara snapped the notes shut and drew his attention back to Silas. "I've had the sign-off from neuro, physio, and cardiology. They're all happy with your progress."

Silas had known that he wouldn't be able to stay in the comfort of his hospital room forever—he was even starting to crave the outside world again—but this news suddenly filled him with unsung dread.

Desmond could, and would, find him out there. Track him down. He might not be so lucky to end up with air still in his lungs next time.

"Are you sure, Doc?" The machines next to him began beeping a flicker faster. "I don't feel too good."

Dr Takara sat on the edge of his bed, resting a firm hand on his shoulder. "Silas, it is perfectly natural for you to be worried. You have been in this very room for almost half the year. But this is good! We need to get you out there living life again!"

The warmth of the doctor's palm radiated down Silas's arm, calming his breathing and returning the machine to its usual, incessant pace. He took a deep breath and nodded, pushing his fear back down to the dark depths of his stomach.

He was ready. To see Ma, to get back to how things were with Jessica. To go home.

The doctor gave him a pristine smile, slapped his shoulder, and left him alone with the old nurse that had been there the first day he woke up. Her face was warmer than it had been that day, almost glowing with a sense of pride. She gave him a stack of papers to sign, some leaflets about the next steps in his recovery, and a list of numbers to call should he run into any complications.

After waiting a few hours to get his discharge forms processed, Silas was evicted from the hospital and thrown back into civilization.

As he stood in the double doors of the hospital, the winter breeze whipping his face, Silas suddenly felt incredibly paranoid.

He was being watched.

His eyes darted around to spot any of Desmond's underlings, here to finish the job once and for all. Pupils bouncing from person to person, his heart rate soared again. A grey mist of fog limited his pulsing vision, only causing more panic to rise in his tight chest.

A tap on the shoulder had him swinging around so fast it made his head throb. Jessica stood there, smiling tightly, but her face quickly fell to concern as she noticed the panic in his eyes. She grabbed him by the neck and pulled him down into a tight hold, the rhythm of her heart helping to regulate his.

"What are you doing here?" Silas breathed, head still buried in the thick locks of her hair.

"Bea called me to ask if I could pick you up," she replied frankly. "She's stuck with a patient and didn't know that we're not exactly talking right now, I suppose."

Silas wondered if he should be nervous about the coolness of her tone; the voice lower than he'd ever heard it before. But, since he was on the brink of a panic attack before she saved him, he pushed the concern to the back of his clouded mind.

After a few long moments and shallow breaths, Jessica led him to her car, driven by a middle-aged man in a black hat and formalwear, and guided him into the back seat with her. She directed the driver to his address and invited him to rest his head on her shoulder as she dragged a thumb over his temple.

A few seconds later, another tap on the shoulder had him stretching away from her. Through the tinted windows he could see his old apartment block. Nothing had changed but the season around it.

"You fell asleep," Jessica said, voice soft, like she was talking to a newborn baby. "We're home."

We're home.

But this wasn't her home at all. She lived in a manor, with a library, a tennis court outside, and a dozen bathrooms—Artie had counted. Suddenly he felt very vulnerable, like she'd taken charge. She was wearing a black leather jacket and leggings with her hair tied up in a tight knot. She looked different. He was wearing grey sweatpants and an old T-shirt that he hadn't changed for a few too many days.

Thankful for rescuing him outside the hospital but not wanting her anywhere near the inside of his apartment, Silas tried to tell her goodbye before retreating. He got out of the car and started walking towards the front door, but he wasn't too many steps closer when he heard her come up behind him.

"I'll walk you in." Jessica wrapped a tentative arm around his lower back as they strolled towards the door.

"You don't have to do that," he murmured. "I understand if you still want space."

Jessica looked at him for a long moment, and something like guilt flashed across her eyes. It made him unsettled—the seriousness of her expression. He'd never seen this side to her. "I think it's better if I walk you in, Silas."

It took all his might to haul his body up the stairs one by one, fighting off the flashbacks from his fall after the attack. Silas felt his heart rate rise again as memories flooded through his brain, intruding and inflicting pain wherever they went. Jessica had her hand on the small of his back, and the simple embrace helped him to ward off some of the panic, but not all.

His brain was a flurry of emotion as they finally reached the fourth floor, the last of his sanity trying desperately to block out just a few of his demons.

With a sigh, Silas pushed through the unlocked door. Taking a moment to look around, from the tired sofa to the tiny kitchen, Silas let out a heavy sigh. It was no manor, but it was home. *His* home, with his ma. A relaxing sense of relief washed over him as he shuffled deeper into the room.

Jessica turned to him with a heavy smile and whispered, "Your home is lovely." Her eyes had turned glassy, her cheeks flushing.

Something wasn't right. "Jessica, what's going on?" he asked, before spotting Bea in the corner of his eye. His face relaxed as he saw her, stepping back from whatever Jessica was going through and giving Bea a small celebratory gesture for his freedom.

But she didn't return the sentiment. It was only then that he truly took in her red-rimmed eyes, the grave expression. So similar to the one Jessica had worn outside of the hospital.

"Bea?" Silas's elated silliness vanished. "What the hell's going on?"

Jessica appeared behind him and took one of his hands in hers as Bea said, "I'm so sorry Silas, your mother passed away this morning."

A crack thundered through his chest as he fell back a step, like the words had physically hit him. "No."

"I'm sorry," Bea said again, voice trembling slightly but her face unmoving. A true professional.

Silas pushed past her to see for himself, unknowingly pulling Jessica along with him. He loosened his grip on her hand to let her go, but she held on and remained by his side. It brought a distant sense of comfort as he strode through his apartment to his mother's bedroom door, past the nurse.

He knew before he entered her room what he would find. But that didn't make the vision of his beloved ma, lying on her old floral sheets, any less gut-wrenching. A physical pain in his chest thrummed through him, threatening to bring him to his knees. If Jessica wasn't still squeezing his hand so tightly, he might have let it.

Silas didn't know if he'd be able to get back up again.

Ma looked more peaceful than he had seen her in years. The corners of her lips were curled slightly, like she was happy—like she was finally able to rest.

Silas pulled away from Jessica again, and this time she set him free. He stumbled towards the bed, expression chiselled from stone but vision blurry, and ran a finger down the side of his mother's face.

She was too cold.

The tears spilt over his lashes then, and sobs rang out louder than he knew he was capable of. They filled the room, the apartment, the world.

Desmond Rose had done this. He had kept them apart for months, worn his mother down to nothing with stress and worry, and forced her to give up before he could say a final goodbye.

He'd spoken to her…just last night. She seemed fine.

Silas buried his head into the side of Ma's face, hardly breathing against the feather pillow that still smelled so much like her. And he stayed there, weeping hopelessly, wondering how he would ever be able to carry on without her.

CHAPTER TWENTY-ONE

✦

A faint stroke along the shoulder had Silas startling awake. His eyes adjusted to the overhead light quickly, reaffirming him that it hadn't all been a nasty dream. No, he had been resting on his mother's hands, cupped in his, when he'd fallen asleep. The sheet where his head had lay next to hers was damp, his skin clammy.

Silas noticed the world outside the window; it was too dark. The room was even colder than before. The colours seemed less vibrant. Silas knew Jessica was saying something, and yet he couldn't bring himself to focus on the words. All he wanted to do was go back to sleep. Surrender himself to the numbing nothingness.

His eyes were raw, swollen, and rough from salt as he blinked back into reality.

There was a man dressed in a dark suit standing in the doorway with Bea, who looked utterly defeated. Undertakers. Jessica's eyes bore into him with grief, and he nodded. Without another word, she squeezed his shoulder and left, closing the door behind her.

It was time.

Silas drew in a deep breath and pressed Ma's encapsulated hand to his lips.

"I'm sorry, Ma," Silas whispered as bitter tears lined his eyes once more. He kissed her hand again before laying it back beside her rigid body. As he stood, he stroked her cropped hair before planting another kiss on her forehead. He needed to leave. If not now, he never would. "Goodbye," was all he managed before he forced his body out of the room.

He pushed past the undertakers, escaping outside onto his tiny balcony. The frozen railing bit into his palms as he clutched the metal, memories of countless nights spent out here as Ma watched from her chair flooding his brain. Silas stood empty. They would watch the world go by, talking about nothing and everything, watching the stars until they couldn't keep their eyes open.

More tears fell.

A crushing weight of hopelessness threatened to pull him under as he wondered how he could keep on living without her. A desperate laugh pushed from his lungs as he realised a balcony might not be the best place for him right now. His breath jutted around him in a thick white haze.

"Hi," Jessica said, popping her head out of the door, her voice a sweet melody. "Can I join you?"

He should've wanted to say no. Needed some space. The only person he ever wanted to join him out here was dead, currently being removed from her comfortable bed to be taken to a metal morgue.

His grief was turning to a white-hot rage inside his chest, but he bit the inside of his top lip and nodded. Jessica shut the door behind her before resting her forearms on the railing, mirroring Silas. She shifted closer to him, placing her hand on his and giving it a warm squeeze.

The weight of their last interaction at the hospital hung heavily between them, but Jessica didn't bring it up. She gave him the grace of ignoring it for now, allowing him to mourn with her at his side.

"Do you have a favourite?" she offered, following his gaze into the sky. It was a crystal-clear night, despite the frost—perfect for stargazing. The stars twinkled one by one, dancing along the dark backdrop, putting on a private show just for them.

Silas didn't want to talk, especially not about the stars. But he could see that she was trying to take his mind off what the undertakers were doing inside his apartment, and he appreciated her for it. He lifted their hands to brush a kiss along her knuckles in a silent thank you.

"One hundred billion stars in the sky and you want me to pick a favourite?" he asked dryly. It was a joke, but it came out in a tiny, defeated whisper. She didn't comment on it, nor did she give up. Instead, she nudged him with her hip, her playfulness seeming to be just the right amount of comfort he needed without being disrespectful.

"Okay, so what's your favourite constellation?"

Silas considered it for a moment. He pointed towards the brightest light shimmering above them. Jessica traced his arm with her eyes to find the right one.

"See Vega? That's the fifth brightest star in the sky."

Jessica nodded, transfixed on her glow.

"Now, do you see the small diamond of stars next to her?" Another nod. "That's Lyra. You can see another smaller star next to Vega—that's also part of Lyra. The Harp constellation."

Jessica continued to nod as her eyes moved from star to star, linking them together. "She's beautiful." Her voice was almost too quiet to register, like she was worried she might scare the lights away.

Silas hummed in agreement, a small smile accompanying the childhood memories flashing through his mind. It was the first constellation Ma ever taught him. "Yeah, she is."

They stood in silence for a few minutes, Jessica's light touch tickling the back of his clasped hands. His head was becoming clearer with the fresh cool air, and the tension in his chest slackened slightly. Like it was a punctured balloon, slowly deflating from a single pinprick. He liked sharing this side of himself with Jessica.

"See that white cloudy thing over there?" Silas pointed towards another section of the sky and Jessica agreed. "That's the Milky Way."

One more hole pricked into him, allowing another tiny stream of tension to leak out. He let her admire the band of stars thousands of light-years away for a moment, before guiding her to see the Sagittarius constellation. It took her a little while longer to find it, but her eyes lit up as she connected the dots.

"That was my ma's favourite," Silas whispered, wringing his hands as he remembered fondly. "She would joke that it had to be her favourite since it's in the shape of a teapot."

Jessica let out a quiet laugh, and Silas allowed a smirk to pull at his lips. They shared that joy together quietly until the burst of fire naturally fizzled out. She rested the side of her head on his shoulder. He kissed her cold hair. There was nothing left to say, and she didn't force anything. Their breath mingled in the still air before them and Jessica huddled closer for warmth, not letting him go for a moment.

They remained there until the undertakers had finished, only silence surrounding them as they quietly mourned the only constant Silas had ever known—the centre of his entire world.

☆☆☆

Silas stared up at the moth-eaten lampshade hung from the ceiling of his bedroom. He stole a glance at the clock again—4 am. The sickly orange light of the streetlamps bled into the room around the too-small curtains, forcing everything into blistering focus.

He craved darkness. A room so black that he could just *exist* in a void of nothingness. He didn't want to see his wardrobe, the bottom full of tainted money that he'd earned to pay for his mother's treatments. He wanted to escape the view of the dying plant on the windowsill, barely hanging onto life through Bea's fleeting nurture.

Silas didn't even want to look at the sleeping beauty next to him, face perfectly slack in a dreamworld. She was pure sunshine, but all he wanted right now was for the darkest grey sky to consume him whole.

For the hundredth time, Silas tried to close his eyes. They sprung back open with vengeance. His mind wouldn't—*couldn't*—stop racing, desperate to find some way to claw out from this nightmare that had now materialised around him.

Slinking out from underneath the thin sheet, Silas escaped into the living room. He collapsed onto the sofa, the cushion Ma had so often warmed, and closed his eyes. He allowed himself to spiral further into the grief building like explosive pressure within his chest.

But just when he thought he might implode, a call buzzed through his phone. Had it been anyone else, he would've thrown the phone from the window. But he answered, "Artie."

"Early bird, Knight? I like it." Artie chirped through the phone, as if it wasn't the middle of the night. "And don't call me that."

"What do you want?"

"No sleep certainly puts you in a good mood, doesn't it?" Artie chortled, but he must've sensed Silas's rising rage, as he turned serious before continuing, "Richard Morton sold you out."

"That can't be right," Silas said, sitting upright. "He said he didn't care enough to bother with Desmond."

"Don't know what to tell you, Sy. Richard might keep his internet history and cameras clean, but Desmond certainly isn't that smart. I have footage of Richard in

Desmond's office a few hours after your conversation with him. Did you happen to notice Richard leaving the party?"

Yes.

Scarlette and Richard were both missing from the event, which is why the hosting duties had been passed onto Jessica. "He left the party at around eleven." Silas's mouth turned parched.

"Bingo, I have him in Desmond's office at midnight," Artie confirmed, voice laced with the cockiness he exuded every time he cracked a puzzle. "They share a drink after Richard rats you out. Care to do the same?"

"No," was all Silas said before hanging up.

Richard Morton. It had been Jessica's father who sold him out to Desmond, leading to his absence in his mother's death.

A fire of black rage returned to the pit of his stomach. He had to know why. Richard had told him he couldn't care less about Desmond; even giving him the advice to get away from his boss. Only to head straight to the man himself and tell him everything Silas had done.

He needed answers.

Silas snatched his coat and keys from the kitchen counter and fled the too-quiet apartment, quietly closing the door as not to wake Jessica up.

Silas drove all the way to the Morton manor without a second thought. His foot never wavered from the accelerator. He ran red lights, skipped over stop signs. The danger didn't faze him once. He was at the mansion within minutes, slipping in through the gap in the fence and picking the lock into Jessica's room. He picked the second lock to grant him access to the manor's hallway, which was still lit with those dim sconces.

Silas headed straight to Richard's office, not bothering to be quiet. He took a seat in the office chair behind the grand desk and waited, fighting the urge to trash the imperious room.

It didn't take long for Richard to join him, entering the room with a feline grace. There was no urgency in his movements, like this was a planned meeting. Instead of Silas breaking in before sunrise.

"Silas Knight," Richard drawled, straightening the collar of the polo shirt he'd quickly thrown on. "To what do I owe this pleasure?"

Silas smirked grimly, standing from Richard's chair and motioning for the businessman to sit. "I thought we could have a little conversation, you and me. About your meeting with Desmond Rose."

Richard looked from Silas to the now vacant chair and walked around the desk to claim it. Silas did the same with the visitor's chair. "It's business, son. You showed yourself to be unreliable, and your boss needed to know that."

"You have no loyalties to Desmond Rose."

"Correct, but I have loyalties to my businesses, and you informed me that your boss was trying to sabotage them. I needed leverage to get him to leave me alone, and that just happened to be selling out his favourite employee." Richard leaned back in his chair, his smugness radiating from him. "I told him I knew about his plans with Jessica, and he begged me to tell him the name of my informant. Well, he was putty in my hands then. He agreed to never interfere with my businesses again, and I gave him what he wanted."

"My name."

"Yes, Silas. Your name was the price of my empire not being ruined by some lowlife jealous prick. As I say, it's business." Richard shrugged casually.

"But I thought you didn't care enough about Desmond to bother," Silas said, recalling his conversation with Richard at the party. "You wanted Desmond to come face you like a man."

An amused glimmer shone in Richard's eyes as he shrugged again. "It appears I changed my mind."

Silas choked on a laugh. It seemed Mr Morton was just as deranged as Desmond. "You just *changed your mind*," he said, mimicking Richard's shrug. "Just like that."

"Silas, I was fine letting you walk free after our little talk. I wouldn't stand for one of my employees turning on me so easily, but that was Desmond's problem. I wasn't looking to get involved. But," Richard grimaced, sucking air through his teeth before continuing, "that was until I saw you parading yourself around my investors with Jessica. Come on, Mr Knight. You didn't think that would come with no consequences, did you? She's my biggest money magnet! Once the guests caught wind of my daughter having a big scary bodyguard following her around, they started dropping like flies. Do you have any idea of how much money you lost me with that little act?"

"Perhaps it's a lesson not to use your daughter as a prop for your parties," Silas said dryly. He wouldn't apologise for being the only person looking out for Jessica's wellbeing that night.

"Perhaps," Richard mused. "But that money pays for her livelihood. And you took it from me. So yes, I changed my mind. And I gave Desmond the push he needed to teach you a lasting lesson."

Silas leaned forward in his chair, resting his elbows on his knees. "And what if I just killed you now?" he asked so nonchalantly that he even surprised himself.

But Richard just sneered, leaning forward himself. "I've already alerted security to your whereabouts. There are cameras all over this house. If you killed me, you'd be as good as signing your life away."

"What if I told you I didn't care?" Silas asked grimly, the grief still numbing the majority of his body, his thoughts.

"I think someone would—" Richard started, but was interrupted by the office door bursting open.

"Silas?" Jessica asked, running to his side. She looked between him and her father a few times before landing on him. "What are you doing here?"

"Your friend here decided to break in through your room and threaten to kill me," Richard said casually, like that was nothing out of the ordinary. Jessica's face paled.

"Is that true?" she whispered.

Silas didn't take his eyes off the businessman in front of him. "Your father sold me out to Desmond Rose. He's the reason I almost died."

Jessica's head whipped to her father then. "Is *that* true?" she asked him.

Richard shrugged. "I was protecting the family businesses, sweetie. Your little stunt in front of the investors cost me a lot of money, I needed to get Mr Rose off my back before he could hit me while I was down."

Jessica's brow knitted in confusion, but she straightened anyway and took Silas's hand, pulling him from his chair. "I don't believe you—he could've been killed!"

Richard groaned, as if he were completely over the conversation, "It's *business*."

"I don't care," she shouted. "I'm so done with this family, with being nothing more than a centrepiece at your parties. I'm leaving, and I won't be back." Jessica turned to Silas and guided him out of the office.

"Always so dramatic, Jessica," her father drawled as the door closed, his voice darkness personified. "Why don't you ask Mr Knight about his current mission?"

Panic flared in Silas's chest, but Jessica ignored the final comment. She pulled him all the way to her bedroom, furiously packing her belongings into large suitcases. Silas tried to help at first, but he couldn't ignore the worried looks Jessica kept throwing towards the unlocked door. So he stopped packing to guard it.

She flashed him a terse smile. Oh, she hadn't forgotten the conversation they needed to have.

Silas only opened the door to let in a whining Ziva, who was swiftly leashed and put on the list of things leaving the manor with her. As she zipped the final suitcase, she looked at him with wide eyes. "Can I—" she started.

"Yes," he replied, and her shoulders collapsed a fraction. It wasn't even a question. She'd be staying with him.

They packed a few suitcases into the back of his car, squished Ziva into the front footwell, and drove away from the manor. For the last time.

CHAPTER TWENTY-TWO

✦

Once they'd arrived back at the apartment and bundled Jessica's belongings up the seemingly endless stairs, both Silas and Jessica fell onto the sofa together in an exhausted heap. Jessica turned to look at him, and Silas let his head fall to the side, meeting her gaze. She looked giddy, but it didn't take long for unanswered questions to cloud her sparkling eyes.

"We need to talk," she said as she pushed up on her elbow and angled her body to face him. He remained slouched on the sofa, but nodded.

"You came back," he said hoarsely. "Why?"

Her eyebrows pinched. "I said I would." But his silent question still hung in the air, and she sighed before continuing, "I didn't come back just because Bea called me. I was planning on visiting you anyway, when I got that call.

She told me about…your mother, and I wanted to be there for you. I told her that I'd pick you up and she gave me your address. But…I was coming anyway."

Silas nodded, a weight easing from his chest. She came back for *him*.

"But I need you to be honest with me," Jessica continued, taking his hand in hers and squeezing it gently. "I meant what I said to my father—I'm done with him, his business. And that means I'm done with anything to do with it. So if you're still working for Desmond or anyone like him, then I want out."

"I meant what I said too, Jessica. I'm finished with it all." Silas took a deep breath in, savouring the heaviness in his chest for a moment before his next confession. "What your father said, about my current mission—"

But she interrupted him, "I don't want to know, Silas. I've been going back and forth on it over these past few days and I—I don't want to know about what you've done, in the past." He tried not to balk at her wide eyes, full of absolute resolution. "If you're truly finished with the con game, then I don't need to know. I trust you."

Silas squeezed the hand still in his, only now realising how much it was shaking. "Okay," was all he replied as she stood up and started unpacking her things.

Okay, indeed.

☆☆☆

It had been a week since Jessica and Silas packed up her life from the Morton manor and settled into his apartment together. The first few days had been blissful. Jessica brought music and life to the apartment, filling the some of the sad silences with her hope and beauty. He grieved a little less with her around, and she kept him sane as he navigated sorting out his mother's belongings.

But then came the flurry of texts, calls, and letters from her father. Manipulative messages telling her to get back to the manor *or else*. The letters were never addressed, meaning that the sender had been at the apartment multiple times—or at least one of his underlings had.

Jessica didn't voice her worry, but he could see it creep across her face while she completed small tasks around the apartment. She'd suggested going back to keep the peace, but Silas had shut her down firmly. He wouldn't let Richard manipulate her anymore.

Silas settled into a new routine with Jessica and Ziva, the house never fully quiet with them here. But one of his favourite times of day became when she'd take Ziva on her evening walk. He'd curl up on Ma's bed, eat in her favourite chair, and watch crappy Christmas films on TV.

Some nights, after Jessica had finally relented to her exhaustion and gone to bed before him, he'd pretend he was talking to Ma through the balcony doors as he watched the stars slowly die above him.

☆☆☆

Silas woke to an empty bed. *Strange*, he thought. He always let Jessica sleep a few hours after he woke up, taking Ziva for her early morning walk in the pleasant quietness.

He rolled out of bed, eyes still puffy from last night's grief, and headed into the living room. He had to duck under a garland Jessica had hung over their doorway, made from plastic holly and berries she'd found in one of

Ma's Christmas boxes. She'd used every last decoration to completely transform the apartment into their own private winter wonderland.

When she had finally led him back into the room and allowed him to take his blindfold off, unveiling the effort she'd gone to, it was then that he first told her he loved her.

Her face shone. "I love you, too," she hummed.

He took her face in his hands, tilting it to hover his lips over hers. "I have loved you since the moment I met you," he breathed before kissing her deeply.

"I knew that," she returned. He felt her grin grow wider before leaning back into him.

But this morning, the apartment was too quiet. He called out for her, but only the dog answered, shaking her tail slightly less energetically than usual. He gave her a quick scratch behind the ears before checking the other rooms.

Jessica wasn't there.

Silas strode into his bedroom to take his phone off charge, dialling her number. The call went to voicemail straight away. He racked his brain, trying to think of a plan. Jessica hadn't many friends that she'd consider close enough to stay with—at least not without letting him know first.

She'd *promised* him she wouldn't go back to the manor.

Desmond's plan suddenly flashed back through his thoughts—*We're just gonna take her. Borrow her for a bit, if you will, and see how long it takes to sell her back.*

Richard had sold Silas out to Desmond to prevent his boss from messing with the Morton empire…but that meant nothing. If Jessica had cut ties with the Morton dynasty, Richard might just be unhinged enough to give Desmond the green light as some sort of punishment.

Silas called Desmond. He called Richard. He called Bea, then Maria. No one answered.

He continued to call Jessica's number, but it didn't ring once.

Silas walked around the block, drove around town for hours, but nothing jumped out at him as a clue as to where she might be. When he returned home, the sun had long set. Ziva was whining for a walk.

Silas kept dialling the emergency number but hesitated each time his finger hovered over the call button. There were too many pawns at play. Richard undoubtedly had the best lawyers money could buy. Desmond would spin it around to make *him* look guilty. The only person who would end up in trouble would be Silas…somehow.

So he kept calling her number, the last glimmer of hope fading as it continued to cut off before the first ring. Sleep finally claimed him in the early hours as he lay on his mother's bed, his phone still unlocked on Jessica's contact information.

☆☆☆

The phone rang in his palm. Vision still blurred from sleep, Silas managed to see the number illuminating on his phone—*unknown*. Against his better judgement, he answered it.

"Hello?" His voice was rough from lack of use, the words feeling like sandpaper scraping along his throat.

"Silas?"

He shot out of bed, all haziness now gone from his mind. The bitter December air nipped at his skin, and his mind felt stone-cold sober. It was Jessica on the other end of the line—and she was sobbing.

Before Silas could say another word, Jessica spoke again. Her sentences were fragmented through tears, and she sounded frightened. No, she was on the verge of a panic attack.

"Silas, they've brought me back to the manor. He's been telling me how he's making *arrangements*. I don't know what that means but…I'm scared. And now he's booked us on a flight, and he won't tell me where we're going."

Jessica's rasping words and sobs fell through the phone, making it difficult for him to keep up.

"Silas? Are you there? I can hear him coming. I stole my phone back, but he'll know it's gone. Please, Silas—help me!" She squeaked the last two words—the height of her panic catching up to her—before ending the call. Silas listened to the deafening nothingness as he refused to lower the receiver from his ear.

Fuck.

Silas was quickly learning that Richard and Desmond had a lot more in common than he'd first thought. They both revelled in superiority—and would stop at nothing to get it. That, and they were both completely insane.

There was no time to waste. Silas shot a text off to Artie, and despite the time being just shy of 2 am, he received a text back immediately.

Come to my office. Usual price.

Silas bundled the money from his wardrobe into a black duffel bag, threw on the first clothes he could find, and headed to Bluetine Park.

Silas climbed the stairs to Artie's apartment two at a time, using the metal rail to haul himself forward.

Walking into the darkened living room, Silas dropped the heavy duffel bag on the desk in front of the hacker, a few rouge notes spilling from the undone zipper.

"Woah, watch it, Knight! This is expensive equipment," Artie said, but his eyes gleamed.

Silas's face remained expressionless as he sat down in the desk chair next to Artie. One of the screens was tapped into a network of security cameras while the other displayed several black boxes, code running through them in luminous green lettering.

Artie gave Silas a toothy grin as he finished counting the money. "So, what can I do for you? Surely not another one of Dirty Desmond's grand plans; I can't imagine he's very happy with you."

Silas shook his head and told Artie about the call from Jessica, adding that Desmond was not to hear about any of this. The last thing he needed was this mess getting back to his boss.

"Lover boy's gone rouge…I like it," Artie said, a touch impressed. "I always said that boss of yours was bad news."

"And yet, that didn't stop you working for him," Silas said dryly.

Artie cackled at that. "So, you need me to tap into the airline's schedule and see if Richard Morton has booked a flight…for anywhere in the world, on any day, at any time? Am I understanding you correctly there?" he drawled, a hint of amusement dancing across his shadowed eyes.

"Yes," Silas hissed through gritted teeth.

"Alrighty then," Arthur shrugged. "Should be simple enough."

They sat in silence while Artie worked and Silas watched the screens intently, silently begging for something to jump out at him. Within just ten minutes, which had felt like an agonisingly long lifetime to Silas, Arthur had found a match on Richard's credit card and Dreamstorm Airlines.

"Looks like he's taking his private jet to the south of France," Arthur spoke to himself as he continued reading five screens at once. Another few minutes and he had found the name of a hotel Richard had booked two rooms with. "Two Hôtel Aux Pétales Blancs in Cassis." Artie threw up his fists in victory, whooping obnoxiously. "Nothing quite like cracking the code before the sun comes up, eh Sy?"

But Silas threw him such a glare, it had him dragging an invisible zipper over his lips.

The flight was leaving in just a few hours, and according to Artie's livestream of the cameras at Morton Manor, Richard and Scarlette were already instructing their workers to pack their cases into their private limousine.

"Shit," Silas muttered as he kicked the chair out from under him, rushing out the door. "Thanks for this, Artie. I really appreciate it."

"Don't call me that!" Silas heard his associate shout as the door clicked shut between them.

He ran every red light on the way to his apartment, only stopping long enough to pack a bag of spare clothes and toiletries. He bundled a few wads of cash into the bag as well. Enough to get him on the plane, but not too much that would seem suspicious if he were to be chosen for a search. He covered the money loosely with a hoodie and left for the airport.

Dreamstorm Airlines wasn't far from his apartment, so the price of the annoying taxi driver warbling on about their dreams to make it big in the music industry wasn't too high.

Silas sat in silence, trying to drown out the incessant drool pouring from the driver's mouth, watching the red numbers tick up, up, up. By the time they'd arrived outside the airport, he threw the exact change down on the empty seat beside the driver and slammed the door before he could even thank him.

The airport was far too busy for 5 am on a Monday morning. Children ran around shrieking like mini firecrackers, their parents trying desperately to keep them in check. Lone travellers stood lazily with their cases, shielding their eyes with their hands, trying to catch another moment of sleep.

Silas shot a quick text in the group chat he had with Maria and Bea, telling them he had a last-minute business trip and asking if one of them could look after Ziva while he was gone. They both assured him immediately that they'd take good care of her, coordinating their calendars and creating a schedule. Silas couldn't help but smile as he watched their back and forth.

He pushed through the queues, most of the tourists either too tired or stressed to notice him passing them by. A few gave him sour looks or tutted in his direction, but no one said anything. No one dared mess with his ice-cold expression.

At the front of the line, Silas purchased the first ticket he could get to Marseille Provence Airport, the closest to Cassis. The kind hostess behind the desk cocked her eyebrows when she saw Silas pull a thick pile of notes from his bag, but didn't mention it as she took the money and returned his ticket.

With nothing to do but wait, Silas found an uncomfortable airport chair in an empty lounge. He sat, leg bouncing.

Richard had taken Jessica, presumably because of her cutting ties with the family—for him. Every party she failed to attend would cost him more money with investors less willing to loosen their wallets. Silas snarled at the thought.

But why France—what were they planning to do there? Was it just a power move, showing Silas that Richard could up and leave whenever he wanted, carting Jessica around like nothing more than hand luggage?

Silas knew he needed to watch out for Desmond's kidnapping instincts, but he never thought Richard would be the flight risk. To establish his dominance by kidnapping his own daughter…

But he wouldn't put it past Desmond Rose either, if his boss had a child. It's what these people did—Desmond would stop at nothing to get what he wanted, and Richard was doing the exact same.

Silas scrubbed at his face, exhaustion settling onto him like a second skin. *I am nothing like them*, he reminded himself. *Nothing at all.*

☆☆☆

Silas dropped his bag on a bench outside the French airport and looked around. It seemed as though his plan had ended with the flight, and he had no idea of what to do next.

He took out his phone to map his way to the hotel. But at that exact moment, an incoming call from Artie popped up. Silas answered with a grunt.

"Now, is that any way to greet the man who helped you so dearly this morning, lover boy?" Artie's voice crackled through the speaker. "How was the flight?"

"What do you want, Artie?" Silas drawled.

"Don't call me that. I was just going to tell you that I've set you up a reservation under the name Neil Kaufman at the hotel. But if you're going to be such a dick, I might go ahead and cancel it."

"No, don't. Thank you."

"Always one step ahead of you, hoss." Arthur's voice was full of sheer glee. "You owe me for that."

The line went dead, and Silas chuckled to himself as he tucked his phone into his pocket.

Neil Kaufman, indeed.

He hailed a taxi to take him to the hotel. The driver's eyes gleamed green at the thought of such a long journey. Blessedly, he was a quiet man that listened to music through headphones. Silas snoozed in the backseat, desperately trying to regain some rest he'd missed out on the night prior.

Three hours later, they pulled up to the grandest hotel Silas had ever seen. He paid with cash from his bag—

double what the fare had been—and jumped out before the driver realised the notes weren't euros.

The hotel towered high above the surrounding buildings, painted in an obnoxious gold colour, with statues of falcons flying out from it. The steps were made from marble and lined with a red velvet carpet, with doormen dressed in forest green suits and hats standing to attention outside.

Silas walked up to the revolving door as one of the doormen forced a white-gloved hand in front of his chest.

"Sorry sir, entrance is for guests only," the doorman said in his thick French accent. The sneer in his voice ignited a slight heat inside Silas.

"I am a guest."

"*You* have a reservation?" The doorman's eyes trailed up and down Silas's body twice, antagonising him.

His hair was matted and loose, framing his unshaven face. He wore dark blue jeans and an old, faded hoodie. His trainers, which were once white, were now a mixture of grey and brown. His panic hadn't left much time for *primping*. But he stood tall, squaring his shoulders, and broke into a cocky grin.

"Yes, under the name Neil Kaufman."

The doorman watched Silas for a little too long before reluctantly checking the list of approved names. The succeeding joy Silas felt as he watched the doorman's eyes bulge was enough to leave him smirking, extinguishing some of his building rage.

"I am so, *so* sorry, Mr Kaufman." The doorman flung open the entryway and stood aside for him to pass. "Please accept my sincerest apologies."

Silas entered the hotel with a dismissing wave.

The interior was just as magnificent as the outside, with the highest ceilings he had ever seen. The walls were gold and white marble, matching the shimmering floor perfectly. The furniture was red with gold accents, and even the air smelt expensive.

He could still feel the doorman's gaze on him, so Silas tried not to look too impressed as he walked straight towards the front desk.

"Reservation for Neil Kaufman, please," Silas said to the hostess, who gave him a much friendlier reception than the doorman. She handed him a key without hesitation and pointed him in the direction of the elevator.

Silas entered the velour-lined chamber and pressed the button for the eleventh floor. He turned around absentmindedly and waited for the doors to close behind him. Just as they did, though, he spotted a familiar face through the thinning gap.

She wore a jumper three sizes too big for her and cream leggings. Her dark hair was dull and matted in a tangled bun, loose clumps of curls covering half of her gormless face. There were deep, sunken bags under her eyes, bigger than Silas had ever seen on a person—only highlighted by the lack of pigmentation in her skin and the tear stains etched down her cheeks.

Accompanied by an older man and woman on either side of her, both wearing all-black and large sunglasses, they almost carried her to the front desk.

The elevator doors closed just as Silas pieced together what he'd just seen—an almost lifeless Jessica playing prisoner to her wicked parents.

CHAPTER TWENTY-THREE

✦

Silas paced up and down his spacious hotel room as he tried to make sense of what he'd just witnessed. Jessica, looking drugged up to her eyeballs, being pulled around by a parent on each arm. Parents who looked like they were dressed and ready to attend a funeral.

Room 1163 and 1164, just down the hall from yours.

Artie was owed a huge drink after all of this was over. Silas shot him a text as soon as he reached his room, asking him to get into the hotel's database to see where Jessica was staying.

They have two adjoining rooms. I don't know which one she's staying in.

Silas made a plan to wait until dark before checking the rooms out. He'd choose one to sneak into, hope to high hell it was Jessica's, and get her home. Still, that left him with hours to fill while he waited for nightfall.

He paced, paced, paced.

Silas didn't let himself think of anything other than the next few hours. How he'd get Jessica out of the hotel without suspicion, what he'd *love* to say to her parents, and the contingency plan for if he snuck into the wrong room. The best he'd come up with was to simply drop to the floor and roll underneath the four-poster bed.

After he was sure he'd gone over every possible problem he might face that night, Silas finally allowed himself to pull his shoulders away from his ears. There was nothing else he could do now but wait, so he hopped in the shower ready to wash the airport stench off him. He slipped on his complimentary fluffy robe and slippers before falling onto the bed.

The white sheets were even softer than the towels had been, the feathery duvet ballooning around him and cocooning him in a supple embrace. Silas sighed blissfully, finally able to relax somewhat thanks to the protective wall of bedding surrounding him. Exhaustion knocked into him like a tidal wave, daring him to rest his eyes for just a second.

☆☆☆

Silas opened his eyes to bright sunshine beaming through the still-drawn curtains. A single sunbeam hovered across his face, dancing around just enough to rouse him from the best sleep of his life.

His eyes drearily wandered over to the alarm clock on the side table, still hazy from relaxation.

8.14 am. Shit. *Shit.*

Silas threw himself off the sheets that had so deceptively taken him captive for the entire night. He ran to the bathroom, robe flying behind him trying to keep up with his pace. He splashed handfuls of cold water over his face and stared at his reflection, desperately grappling for a new plan.

Ideas swarmed around his loud mind, but he was pulled from his thoughts by muffled voices in the hallway outside his room, quietly drifting in through the cracks of the door. There were two voices—one low whisper and one exasperated, desperate shout.

Silas looked through his peephole, the bowed glass allowing him to see the Morton family standing right outside his door, all in the same outfits as yesterday. Richard gripped onto Jessica's arm so tight it looked like he could snap it in an instant, while she tried to kick his legs from under him as they stumbled down the hallway. Scarlette walked behind the pair, silently watching with lips so pursed they were completely devoid of colour.

Richard let out a tiny yelp as one of Jessica's kicks caught him in the shin. "That's my girl," Silas muttered as he smirked grimly from behind the door. Richard didn't find it amusing. In one swift motion, he had her pinned up against the wall by her throat.

Silas snarled as he saw the fear in his lover's eyes, her father spitting threats into her ear so quietly he couldn't make them out. After poisoning her brain with a few more insults, Richard released Jessica's neck and yanked her forward. She didn't put up a fight this time, allowing them to walk out of his eyesight and toward the elevator.

Springing into action, Silas bundled all his belongings into his bag—including his new robe and slippers—and threw open the door. But before he reached the elevator, his phone buzzed and Artie's name flashed across it.

"What do you want?" Silas snarled down the receiver, jabbing the elevator's call button incessantly.

"Wow, good morning. Nice to know even sleeping in a bed fit for a king didn't help your mood."

"What do you want, Artie?" *Where was the damned elevator?*

"Don't call me that. I just wanted to let you know that I managed to get into the hotel's camera system last night—you're welcome—and I've been monitoring your floor. Richard left his room every two hours last night to take a phone call, on the hour. He was downstairs for twenty minutes at a time. So, if you're looking for an opportunity to get your girl alone, I'd say I just gave you a perfect in."

Silas considered slamming the phone down on the tiled floor, just to get away from Artie's smug tone. The elevator doors slid open in front of him. He let them close again. "Who's he on the phone to?"

"Who am I, his network provider? I don't know. But I've been looking into his connections and dealings, and you cannot underestimate him, Silas. I might not know why he's taken his family to France, but I would bet it's not just for a holiday."

"Why are you wasting my time, then? I could have caught up to them by now."

"And make a scene with the Richard Morton in the middle of the street? In broad daylight? Come on now, Sy. He'd have you locked up and shipped back to the UK before Jessica would even recognise you. Even I know you're not that stupid—although this girl is doing something to your brain, that's for damn sure."

Silas blew an irritated sigh out of his nose. He knew Artie was right. "What would you do then, smart guy?"

"Oh, I'm so glad you asked!" Arthur chortled. "It's a simple plan really—I'll let you know when Ritchie heads out for his phone call, you go and retrieve the girl, and I'll guide you to the back exit where you can make your escape into the sunset. You'll make sweet, sweet love beneath the moon and I'll be here, dreaming of how I'll cash in all the favours you'll owe me."

Silas threw up an obscene gesture at one of the cameras.

"Love makes the man cruel," Artie crooned. "Do you want my help or not?"

"Yes, I want your help."

"Magic word?"

"Fuck you."

"Oh, so close. Try again?"

"Artie…"

"Don't call me that. Magic word and I'll help you."

"*Please*." Silas spat, much to Artie's glee.

"Smart man. Oh, and I thought you should know that Desmond's men have been asking about you. They've been all over town looking for you, saying something about how much you owe the boss. Tsk, Silas. And here I was, thinking you were the golden child over there. Tell me, was it Jessica that poisoned your soul and turned you *bad*?"

Artie had lost the ability to talk about anything seriously a long time ago. "Do you ever get tired of being such an annoying prick?" he asked flatly.

"Nope, not at all."

Silas sighed. "Don't tell Desmond anything. I'll deal with him when I get back."

"And I'm sure you'll need my help with that, too," Artie drawled.

Silas ignored him, ending the call with the understanding that he would wait for the all-clear later that night, where they'd work together to get Jessica safe and away from her wretched family.

☆☆☆

Silas spent the rest of the day pacing, ordering room service to be charged to Artie's card, and flicking through French television channels. He watched Jessica and her parents return through the peephole, Richard still dragging his daughter along with a predatory grip. Silas wanted nothing more than to be able to jump out then and there and rip Richard's head clean off.

But Artie's plan was good, and he could do with all the help he could get.

So, he waited as the minutes trickled by slowly, each hour feeling longer than the last. With nothing to do, thoughts of Ma crept back in, and he struggled to fight them away. He was here on a mission. He needed his head clear to save Jessica and put as much distance between her and Richard Morton as he could.

Still, it wasn't until midnight when a text pinged through from Artie.

Coast is clear, lover boy.

Silas had bitten each nail down to a nub by that point, and it stung to type back.

Where the fuck have you been?

I needed to check if he was going to repeat the same pattern from last night. Yep, it's still a twenty-minute phone call each time. So stop snapping at me and get a move on! Room 1163 is hers.

Silas slipped the phone into his back pocket, slung his bag over his shoulder, and left the hotel room silently. The hallway was lit with warm sconces between each door. They wouldn't help his escape later, but at least he wasn't squinting to find Jessica's room. He arrived at the door seconds later, but before he reached the handle, the light on the electronic key reader flashed green. A resounding click followed as the door unlocked.

Silas knew Artie would be giggling like a schoolchild at that little party trick.

Slipping into Jessica's darkened room, he took a second too long to admire her sleeping body. She looked peaceful, if not frightened—even in her dreamland. He was just relieved she was in one piece.

"Jess?" Silas whispered, gently shaking her thigh through the duvet. "Jess, we gotta go now."

She stirred, peace lasting for only a second as she whimpered in terror once she noticed his dark shadow, clutching her legs up to her chest and scooting to the far side of the bed.

"Jess, it's me—Silas," he whispered, shining his phone light over his face to prove it.

"Silas?"

"Jess, it's me. Your father is outside making a call right now, and we have to go. Are you okay to walk?"

Silas felt tears stinging his eyes as he took in the full extent of her. Even under a veil of darkness, with only the moonlight casting a watery light over them, he could see how pale her skin was. How her eyes were swollen from crying, her hands shaking beyond her control. He wanted to hold her, bring her back to life, and protect her from the world outside.

But he couldn't. They were wasting too much time.

Silas helped her get changed, pulling her leggings over her shaking limbs. He slipped her sandals on and gently stretched a jumper over her head. She stared ahead while he did so, glossy eyes not focusing on anything. Once the jumper was on, he took her face in his hands and rested his own in the crook of her neck, suddenly feeling a desperate urge to never let her out of his sight again.

He was about to break away and continue packing when he felt her arms clasp around him, fingers digging frantically to anchor into him. He returned the embrace, keeping his hands light and gentle across the small of her back. They remained there for too long, but he could feel her fear melting into relief the longer their bodies pressed together, so he silently counted the seconds as she returned to him.

Several vibrations signalled multiple frantic texts from Arthur, and Silas reluctantly loosened his grip.

"Jess, please. We really need to go now. Do you trust me?" Silas pleaded, trying to hold her gaze, which was still hazy but more alert than moments prior.

She nodded and he held out his hand. She grasped it tightly. They were about to escape when light spilt into the room.

Adjoining rooms.

That's what Artie had said when they'd all first checked in. Silas didn't let go of Jessica, and her hand squeezed him even tighter. So tight that he didn't think she'd ever be able to let go again. Not that he'd let her if she tried.

Scarlette's eyes peeked around the door, widening as she pieced together the vision in front of her. Silas opened his mouth to speak, tucking Jessica slightly behind him, but he didn't get the chance. The weary woman looked between the pair, expression almost as broken as her daughter's, before the door snicked shut.

Silas and Jessica shared a quick glance in the once-again darkened room before resuming the escape plan. Silas opened the main door a fraction as a text came in from his partner.

> *So when I said you had less than twenty minutes, did you think that was a mere suggestion? Remind me to kick your ass later. Take a right out of that room and follow the hallway to the end.*

Silas obliged. They walked quickly through the hallway, glancing around them as the sconces danced and flickered. Shadows bounced, taunting them. They reached the end of the hallway at the exact moment another text came in.

> *R is on his way back up, so you need to be quick. See that door to your right? Take the stairs down to the first level.*

The door to the right of them, labelled *Staff Only*, unlocked with an obnoxiously loud click. Silas pushed through it and led Jessica down the winding stairwell, the acidic smell of cleaning products getting stronger the closer they got to the bottom.

By the time they reached the first floor, Silas's legs were on fire. Jessica was panting and holding her side.

> *Okay, see that fire door? That will take you out onto the staff balcony. The fire escape will get you to the main road. Taxi's waiting for Neil.*

The fresh air attacked their faces as they broke out into the icy night. Sure enough, a steel ladder reached down towards the street below them. But as Silas tested out the first rung, his palm slipped. A layer of invisible ice coated it. He wanted to scream. Instead, he clamped his teeth down on the inside of his cheek and sent a text to Artie.

> *It's covered in ice. Surely there's another way?*

> *Not unless you want the staff to spot you, sunshine. I've been splicing the footage of you leaving so no one can follow you,*

but wiping the memories of hotel bellboys is a little out of my expertise.

Silas was in no mood for sarcasm, and Jessica was shivering even worse than before. He pulled her towards him to share his heat, but it didn't help much.

Then how the fuck do you expect us to get down?

Use your imagination. Hope for the best? I don't know. Good luck, though.

Silas growled—the only outlet he allowed for his festering rage. He looked back to Jessica, who was staring at him hopelessly. He brought her hand, still interlaced with his, up to his mouth and kissed the back of it.

"I'm going to climb down and wipe as much of the ice off as I can. Once I get down, I'll signal for you to follow, okay?"

Panic froze her expression in place. "No, Silas. No, you can't leave me up here," she begged, tightening her grip on his hand. "Please, he'll find me. I know he will…Let me go down first, *please*."

Silas took her face in his large hands and kept it still, locking their eyes together. "Jessica, listen to me. I'm never going to let him hurt you ever again. But I need to get down first to wipe the ice away. You can barely walk in a straight line you're shaking so much, and I need to be down there to catch you if you slip."

She didn't look convinced, opening her mouth to argue. But before she could, he leant in and kissed the words away. It was frantic, frenzied, and over far too quickly.

With her face still sandwiched between his grasp, he asked, "Do you trust me?"

She nodded—without hesitation.

So he leaned in again before letting her go and swinging his leg over the side of the balcony edge, not giving her the time to change her mind.

The frozen steel burned into his skin as he shimmied his way down the groaning ladder, wiping the sticky ice off every rung. His hand melted the ice quickly, and it only took him a few minutes to make the final jump down to the pavement.

He looked up. Jessica was still staring down at him from the balcony. His chest exploded as he let out the breath he'd been holding. She was still with him, right where he left her. He fanned his hand to signal that it was safe for her to climb down, and she practically skipped over the railing after him.

Silas held onto her hips as she made the jump from the final rung.

Then they ran like hell to the only taxi waiting in the parking bay outside of the hotel.

"Neil Kauffman?" Silas asked the driver as he bundled Jessica into the back of the car, quickly following her before slamming the door. The driver nodded, throwing his magazine into the passenger seat and speeding off before they had even clicked their seatbelts in.

> *Make sure to mention me in your wedding vows. I made sure that you're not on any of the security footage, and R hasn't*

left his room again. Your flight is in four hours, emailing you the tickets now. You're welcome! I'm going to sleep.

Silas sputtered a desperate laugh at Artie's final message. He sent a quick grateful response before turning back to Jessica, who was staring out the window, shoulders hiccupping with emotion. He squeezed her hand. She turned to him, tears trickling down her rosy cheeks. But she was smiling. A small, desperate smile. Her tears were of happiness. Emotions of his own rose in his chest and he had to fight them back down to stop himself from joining in on the waterworks.

Jessica tried to speak a few times, but no words ever made it past her lips. Silas stroked an obsidian curl behind her ear, then wiped the wetness from her cheeks. She caught his hand and kissed the palm, holding him to her lips gently.

After long moments of staring at each other, perhaps to convince themselves they were both real, Jessica was the first to close her eyes. Silas dared to do the same.

They were free—they were on their way home. Richard hadn't caught them; Scarlette hadn't told on him this time. They were *free*.

"I'll never let them hurt you again," Silas vowed quietly into her hair as he held her close. Her only reply was the smallest nod into his chest.

Neither of them considered letting the other go, not even when they were safely on the plane and above the clouds.

CHAPTER TWENTY-FOUR

✦

A full week had to pass before Jessica and Silas were able to feel any semblance of normality once home. After the taxi dropped them outside the apartment, neither had suggested doing anything but hiding out, front door barricaded and curtains drawn, while they came to terms with the ordeal they had just faced.

It took Jessica three days to string a coherent sentence together, and Silas faced a panic-stricken urge to hold her every second of each waking hour. He didn't want to spook her, though, so he settled for quick touches as often as he could. A quick tap on the shoulder, interlacing their fingers, a stroke along the small of her back—to remind him that she was real, she was safe, and she was with him.

Bea brought groceries over but left them outside the front door without knocking. Silas grabbed them while Jessica took a daytime nap, taking care not to make too much noise as he pushed the dresser away from the door.

The police had been over twice in the past seven days. Silas tried to keep them away, but after a few threats of them breaking down the door, he obliged and let them in. Like it or not, Richard could build a good case against him to charge for kidnapping.

The first visit was shortly after Silas had carried a still-defeated Jessica into the apartment. The plane ride was traumatic enough, and she was coming down from whatever tranquillisers her parents had been pumping into her. He'd just managed to settle her in his bed when pounding on the door echoed through the entire apartment.

Silas answered the calls and was greeted by two muscular policemen, one wielding a battering ram, the other twirling handcuffs around his pointer finger.

They had been visibly surprised when Silas cooperated with everything they'd asked of him. He'd remained calm throughout the questioning, and even held his arms out ready for the handcuffs.

It was Jessica who had been the uncooperative one, freaking out as soon as she'd seen the hardhats and cuffs tightening around his wrists.

She started shrieking about the justice system, pulling his mother's armchair in front of the door and standing on it. She didn't blink once while the officers considered their next move, her eyes red-rimmed and bruised with exhaustion. Luckily for him, the officers gently agreed to hear her side of the story before taking Silas down to the station.

She told them everything.

The two officers stole glances at one another throughout her ramblings, silently contemplating her obviously manic state. One even shot a look of doubt at Silas, who remained stoic as he heard the intense details of what Richard had done to her. She hadn't wanted to talk about it before then, so her revelations had him wanting to burn the Mortons to the ground. If there weren't two officers standing in his living room, Silas might have done just that.

After an hour of Jessica recalling every single minute detail of how Richard had stolen her from their bed in the dead of night, drugged her and shoved her on his private jet, she broke down. Her palms barely stifled her cries as she wept, so Silas guided her by her shaking shoulders back to the bedroom.

She called back, through shattered sobs, that she would be pressing charges against her father instead. She'd shown them the bruises, the puncture marks littered across her limbs from when god-knows-what had been pushed into her. Silas tensed his entire body at the sight.

Once Jessica was tucked back in bed, Silas returned to the living room, apologising for her outburst and pushing the armchair aside to let the officers pass.

They were both clearly dumbfounded, unsure of what to do next. They muttered something about talking to their superior, but to not leave the country—with a stern threat that they would be back.

The second visit was two days after the first. The same officers arrived at the door, less cocky this time, visibly wary. They explained that Richard was willing to drop the charges on Silas—if Jessica would do the same for him.

Anything to save his public image.

"I don't want to drop the charges," Jessica said definitively, pacing around the room as the officers stepped out to give them a moment to talk. "I want him to feel even a fraction of what I felt when he took me. I want *him* to believe he was about to lose everything."

"I know, Jess." And he didn't blame her. Nothing would've made Silas happier than to see Richard Morton beaten down to the knees for what he did to her. "But he probably has his lawyers on the case right now, finding a loophole to make me look like the guilty one. Like it or not, I technically *did* take you from his hotel room in the dead of night."

"They'll listen to me," she started.

"Not when they find evidence that I drugged you, planted by his lawyers. Not when character witnesses, that we'll have never heard of before, stand up to say what a terrible person I am."

Jessica stopped pacing at that, sitting on the sofa next to him. Silas pulled her in, tucking her underneath his arm as he whispered, "If you want to go through with this, then I'll back you every step of the way. But if it came down to the Mortons vs the Knights in a court of law, I think we all know who would win."

"The Knights," she hummed quietly. "That has a nice ring to it."

Silas smirked, kissing her curls.

But Jessica stood down, telling the officers that she was willing to drop the charges against her father.

Scarlette and Richard hadn't even tried to contact Jessica since they'd all set foot back on English soil. For the best, he knew. But that didn't stop the anguish from hardening Jessica's face. Her expression was tougher, fouler—every waking hour, and even as she slept.

☆☆☆

Each day brought a slither of the old Jessica back. The bruises littering her arms turned a peachy-yellow colour, and her voice stopped rasping so much. She started humming again. The night terrors still forced her from sleep every single night, but Silas was there to hold her tightly, rocking her back and forth in the darkness until she was able to stop herself shaking.

Still, the sleepless nights didn't wreck her peaceful mood in the daylight. Silas began taking Ziva on walks, but Jessica didn't feel comfortable leaving the house yet, so she set to work on the apartment. The cupboards were reorganised, shelves rearranged, and Ma's blanket was reupholstered into a throw, now perfectly folded along the back of their freshly cleaned sofa.

Although she wouldn't say it to his face, Silas knew she was looking for anything to keep herself busy, away from the outside world, tucked into the safe cocoon she'd been building them.

The selfish part of him didn't care—he wanted her close, safe.

So he played along, pretending that they were the only two people in the world.

They spent their evenings cuddled up together on the sofa, watching TV under the comfort of their new throw. It still smelled like Ma—lavender with a hint of emollient. He liked that. While his mother's scent was quickly fading around the apartment, being replaced by Jessica's own, this throw remained a constant. A lifeline for when the grief became too consuming.

The evening of Christmas day, Silas and Jessica lay together on the sofa underneath the blanket watching *A Christmas Carol*, Ziva resting her head across his ankles. He inhaled deeply, remembering fondly the traditions Ma upheld each December, as he drew idle patterns along Jessica's back.

"Do you think your mother would've liked what I've done with the place?" Jessica asked, her voice thick.

Indeed, it looked completely different from just a few weeks ago.

"Oh definitely. She never liked my style," Silas said, vision blurring as he fondly remembered the incessant complaints about the bareness of the apartment. "She'd love it. And she'd love you. *I* love you."

She looked up at him then, crinkling her nose and giving him an overexaggerated cheesy grin, which he mirrored. "I love you too, honey."

He leant down to kiss her. She tasted sweet—oh, so sweet. Like the ripest, juiciest berry in the punnet. He knew he'd kiss her all day, if she let him.

But she sat up, breaking them apart as she reached over the arm of the sofa. "I didn't know when I should give you this," she said, still rifling through her bag behind the chair. "I've been holding onto it for a while and...it just seems fitting tonight."

Jessica finally turned back to him, placing a box in his hand, delicately wrapped in deep green tissue paper. He looked at her, brows furrowed, but she just waited with a massive grin on her face.

"Jess, you shouldn't have," he said, turning the present over in his hands. The wrapping was almost too pretty to disturb. "We said no gifts."

"Oh, like you did so well with that," she smirked, waving a hand to her new easel and paint supplies he'd bought her. "Just open it already!"

Silas chuckled but obeyed. He gently tore one of the folded edges from underneath the tape, the paper falling away. He turned the gift around and gasped.

There, laid in his hands, was the first edition copy of *A Christmas Carol* they'd spotted at the market, on the day they first met. "Jessica..." Silas started, but he didn't know what to say. He was too stunned to form a sentence.

Jessica was still grinning. "I went back and bought it when you were inside getting my bag," she said. "I was waiting for the right time."

When Silas finally looked back at her, his vision was misty. "Thank you," he whispered. "But it's too much. I should pay you back."

He stood to retrieve the money from his wardrobe, but she grabbed his arm and pulled him back onto the sofa.

"You will do no such thing," she said definitively. "It's a gift, Silas. Let someone take care of you for a change."

Silas looked from her to the book, then back to her. "No one has ever done something so generous for me before," he admitted. "Thank you."

Jessica gave him a sweet smile and tucked a lock of his long hair behind his ear. "I knew you were going to be special—from that very first day."

She'd known.

Even when Silas hadn't believed himself worthy of anyone or anything, Jessica had seen him. Bought him this book, because she knew he was hers from that first meeting. And then kept the book, waiting for the right time to give it to him. Because they'd have time. Together, he'd make sure they had the long years they deserved.

She didn't know that their first meeting was engineered by him; she didn't want to know. The guilt ate away at him, but she hadn't asked about his old career again. He was finished with the con game, and she trusted him enough to leave it alone.

Silas reminded himself of the vow he'd made in hospital, to never stop trying to earn the trust she so willingly gave him.

He'd start by making sure he never got caught up in that dark business again. Desmond's final message still sounded clearly in his mind, and he would deal with his old boss when the time came. But right now, here with Jessica and Ziva, Silas had everything he'd ever need.

☆☆☆

After half a month of remaining in the comfy confines of their tiny apartment, Jessica had been braving the great outdoors in little bearable moments—with Silas next to her every step of the way. A trip to the market, a walk along the beach with Ziva. Bitesize pieces of reality to convince her that Richard wasn't out there waiting for them.

Silas often found himself needing the reminder just as much as her. He'd been trying to ignore nagging thoughts of his old boss, and how long it'd been since he'd heard from him. *Game over.* At what point would Desmond cash in on that lost life?

"How about a picnic at Emsterel Thicket?" Jessica asked as they lay in bed, throwing out ideas of what to do that day.

"It's the middle of January," Silas said dryly. Sheets of frost still lay thick on the pavements. She looked at him expectantly, so he continued, "It's freezing cold outside."

"It's not so bad in the afternoon sun."

And that was that.

Silas packed them a picnic and drove them down to Emsterel Thicket. Plenty of people were busy bustling around Bluetine Park's square, but the entrance of the thicket was a ghost town. *Mercifully.*

"Aw, remember the first time we were here?" Jessica gleamed up at the gates as Silas fetched the basket from the back seat.

He mumbled something incoherent as he remembered that day in horrifying detail.

Too many wasps, a sprained ankle, the sticky summer heat.

Jessica in a bathing suit, her sunshine smile, the way she kissed him.

"Oh, come on!" Jessica laughed. "You had fun really."

Another grunt, but this time matching her teasing tone. Jessica playfully hit him on the arm as he looked up, spotting a stout man walking towards them. His shoulders fell as Barney grew closer, eyeing the pair with his arms outstretched and a great big goofy grin taking up half his face.

"Silas, mate! How have you been?" Barney's high-pitched voice whizzed through the air around them. His hair was as red as ever, but his eyes were surprisingly not. Actually, he looked happier and more at peace than Silas had ever seen him.

"Alright, Barney?" his voice strained. Silas had no intention of seeing the man he'd conned so many times ever again. He was done with Desmond's shady little schemes. He had half a mind to give all the money back to the man in front of him. Perhaps he would have done—he had a few stacks in the trunk of his car, after all—if he didn't know what Barney would blow it on.

Silas made a note to send some cash straight to Marlene's home address, as it was Barney's wife who'd lent it all to him in the first place.

"Man, it is so good to see you," Barney beamed. He really did look on top of the world. *Were those veneers?* "And who's this?" he asked, standing back to admire Jessica in all her glory.

Jessica, who was silently shifting her weight from foot to foot, introduced herself sweetly. She gave the stranger a dazzling smile, warm skin glowing in the winter sun.

Damn it, Silas was smitten. *Unbelievably* so.

A few more pleasantries were shared among them, but Silas excused them quickly. Barney didn't put up a fight and walked back towards the betting shop. No, he wasn't walking—he was *swaggering*.

Silas took the picnic basket in one hand and Jessica in the other. He guided her to the entrance of the forest, the path still only big enough for one person at a time. As they ventured further into the woods, the hum of Bluetine Park's crowds fizzled away until they were left in silence. The only sounds were the crackling of dead wood underfoot and the relentless insects flying around their heads.

The forest had become incredibly overgrown since the last time Silas had stepped foot here. Low-hanging branches tickled his neck as he tried to shift around them, nettles nipping at his ankles with every step.

Even the winter frost wasn't enough to kill these evergreen bastards.

They walked for half an hour until they got to the lake that they'd visited last summer. The greenery around it was half wilted, half decaying. But as Silas laid out the blanket and started pulling foods from the basket, he noted the gorgeous look of wonder in Jessica's eyes.

He helped her down onto the blanket and they sat in silence, Jessica marvelling at the nature around her and Silas enjoying the view right in front of him.

A twig snapping in the distance pulled them both away from their serenity.

"What was that?" Silas asked, instantly on high alert. He swung his head around to spy anyone encroaching on them.

Jessica gave a quick shrug before tucking into the strawberries, a hint of amusement flashing over her face. "Probably just a dog walker or something," she dismissed, but after seeing his rising panic, she rested her hand on the back of his. "Don't worry, honey. It was nothing."

"Yeah. Maybe," Silas returned with much less conviction. He turned most of his attention back to their date, but every few seconds he would steal a glance into the tree line surrounding them.

He couldn't see anyone.

So why was his stomach twisting around over and over, wringing itself dry?

☆☆☆

After they'd finished their picnic, Silas invited Jessica to lie down on the blanket with him, giving them the perfect view of the sky between the leafy frame above them. Jessica curled into his side and he traced the line of her arm with the tip of his finger.

In that moment, Silas felt a resounding peace unlike any other. A physical warmth washed up through his body, forcing his lips into a smile and heating his cheeks. He was content. No, he was happy. He was *proud*.

"How did I get so lucky?" he asked the clouds above them.

Jessica leant up on her elbows and offered him a genuine smile. "What do you mean?"

"How did I end up here, with you, our entire lives ahead of us?" It was a rhetorical question, but he still craved the answer. After all the terrible things Silas had done to earn money for his mother's medical treatments—and he had done some *heinous* things—why was he granted such promise and beauty before him?

"We're free, Jessica. We could go anywhere. Just pack up the car and get the hell out of Fayette Bay, away from your parents and my old boss. What are we waiting for? Seriously, let's go—you and me." He squeezed her hand, genuinely excited about the prospect. "Let me grant you that wish."

Jessica's smile widened, baring her perfect teeth. "You're a wonderful man, Silas. I'd follow you anywhere."

Such a line would have made him cringe before—in another lifetime—but before he could protest, she leant down and kissed him so firmly that any notion of disagreeing with her completely fell out of his head. She tasted like strawberries with a hint of cool sweat from the walk.

She tasted *wonderful*.

Jessica broke them apart, but she didn't get very far before he wrapped his hand around the base of her skull, pulling her in for a deeper connection. A soft hum drifted into his mouth, dancing along his tongue and making him crave her closeness. She must've felt the same, as her hand slid down his chest, stomach, and underneath his T-shirt. It lifted slightly, the cool air kissing his bare skin.

"Wait, there's something I need to tell you," she said onto his lips.

But a roaring fire had awakened inside him. "It can wait," he growled, flipping them over so he was towering above her. She was breathless, her eyes hungry. After a quick moment, she nodded, shaking off her coat. He dipped down, creating a string of kisses down her cheek, neck, chest, arms—any skin he could find. She arched. He moaned. Thoughts of anyone around them disappeared.

It was just them, together. Forever.

The heat between them melted any chill in the air away, neither of them noticing the dark clouds masking the watery sun high above them.

It was only when Silas finally lay down next to Jessica and returned to reality that they felt the icy droplets of rain starting to splatter against their bare skin. They jumped up unceremoniously and pulled their clothes back on, straightening up as best they could before the true downpour began, instantly flooding the picnic basket and empty boxes their fruit had been in. Silas whipped up the blanket and wrapped around Jessica's head and arms.

She giggled, giving him a lasting kiss as the rain drenched them. She nipped his lower lip, and if his sodden clothes hadn't been grounding him to their stormy reality, he might've laid her straight back down again.

"Quick!" Silas shouted over the crashing weather once she released him. She led the way, awkwardly walking as quickly as she could over fallen branches and thick roots protruding through the uneven ground. Thunder cracked above them, the thick clouds working with the tall trees to block out almost any light around them.

"Fuck!" Silas rang out, pain blistering up his foot as it rammed into something solid. Jessica turned to walk back to him, but he shouted at her to keep going. He'd slipped her the keys at the lake so she could get in the warm confines of the car and wait for him. She hesitated before nodding, continuing towards the forest's entrance.

Silas shifted all his weight to the damaged foot, hoping to press out the pain. He'd dealt with a lot worse than a stubbed toe. Looking up to the crying sky, he sucked in a deep breath, allowing water to seep past his parted lips in an attempt to cool his burning anger. Rolling his shoulders back, he set off again, cursing out whatever had just obliterated his foot.

He only managed a couple of rushed steps before a blinding pain shot across his face.

Yelping, Silas leapt back. His hand cupped his nose and instantly filled with a warm fluid. Another crushing impact to the face sent him to the floor, keeling over and sinking into the marshy ground.

The rain was still falling hard, droplets crashing into leaves and muffling the sounds of gruff voices shouting at each other, dancing around him as he scrambled desperately for a plan. Footsteps approached quickly from behind him, so he thrust himself upwards and swung the picnic basket over his shoulder.

The invader growled at the impact. "You'll pay for that later, Knight."

Hands grabbed the basket and ripped it away from his touch, discarding it far into the forest. Rough fingers gripped his wrist to keep him steady as another fist ricocheted off his cheekbone, blasting pain up into his temple.

Another hand grappled onto him, squeezing his forearm so tight that he could feel the nails cutting through the top layers of skin. Both men forced his arms behind him, a sharp pinch digging into his wrist as they bound his hands together.

Silas kicked behind him with as much force as he could summon, feeling a good connection between his sodden shoe and one of the men's knees. The victim crashed to the floor, squealing in pain.

"Get up!" the other snapped, embedding a rubber sole into Silas's stomach. He doubled over, his lungs wheezing free of any wind they'd previously held.

Without his hands to break the fall, Silas barked out as his face smacked into the rough mud beneath him. A firm stomp to the spine had him collapsing onto his side, pain searing through his bloodstream.

"Get the bag!" he heard one of the assailants scream at the other, followed by sloshing footsteps.

Mud mixed with sweat and blood flooded his eyes, taking away almost any vision he had left within the dark forest. The grim concoction seeped up his nose and into his mouth, making it near impossible to breathe.

The still-present man was busy trying to tie Silas's ankles together as he thrashed them apart. Silas felt a few good impacts land, but that only made the assailant mad. And once that anger turned to white-hot fury, he took out a blade and rooted it into Silas's calf without a second thought.

Blinding agony raced up his veins from his fresh wound, pulsating with every convulsing movement. He didn't stop kicking his legs, despite every strike creating a new explosion of pain.

"Look, I tried to play nice," a growl purred into his ear, the bitter stench of the man's breath burning his nose. He didn't say anything else, but the evil sneer that followed told Silas everything he needed to know. And when he felt that bee-sting sharp scratch enter his neck, he wasn't even a little surprised.

The second-in-command came running back just as Silas was beginning to drift into a hazy sedation. The two men took an arm each, hauling him up and forcing him steady. He leaned on the shorter man's shoulders while the other pulled a thick canvas bag over his face, turning the world black as his bones turned to dust beneath him.

CHAPTER TWENTY-FIVE

✦

Colours spiralled before his eyes.

Silas blinked, blinked, blinked, willing the rainbows to stop spinning.

But as his eyelids shuttered open, he saw…nothing. No more than the vibrant swirls creating his own private firework display.

Silas knelt on the ground, wrists still tied behind his back. A quick test confirmed that the two men had indeed managed to bind his ankles as well.

His entire body ached as he tried to force his feet free, knees scraping along the cold, uneven floor. A million questions flickered through his mind.

Where was he, and who had done this?

Was Jessica okay? Was she looking for him?

It had to be Richard. His men had seen them the first time they'd visited Emsterel Thicket, and they knew it was one of Jessica's favourite places. It'd already be on his radar as a place of interest.

But Richard would have to know that once Jessica caught wind of what her father had done, she would press charges for their France trip and the Morton empire would be brought to its knees. He couldn't be that foolish, could he?

What about Desmond—the man he'd been alienated from for weeks, tentatively aware of how the *game over* threat remained unfinished. With everything that had happened with Jessica this past month, his boss had been the last thing on his mind.

The internal debate was answered immediately when the thick iron door opened with a ferocious squeak of the hinges.

Muffled murmurs sounded, then rustling as the fabric bag was ripped away.

Squinting from the intrusive blinding artificial light, a mixture of dried blood and dirt crumbled away from his eyelashes. His vision wouldn't focus on one single thing. Everything blended together.

The strip bulbs hanging along the corrugated ceiling buzzed. The walls, lazily painted midnight blue, glinted as the fluorescent light flickered over them.

The two henchmen responsible for capturing him sauntered past, grim grins plastered across their faces. The short one led while Lanky followed closely behind.

Idiots.

Sucking in a deep breath, Silas spat a hock of saliva towards them, but they didn't flinch. The underlings just pointed and cackled as they leered at him, the way a child would a caged animal trapped in a zoo.

"Silence," a booming voice ordered, sending the kidnappers into instant panic-stricken paralysis. The owner of the voice emerged through the door, using his foot to kick back and swing it shut again. The metal clattering together with such force made the room quake, almost knocking Silas from his knees.

Designer dress shoes clipped along the concrete, tartan trousers tickling the wearer's ankles as he sauntered nearer. Richard really knew how to dress to make an entrance. The royal blue and emerald stripes of his suit almost shone in front of the peeling walls. He still looked as rich—as important—as ever underneath the cheap buzzing lights.

"Ah, Silas. You're awake at last," Richard's voice bounced off the thin walls, travelling all the way around the room. "I was wondering when I'd get the pleasure of meeting you again."

"Richard. Whatever you're thinking of doing, don't. Jessica will—" Silas started, the threat ice cold as it escaped his lips.

"Do not," Richard spat the sharp words in a quiet venom, "speak of her to me. You ruined her."

He only deigned to look at Silas directly on the last word, pure hatred darkening his eyes. His face had aged considerably since the last time Silas had seen him—his skin was pinching together around his eyes, he hadn't shaved properly so grey stubble peppered his jaw, and his hair was too long for its usual style.

And yet, Silas thought, *he still looked a hundred times better than Desmond ever could.*

"You took my little girl away from me." Richard edged closer, the rage within him so strong it was almost bursting out of his cashmere suit. "She needs me; she *needs* her family. Who will support her once your blood money runs out, Mr Knight?"

"You made her parade around in front of your friends like nothing more than a party favour," Silas snarled. "I'll support her better than you ever could."

Richard's eyes flashed as he took in a sharp breath. "We all have a part to play in our investor functions," he said. His voice was low, lethal. "She knows that."

"You heard her Richard. She said it herself, that she's done with you. She doesn't want anything more to do with your *business*," Silas gasped the words, struggling for breath. "And who could blame her?"

Richard snarled, examining the shimmering rings adorning his knuckles. "Jessica doesn't know what she wants, Silas. As soon as she sees you for who you truly are, she'll come running back to me. I'm only fixing the mess *you* started."

Silas growled at Richard, looking up at him through a predator's gaze. "There is nothing to fix. Jessica is kind, she's wonderful. She's a fantastic woman. Despite your best efforts, she's the best person I know. *You* are the one that tried to ruin her." His tone turned mocking, "But you failed."

Richard glowered at him, but then sneered. With one swift movement, he delivered a firm slap right to Silas's jaw, knocking him off balance. His face smacked into cool concrete; the rest of his body powerless to protect him.

Face smarting from both impacts, Silas cursed colourfully into the rough floor. His jaw cracked with each word.

"Get him up," he heard Richard order the two underlings. They obeyed, hauling him up together, resting him back on his numb knees. They returned to their original position in the corner of the room, snickering.

They needn't have bothered, because as soon as they'd resumed their places, Silas was hit straight back onto the unforgiving floor and they were ordered to pick him up again.

After a few more knocks—*eight, nine, ten*—Richard knelt beside his convulsing body and grabbed the neck of his T-shirt, jerking him up so that they were face-to-face. Silas felt a burning line trace around his features as Richard studied him.

A vicious grin swept over the powerful man's face before he hissed, "I'm going to enjoy this."

Before Silas could think of a smart reply, Richard lifted his free fist and brought it thundering down onto his skull, a deafening crack instantly powering through his head. Richard kept him close with his bunched T-shirt, raining punches down again and again and again.

The attack must have lasted no more than five minutes before Richard gave up, massaging his crimson knuckles now covered in blood. *His* blood. One of the onlookers offered him a towel for the mess, but the businessman refused.

Silas lay on the cool concrete, head surrounded by splatterings of his blood, body convulsing as it became harder and harder to breathe. "Just kill me," he managed to gasp out, sounding much more pathetic than he'd hoped.

Without looking back at him, still polishing his gold rings back to their original pristine state, Richard sneered, "Well, we'd all love to see that, wouldn't we boys?" More sniggering from the edge of the room. "Unfortunately, I was told I couldn't." The three stooges started retreating through the door. "Not yet, anyway."

Silas was left alone in a pathetic, bloody heap on the floor. His face pulsated against the uneven ground. With his arms still trapped behind his back, he pulled his knees as far up in the foetal position that he could get them.

He could feel the beginnings of the familiar darkness setting in, and he wondered whether it would be best just to allow it to pull him under.

But...he couldn't, not without knowing Jessica was okay. He didn't even know if she'd made it back to the car.

What if Richard had her in another one of these metal boxes, on his way to pay her a visit next? No, Silas would not allow the blackness to take him—no matter how tempting it seemed.

Through shaky breaths, he thought of any possible way to escape. His limbs were bound, but if he could break one of the ties restraining him, then he'd at least have a chance of getting out.

Rolling onto his front, Silas tried to thrust his legs apart. His bursting wounds scraped along the gritty floor as he did so, sending little shocks of pain radiating through his muscles. With no momentum or strength behind his ankles, it was a pitiful attempt at best. His legs weren't going to help him escape.

His hands it was, then.

A survival tip he'd seen some of Desmond's men practising outside the shop swept through his mind, like an angelic lifeline. They were binding themselves together with cable ties, giddy each time they burst free of them. Silas demanded they show him how to break them.

The escape method was simple enough. All he needed to do was fist his hands and pull them back into his body as hard as possible. The flicker of relief quickly snuffed out, though. His hands were bound behind his body, when they'd taught him how to break out of forward bounds. Was it even possible to generate enough force to snap the bands behind him?

There was only one way to find out, and he was getting hungry for his escape.

Resting his useless legs back on the hard floor, Silas balled both hands into fists so that they were flush behind his back. Lifting them as high as he could—which wasn't as high as he was hoping—he thrust his wrists down into his spine, pulling them apart with all his might as they landed.

Nothing.

Well, apart from a wicked zing of pain radiating up his forearms as friction irritated his welting skin.

Silas tried again, and again. And again, once more for luck. He was granted no such thing.

Screaming—out of agony, anger, and a little self-pity—he tried one last time. He used every single last scrap of energy he had left in him, pulling his arms up way higher than before, shoulders grinding at the strain, and threw his wrists down with an almighty roar.

The tie pinged off.

Silas's fists crashed into the concrete beside him. His bones turned to liquid, an instant numbing buzz spreading up his fingers, wrists, arms.

No time. There was no time to acknowledge the pain.

He hooked a finger through the cable tie across his ankles. With a little force, he managed to loosen the lock just enough so that another digit could fit next to the first. Sharp plastic cut into his swollen fingers as he pulled, willing the tie to snap just as the first had.

But as it carved deeper into delicate skin, the cable tie resisted his depleting strength.

Pulling his throbbing fingers out from underneath the plastic, Silas desperately searched the bare room. There was nothing in there with him.

Nothing except *something* glinting on the far wall under the yellow light. Desperate for any help from a higher power, Silas scooted over to the wall and almost wept. The light bounced off a piece of rouge metal.

A jagged, rough square jutting out from the wall.

If he wasn't so focused on getting the hell out of his dungeon, Silas might have laughed. He might have even thanked whoever decided to throw him a bone in the sky.

No time.

So Silas lay on his back and thrust his legs high into the air. His abs strained under the weight, forcing him to drop them sloppily on the metal. Pain soared through his calf and up his leg as the rusted material landed half a centimetre to the right of the cable tie, piercing through skin instead.

He grunted, blew a heavy sigh up his face, and swung his legs back up above the weapon. This time, ignoring the burn in his lower stomach of muscles threatening to burst, he kept his legs steady until he was sure the metal was positioned precisely below the cable tie.

Squeezing his eyes shut, Silas slammed his feet down.

The plastic tie flew away with ease and his legs splayed apart, grateful to have their own space again. He stole another quick moment of relief before he rolled over and rose to his feet.

Anger coursed through his veins and forced him to the rusting door. It was unlocked.

A second of uncertainty stopped him from pulling the door open right away, panic freezing his hand in place on the handle. He didn't know what he was walking into. Weapons, more lackeys, Richard's unwavering supporters? Begrudged investors convinced he'd stolen Jessica away from them as well?

He was safe here—for the time being. In his private metal morgue. Alone.

But Jessica was out there.

With her warm smile. How she made everything feel okay.

Deep. Breath.

Silas ran a hand down his face, which was still slick with blood, before pushing the door open. Beyond the door was a dark room, walls made of metal, the roof corrugated. The floor was still concrete. The only difference between his room and this one was that there were no lights turned on. The light from his room trickling in through the open doorway was the only aid his sight had.

He could make out another door across the room. So Silas shut his behind him, thrusting himself into complete darkness before making his way across the room.

Reaching out to feel for the wall, cool steel eased the pain of his pulsing fingertips. Silas resisted the urge to press his face to it, his wounds almost thrumming at the thought of some cooling relief. But he pushed on, continuing to make his way around the metal box until he felt the indent of the next door frame.

This time he did allow his face a brief embrace with the metal, listening for any movements beyond it. His rage had relented some control back to his brain now, and bursting through squeaky doors without knowing what was waiting on the other side was not how he wanted to die.

But the silence beyond beckoned him through. More darkness. The only sound was his rushing blood drowning his eardrums, his heart threatening to burst from his chest. He started to make his way around the wall again, but his fingers were intercepted by a plastic intrusion. Tracing a line around the square shape, Silas flicked the middle lever. Sure enough, a familiar strip of light flickered on above him.

He stood at the edge of another identical room. Third in a row.

Silas slipped through the door on the right-side wall of the current metal container. It led to another room. *Again*, it was identical. So was the room behind the next door. And the one after that. He stood in the middle of the cheap metal maze as it clicked.

"No fucking way," Silas drawled before screaming, "No *fucking* way!"

The words bounced from one wall to the next, surrounding him with his own realisation. Then he cackled, filling the room with its shrill ring.

He turned around, looking for the next door when a loud crunch filled his ears and searing pain jolted down the back of his head to the base of his neck. The edge of his vision was quickly fading to black as he looked up at the man above him, swinging a bloodied baseball bat with a pathetic smug grin tattooed on his face.

"You—" was all Silas managed before everything around him fell away.

CHAPTER TWENTY-SIX

✦

Ringing.

Oh, such incessant ringing filled his ears. Beads of bitter liquid rolled down his face, seeping into any crevice they could find. Silas wished for the silence to take him once more. He refused to open his eyes, uninterested in the horrors surely waiting beyond them. *Why bother?*

Couldn't the vermin just get on with it and put him out of his misery already?

His arms ached as they stretched above his head, thick rope burning the already tender skin of where the cable ties had been. His wrists were holding most of his weight within the bound ropes, and his shoulders threatened to pop out of their sockets at each of his swaying movements.

Tied up, *again*.

Someone loudly cleared their throat in front of him. Probably the same person that had been thumping his metal pipe onto the steel walls for the last ten minutes.

"Come on, Silas. We all know you're not *really* dead."

The voice was thick with superiority. Silas could feel the haughty look on his greasy face boring through his closed eyelids. He had no intention of giving his captor the satisfaction of seeing his bloodshot eyes and weakened demeanour. He wouldn't allow him to see how much damage his men had inflicted upon him.

That was until the end of the bat pushed into his calf, the stab wound still fresh and pulsating.

In a feeble attempt to keep his scream locked behind his clenched teeth, Silas screwed his face up so tightly that a tear leapt free and ran down the obstacle course of dried dirt and blood. Liquid oozed from the puncture wound behind his trousers.

Another blow to the calf eventually brought his eyelids wide open, his vision swirling before him. His stomach lurched.

"Ah!" the weapon wielder cackled with too much enthusiasm. "He's awake. Everyone! See our dear friend Silas has decided to join us at last."

Silas tried to blink the haze away to make out who this *everyone* was. His eyes adjusted, painfully slowly, just enough for him to see the man standing right in front of him. Batton in hand, decaying teeth bared in a twisted grin, a white vest covered in years of sweat stains and tar.

"Desmond," Silas spat as venomously as he could, spittle flying towards his haggard yet gleeful boss. "What the *fuck* are you doing?"

Desmond's all too familiar triumphant chuckle bounced off the walls, encapsulating Silas in a relentless whirlpool of horror.

"Silas, my son, I love you dearly. But you missed one too many deadlines—you ratted me out to my sworn enemy! You chose your lady-friend over me. I think I gave you more than enough chances to see the light, didn't I?" But Desmond wasn't asking him. He turned and laughed with one of his accomplices, who was still hiding in the shadows along the wall where the single lightbulb couldn't reach. Desmond's voice turned darker as he continued, "I told you it was game over."

Silas barked through gritted teeth, "How was I supposed to get into the Morton manor without Jessica, when your new *friend* was busy having her shipped off to France."

"A test, Silas. That you failed. With the Mortons in France, you had the opportune time to break in and get those documents for me, but you chose to run after Miss Jessica instead." Desmond shrugged. "From then on, I knew where your loyalties lay. And I enlisted my new apprentice to do the work that was *obviously* too difficult for you," he crooned, beckoning someone over from behind him.

The man walked around the wooden frame that Silas was shackled to, purposefully hiding his face until he was safely three paces behind Desmond. But Silas knew that slick ginger head of hair anywhere.

"Fucking hell, Barney. Really?" Silas thrust his body towards his old client, the man who'd begged for his friendship for the best part of a year. The rope ripped through delicate skin. He didn't get very far—certainly nowhere near the duo in front of him—but he still got a hint of satisfaction as Barney cowered back further behind Desmond in panic. "Spineless, as usual. Where does Marlene think you are right now?"

Desmond ignored him, but Barney looked away, suddenly very interested with his dusty shoes.

"Indeed, but even Barney was able to do what *you* couldn't," Desmond drawled, sneering, running the cool tip of the bat down the side of Silas's face. It felt surprisingly reassuring against the welts along his cheeks and chin. "While you were busy chasing a girl overseas, Barney was doing your job, infiltrating the manor for me. Who do you think planted the idea in Richard's head to whisk her off to France?"

Silas considered it. "Richard told you about what I said to him at the party to get you away from his businesses, but you double-crossed him."

A sneer. "Bingo! I agreed that I wouldn't interfere with his *businesses*, but I didn't say for how long. I gave him six months before setting a new plan in motion. Pretty reasonable, if you ask me." Desmond looked to Barney, who nodded eagerly.

"I needed the Morton family out of that big house for a while, and it seemed that you'd already pissed Richard off enough that he was considering killing you himself," Desmond mused, strolling around the room before him. "Well, call it loyalty to my workforce, but I didn't want him to kill you. You were mine, anyway. So I told him to take Jessica off to France—they'd get a nice family holiday, and you'd get an idea of what he was capable of. It's not my fault he went rouge and started planning a new life out there for her, or whatever he had up his sleeve."

"You're evil," Silas growled. "Do you have any idea what that did to Jessica?"

"Oh no, Silas. What *you* did to Jessica. All roads lead back to you, sunshine!" Desmond whacked the metal weapon on the wall for emphasis, the almighty clang ricocheting through the room. "You thought you could save her, but you ruined her life. Should we all take a moment to acknowledge our mistakes?"

Another growl escaped Silas's lips, forcing Desmond's cocky expression to turn sour. It only made his anger burn brighter.

"I'd do it all again," Silas spat. "I did it all for her."

Desmond hummed a laugh, backing into the shadows, his eyes shining brighter than ever. Making room for someone else to speak.

And that they did. "Is that right, Silas?"

The new voice drifted from the shadows behind the two men, its tone much more sinister than he'd ever heard before. Heels clicked along the concrete floor as she descended from the darkness. Her obsidian hair was tied back high on her head. She wore all black with her leather jacket. Even her makeup was darker than usual.

"Jessica?" Silas asked, squinting his weary eyes, willing this to be nothing more than his imagination playing a terrifying trick on him.

"That's right, Knight—our very own Jessie!" Desmond clapped his hands together, bat tucked underneath his armpit.

Silas tried to comprehend what the *fuck* was playing out before him. Barney, sure. Desmond, obviously. But *Jessica*?

"Jessica," Silas rasped. "What's going on?"

She had her winning smile on, running the tip of her tongue across her lips. She looked like she had been caught playing a mischievous game, not unveiled to be one of the masterminds behind his capture.

"Oh, Silas…" Jessica's voice sang around him, somehow still soothing a fraction of his pain. "My poor, sweet baby Silas." She walked up to him, pressing her body to his as she wrapped her arms around his waist, resting her head on his thumping chest. She embraced him for a moment too long before looking up at him and meeting his gaze, her doe eyes as adoring as the day he'd first woken up in hospital. He wanted to beg her not to move. He couldn't bear the distance, even as her next words sliced his wretched heart into bloodied ribbons. "I told you I'd get out of there one day."

She dropped her arms and strutted back to a cackling Desmond, her poisonous tone still burning its way through his veins. Desmond applauded her as she took her position behind him, pretending to bow at her performance.

And what a performance it had been.

"Will someone tell me what the fuck is going on?"

The trio looked at each other wide-eyed, like they were in some damned comedy sketch, and burst into fits of giggles.

Despite himself, Silas joined in. It *was* all so laughable, really—how could he not? As he hung there helpless, he watched the girl he was hired to trick into falling in love with him, gleefully celebrating a mission accomplished.

But it wasn't him who had made her fall in love.

No, she had played *him*. Jessica, who had made him feel safer than he ever had before. Who was there for him when Ma died, after Shingles robbed him of his strength and confidence.

But the waterfall, the market.

The beach, the sunset, the manor.

Her bedroom, the forest.

Was it all a lie?

It didn't make sense. It *couldn't* make sense.

The feelings he'd caught, that she'd nurtured…had all been a lie?

No. *No.* It couldn't have been…

And yet they were. Because they were there, stood in front of his wrecked frame, laughing together at *him*. When had he become the punchline to their inside joke?

Their laughter finally settled when Desmond let out a long sigh. As if it were a silent dismissal, Jessica and Barney left the metal box. Silas watched her leave, and she deigned him a final glance back. Her face was gleeful, but her *eyes*—he knew her well enough to know what was going on behind them.

Or did he? Had he ever known the real Jessica at all?

His boss pulled up a metal fold-away chair to sit on backwards, perching his chin on the backrest. He looked as though he couldn't give less of a damn that it was his closest confidant tied up before him, festering wounds stinking up the humid room.

Desmond took a pack of cigarettes out of his dirty jeans pocket and lit one, taking a long exhale before speaking. "Our story began one fine June day, when I asked my *best* worker—" He used a theatrical hand movement to signal towards Silas, "—to perform a simple task for me. It wasn't anything he hadn't done before, and he was a good egg, so I gave him the opportunity. I never thought that he would let me down, especially so *damn* bad."

Smoke tendrils danced slowly in the still air, swirling across the space between them.

His boss began laughing again, more grimly than before. Without warning, he flung the chair out from under him. It collided against the wall with an almighty clap of thunder.

"See, Silas—your job was *simple*." He drew out the last word as he thrust himself closer, squaring up to rest their foreheads together. "All you needed to do was get some intel on my pal Rick. I would have handled the rest." Desmond shook his head dramatically. "I was rooting for you, Knight."

"Where do Jessica and Barney come into all of this?" Silas snarled. He knew he'd failed his job—he didn't need reminding. No, he needed to know when the past seven months had become a lie.

Desmond's beady eyes lit up. "Ah, sweet little Jessica. I can see why you like her. She's very...*willing.*"

Silas jerked against the ropes so much that Desmond jumped back, fear washing over his expression as he waited for the restraints to give way. The glimmer of panic only lasted for a fleeting second before it returned to fury.

"She came to me, my boy. After I'd thought that Shingles had taught you a lesson and I hadn't heard from you for almost six months, she rang me up. Trying to get answers out of me as to *why* I would've done this. Well, it was only fair of me to ask her to stop by." Another hungry grin. "It was the perfect opportunity, since my employees weren't helping me any. I told her all about Rick's unsightly business—the tax evasion, the torture, the *women*—turns out she knew all along. I think Jessie might have hated her father even more than I did!"

Silas tried to make sense of it all, but words just kept tumbling out of Desmond's mouth. The only pauses were when he stopped to suckle on his second, third, fourth cigarette. He flicked the butts onto the floor near Silas's feet each time one burned down to the filter. Ash sprinkled around the room like fairy dust.

"Our Jessie was obviously upset about your mission. Of course, I had to tell her everything. It wouldn't have been right to keep things from her at that stage, right? I told her about your engineered meetings, the spying on her with Arthur. She looked devastated at the end of that conversation, Knight. If it's any consolation, I think you truly did trick that sucker into falling in love with you!"

"Don't talk about her like that."

Desmond ignored him. "Anyway, I struck a deal with Jessica—well, she was more than willing to work together. She wanted away from the Morton name, and I wanted to have some *fun*." He poked his yellow tongue out at Silas. But when he didn't receive the laughter he wanted, Desmond rolled his eyes. "Not like that, my dear boy— don't you worry yourself. See, at this point, you'd sold me out and ruined my game to win Richard's money. And when I found out that you weren't dead from my initial orders, I wanted to teach you another lesson—one that might stick this time. I told Jessica that if she could make you fall in love with *her*, then I'd get her away from Slicky Ricky for good."

Silas scrambled inside his head, reliving that last encounter at the hospital.

"I was already in love with her," he whispered.

Desmond almost looked pitiful. "Yes, she knew that. But I told her she needed to *keep* you loving her. See, I needed you in Fayette Bay so I could get my hands on you after your stint in hospital. And her admitting she knew everything would only force you further away from me. I didn't feel like chasing you over the country, so I used Jessie to anchor you here, just a little while longer as I made arrangements. But I wanted you to know I knew *everything*, so I told her to pass on my message."

Game over.

Jessica had visited him after all this to tell him she needed time away from him, to think about everything. But she still promised she'd come back…

"Why wouldn't she just tell me she knew about the mission?"

Desmond sighed. "My best guess is that she was hurt, and she didn't want anything to do with you after that. Terribly sensitive, that one. But she needed my help getting away from Richard, and she knew the only way to keep you *in love* with each other was to ignore it. Maybe she wanted to give you a taste of your own medicine."

"But she cut ties with Richard herself," Silas realised, "after she found me in his office."

"That was just a bonus for me," Desmond cackled. "A free worker! Never turn your nose up at that, Knight."

Desmond laughed a while until the joke died out, returning the room to a horrifying silence. Desmond took that as his time to leave. "And that concludes our story time on how you were played by Little Miss Priss. Any questions?"

Yes, plenty.

"How could she do this to me?"

Desmond snorted. "Does the pot call the kettle black, Silas? She did nothing worse than what you were doing to her. You *both* had your reasons for teaming up with Dirty Des—she simply came out victorious." His boss started to leave, scraping the batten along the floor as he did so. "Don't cry yourself to sleep about it, Knight. Shit happens. I'll see you in the morning, sunshine."

And just like that, he was gone. A click of a lock sounded, and Silas was alone. A large moth danced around the flickering light bulb before him, *taunting*.

He took stock of his injuries. Hell only knew how many cuts on his face, a stab wound to the calf, burning welts along his wrists and ankles, and maybe another broken nose.

He couldn't count all his injuries without freeing himself. But Silas did know one thing—he would be lucky to last much longer without any medical attention.

CHAPTER TWENTY-SEVEN

✦

As he drifted in and out of consciousness, Silas swung lazily from his rope bonds, unable to stop the intrusive thoughts plaguing his mind. The life he'd allowed himself to dream about with Jessica—the one she told him she'd *wanted*—had all been a lie. But he couldn't stop dreaming of it, of her, during the long days and even longer nights in his dungeon.

Because an entire lifetime with her? It was more than he deserved, and a con he'd happily turn a blind eye to.

He would've lived that lie forever, if she'd let him. And it would've been the sweetest con the stars had ever seen.

☆☆☆

Silas whimpered awake, raw blisters instantly stinging beneath the frayed rope. He had no idea how long he'd been tied up in this storage container, but judging from how many times Barney had been sent in to feed him a bowl of liquid slop, it had been a few days. Trying to stay awake for as long as possible proved to be futile—his entire being was exhausted, depleted.

The infections coursing through his bloodstream weren't helping, either. Each hazy slumber became longer, with just fragments of reality breaking up his dreamless sleep.

Silas rolled his neck weakly, desperately trying to focus on the person sitting in the corner of the room. His eyes betrayed him, thick blurriness coming like waves crashing to the shore.

But in a fleeting moment of clarity, he saw her. A head wrapped in a floral silk scarf and a gorgeous smile that Silas would recognise anywhere.

"Ma!" Silas croaked, throat hoarse from dehydration. "It's me, Ma!"

The woman sat motionless in the corner for a few moments before slowly rising from her favourite chair. Someone must have brought that green sofa from his apartment for her. Jessica still had a key.

"Can you see me, Ma? I've missed you so much."

The woman continued walking towards him, ever so slowly, only stopping when she was right in front of him. He could see every line on her face, the twinkle in her eyes he'd craved to see shine again, and her thin lips she kissed him with every chance she got.

She cupped his raw face with both frail hands, tucking his matted hair behind his ears. Her touch melted into his skin. In that moment, all pain faded away. He leant into her warmth. She gently pulled his face down and placed a hard peck on his forehead. And when she moved back so he could look at her again, molten tears streamed down his cheeks.

"I've missed you," Silas repeated, this time much quieter as he sobbed like an infant.

"I've missed you too," she whispered back, the words drowning within his heavy howls.

Ma placed his head onto her chest and stroked his sodden cheek. She stood with him, silently soothing his broken being, until he regretfully slipped back into his familiar nothingness...

The metal door swung open and crashed against the wall, startling Silas into reality once more. His eyes darted around the room, but Ma was gone. Her green sofa had been moved from the corner, too. Desmond barrelled into the room, Jessica hot on his heels.

"Silas, my friend!" Desmond's voice was far too loud for his fragile brain to manage, a piercing pain soaring from the front of his head to the back. "We have *divine* news for you."

"Your wounds are looking a little weepy, honey. So, we called in the best of the best," Jessica took over, her voice as sickly sweet as ever. "Get in here!"

Silas peered up through his top lashes as Bea entered the room, hands clutching a plastic bag in front of her. Her nervous expression turned to horror as she saw him in all his glory—hung up like a dead animal, the ropes now holding the entirety of his weight.

His arms had gone numb a while ago, and Silas wasn't even sure if they were still attached to his shoulders. His head was slumped, chin still resting on his chest where Ma had left it, without the energy to lift it again.

Desmond gestured towards Silas, granting her access to approach him. "Sorry about the smell, dear. It is rather hot in here." Desmond laughed with Jessica, who followed along after a brief pause.

"He needs urgent medical attention!" Bea hurried to Silas, hands trembling.

She's just a specialist nurse for the elderly, Silas thought. *She's out of her depth here.*

"He's fine! Just patch him up a little," Desmond drawled, waving his hand in dismissal.

"Come on, Bea. I know you can do it." Jessica's voice turned comforting and supportive—much closer to what he'd come so fond of these past months. Was it only Silas that she had been lying to all this time?

Bea took a long, stuttering breath in and out to calm herself. She opened her plastic bag of supplies and got to work dabbing his face. "I need antibiotics. Lots of them—and *quickly*."

A grumble from Desmond. "Jessie, would you be a gem and tell Barney Boy that he needs to get us some antibiotics as soon as possible?"

Jessica's face fell a fraction. "Can't you do it? I should stay here with Bea. She knows me, she'll be more willing to work on him if I stay."

"It's best if I stay, in case either of them gets any funny ideas about freeing him."

"Do you not trust me, Desmond?"

"Of course I do, but—"

"Then let me stay," Jessica said as she folded her arms definitively. A challenge.

"Jessica…" Desmond snarled.

"Look, if you don't want to see him die within the next few hours, I'll need those antibiotics yesterday," Bea shouted, never taking her eyes off Silas. "I don't care who stays, just get me what I need!"

That, along with a stern glare from Jessica, had Desmond shuffling out of the room with his tail between his legs.

"What the heck is going on here, Jess?" Bea pleaded, still not peeling her attention away from his injuries. She was at his calf now, prodding the swollen, decaying skin around the old stab wound. After giving it a quick clean with something that burned his exposed nerves to his very core, she began stitching it up. He felt, with every hole the needle made in his skin, more rancid liquid escaping and trickling down his leg. As much as she was trying to hide it, Silas could hear each subdued groan Bea made at the putrid injury.

"It's better you don't know."

An icy quiet fell over Bea at that. She swung around, dropping the needle so that it softly bounced off his muscle. From the way Jessica suddenly fell back a step, he could only assume that Bea was shooting venomous daggers at her.

"Tell me right this instant what is going on."

A brief pause settled between them before Jessica said, "I'm dealing with it."

Bea turned back to his leg and resumed the stitches. He could see tears lining her eyes as she blinked them back, begging them not to fall. A thick bandage was secured over the mutilated skin to keep the threads in place before she moved onto his ankles.

Bea sat cross-legged on the floor and lifted his trouser legs. She grabbed the bottle of liquid fire before she froze. Turning back to Jessica, she whispered, "Jess…is he the bad guy?"

Ouch.

A fair assumption to make, given how he'd never had a relationship in all the years she'd known him and his obviously suspicious line of work, but still, that question hurt.

"What do you mean?"

"Did he hurt you?" Bea dug deeper. "Is that why you're doing this to him?"

Silas almost expected Jessica to go along with the assumption—it would automatically make him look like he'd deserved this and her look like the helpless victim who heroically got away from her abuser.

So when Jessica shook her head instantly and said, "No," he felt a tinge of hope.

"Then please tell me what is happening," Bea whispered thickly. "He's my friend."

Jessica cleared her throat, bouncing around like she was nervous. Silas managed to perk up slightly—he wanted to hear this.

"I did something bad, Bea. I—I don't know how I ended up here…it's all my fault." She started sobbing into cupped hands. "I'm sorry, Silas. And I'm sorry to you, Bea, for dragging you down here. I've been trying to get Desmond to take him to hospital since my father brought him in."

"He does need to go to the hospital," Bea agreed. "Desperately."

"I know! But I'm scared that if I push too hard, Desmond will realise that I'm not on his side. That's why I convinced him to let me bring you here, so you could help."

"Help with what? He's dying!" Bea almost shouted. *Again, ouch.*

"To keep him alive so that we can both convince Desmond to take him to the hospital!"

"Why would he do that?" Silas heard himself saying, his voice nothing more than a low rasp. "He'd rather see me dead."

Jessica looked at him in the eye then, tears welling in her own. She shook her head, "He doesn't want you dead. He keeps telling us that you're just confused, that you'll come back to work for him." A humourless laugh. "That's the real reason he used me to bring you here. He thinks that if you know I was faking our relationship, you'll go back to working for him. He's *so* close to taking you to hospital so he can be the hero, Silas. You just need to hold on for a little while longer."

Silas didn't know what to believe as Jessica walked over to him, standing beside where Bea was sitting, and stroked a gentle hand down the side of his face. "I am so sorry, Silas. *Please* hold on—for me."

"Was it all a lie?" was all he could say before the door swung open and Desmond sauntered back in. Jessica jumped away from him, reverting to her cool exterior. Her face remained flushed as she kept her eyes on the ground.

"Barney Boy apparently has no idea what antibiotics are, so he grabbed everything he saw," Desmond said, shoving the box at Bea's side.

Silas never knew Desmond's insider contacts were so *fruitful*.

"Thank you," Bea murmured as she got to work. She filled a sterile plastic bag with liquid and hung it onto the wooden beam his hands were tied to. "This might sting a little," she warned him quietly as she poked a needle through his skin into his vein.

Silas barely noticed.

He could barely concentrate on anything through the intense shivers convulsing their way along the entirety of his skin. He clenched his teeth to stop them from chattering.

"He's seriously dehydrated, malnourished, and has infectious wounds all over his body," Bea said to the room. "He needs to go to the hospital."

The notion was swatted away with another dismissive palm from Desmond. "He doesn't need a hospital, sweetie. He needs you to keep him alive—what's so difficult to understand?"

As Bea continued tending to his smaller wounds, Silas felt the pent-up frustration humming off her, quickly boiling to the surface. Soon she wouldn't be able to hold the positive demeanour she tried so valiantly to keep up.

"This isn't my area of expertise, Mr Rose," she said, voice trembling. "He needs a real doctor."

They argued for a while longer until Desmond stormed out of the room and Bea was left silently crying into his bandages. Jessica dared to comfort her for a moment with a swirling hand on her back. She stole a glance at Silas, who never took his eyes off her, and whispered, "None of it was a lie to me."

And then she was gone, the door swinging shut behind her.

Bea shot up and wrapped her arms around him, hugging him far too tightly for a man in his current condition. Like she read his mind, she jumped backwards, arms in the air.

"Sorry, I'm sorry!" Bea grabbed for the ropes around his wrists, the jerky movements sending snakes of pain slithering down his forearms. "Tell me how to get you out before they come back."

"No," he barked, although his voice was barely decipherable through dehydration and lack of energy. "He'll kill you if you loosen these ropes. Leave me, Bea. I mean it."

Bea recoiled with a sharp intake of breath, but reluctantly took her hands off the rope. "Don't give up, Silas. You heard Jessica, we'll get you to hospital."

"Quickly." His larynx was running on fumes at this point, the sound threatening to die out altogether. "I don't want to die here."

Bea just nodded, chewing on her upper lip.

Over however long he'd been decomposing in his metal dungeon, Silas had been devising a plan. It wasn't his finest work—he knew that. But he was out of options here, still unsure of what Desmond's end goal was. Jessica said he didn't want him dead, but that didn't mean that he wouldn't have some *fun* with him before healing him properly.

His plan required being well enough to actually talk for longer than a few sentences, and he needed to get Jessica alone. At this point, through all the torture he had endured at the hands of his ex-boss, Silas didn't know what life would be like after this.

But he needed to be alive to hear the answers he so desperately craved, and to put an end to this hell once and for all.

CHAPTER TWENTY-EIGHT

✦

Bea was being kept in the makeshift dungeons, too. She wouldn't ever tell Silas where she went after being dragged out of his storage container night after night, but he knew that she wasn't going home. She wore the same outfit—a threadbare jumper and black leggings, which were now almost grey from the amount of dust they'd picked up from the concrete floor. Her once shimmering hair was now dull and dishevelled, and flakes of black makeup clutched onto the puffy skin below her eyes.

He hated that he'd forced his friend into this disaster, but selfishly felt relieved at her company. Bea was good. Too good for his mess.

It had been a few days, she told him, and he was starting to feel a little better. Whatever liquid was being pumped into his arm was working.

And it was *delicious*.

The room stopped spinning, his vision returned to some form of normalcy, and the smell of blood was slowly fading. The hot flushes had become less frequent, and he was beginning to feel his stretched arms again. *That* wasn't such a bonus.

His nurse wasn't so sure of his progress, though. Each time she changed his dressings, she would mutter a string of medical jargon under her breath. The words went right over his head, but he didn't dare ask her to elaborate. Each night, after they'd been ripped apart, he heard the heated debates between Bea and Desmond ringing through the walls.

"He isn't getting better, Desmond," her soft voice rang loudly through the corrugated metal. "*Please*, it's Silas! He's going to die without urgent medical attention."

On the third night of pleading, she added an explosive finisher. "He will be dead by sundown tomorrow if you keep him here."

Harsh words, especially considering Silas didn't know if they were true or if she was just trying to play on Desmond's desperate need for power. To convert him back to a blind follower, loyal to nothing but the business.

But Bea must have made some impact, as the next morning Desmond and his gang burst into his room. "Road trip!" he sang, offkey and as shrill as ever. He walked straight up to Silas and whacked him on the back with all his might. "Let's get you patched up, son."

Barney untied the ropes from his wooden beam, letting Silas's arms fall lifelessly before him. It was an effort not to lose his balance altogether and collapse to the floor, but he managed to stay upright, swaying without the support of his constraints.

Jessica stood close to Bea, her face unreadable. Desmond pranced around like a fool, singing a silly nursery rhyme about hospitals.

Unable to take an unassisted step, Barney and Desmond dragged Silas to the white van parked outside the main door. He released full control of his body, forcing as much strain on the short men as possible.

Before they bundled him in the car, Silas stole a moment to marvel at the outside world. The bitter air kissed his frail skin, the smell of fresh air caressing his lungs.

The cool winter sun shimmered down on his deprived skin, warming him ever so lightly. The tiny jolt of vitamin D was enough to lift his spirits for a moment before he was thrown onto the dirty floor of Barney's van.

Desmond and Jessica took the front seats while Bea and Barney were demoted to the back. They crouched down beside Silas, who still wasn't making any effort to move.

No one talked. Silas listened to the rattling of Barney's chest as he fought to catch his breath. Apparently, he wasn't used to hauling hostages around.

Why him?

What purpose did he offer Desmond?

Barney, although well-mannered and desperate to please, was a laughingstock. He would crack under the pressure in a moment, so why was Desmond even bothering with him? Was Barney so foolish to get involved with someone so instrumental in his downfall?

In that moment, Silas wished nothing but the worst on his *replacement*.

☆☆☆

Desmond called ahead to his contact inside the hospital and got Silas the "best of the best". He was given stronger antibiotics, better painkillers, and more food than he'd received the entire time he was in his dungeon.

However long that had been.

Although he had finally agreed to get Silas the medical attention he so desperately needed, Desmond was more paranoid than ever. They all—Desmond, Barney, Jessica, and Bea—remained in his room until they were almost forcefully removed by the night nurses.

"Someone needs to stay with him," Desmond hissed as they gathered their things painfully slowly, biding time. "What if he rats, or escapes."

"Look at him, Des. I don't think he's going anywhere," Barney reasoned as Bea nodded in agreement.

Jessica shuffled her leather jacket back off her shoulders. "I'll stay," she determined. "I was here every day of his last visit. I'm sure that they'll believe we're engaged." She slipped a ring from her second finger to her fourth. "Family can stay, and I'm the closest thing he has now." Her careless shrug made him want to snarl.

Desmond snickered. "I knew there was a reason I liked you," he said, voice low with lust. Silas thought he might throw up if he wasn't pretending to be asleep in his sterile hospital bed. The sheets might have been scratchy, but it still felt damn good to be laying down. He felt like he was floating on a weightless, pristine cloud.

Jessica ignored the flirtatious comment and waved them off before the nurse had a chance to come back and reprimand them again. She made herself comfortable in the hospital chair, legs crossed as she picked a loose thread on her sleeve. She angled herself away from him, giving her the perfect view of the long strip window.

"I know you're not asleep, Silas," she said, her voice quiet and thick.

But he didn't open his eyes. He needed some time to think things through without fear plaguing his every thought. Jessica *had* got him here, through Bea. But she'd still led him to the thicket for Desmond, into the trap laid out by Richard.

Silas didn't know what to think—to believe. So he remained still, eyes firmly shut, thin pillows deflated underneath all the weight of his heavy head.

Minutes passed. Then an hour. The only sound that broke the deafening silence was Jessica explaining their fabricated relationship status to the nurse. The nurse agreed to let her stay and brought her a blanket for the night.

Silas had lost track of how much time passed before he heard another sound. A sob. It was almost completely silent, but he still heard the muffled gasp. Another one, and then another followed as she tried so hard to keep her emotions away from his ears. But he heard them all, and despite all his instincts, his stupid heart softened.

"Jess," he muttered, almost as quietly as her crying. She remained facing away from him, but she sniffed harshly, not bothering to hide now.

"I don't know how I got into this," she finally gasped, tears falling thick and fast.

"What do you mean?"

Jessica threw her hands into the air in exasperation. "What am I doing here?" she asked the world out the window, as if the stars might have a better insight.

"Why don't you walk me through what Desmond told you, and maybe I can help." He didn't know why he was offering, but perhaps it was because he still wanted to believe that this was all a stupid misunderstanding.

Jessica nodded, throat bobbing as she held back her sobs. "I called Desmond because I wanted answers. I wanted to be able to tell you who attacked you, and why. He told me he'd tell me everything if I came to his office, so that's what I did. I went down there, and he talked for ages about how much my father apparently owed him; how much of a bad guy Richard is. All I needed to do was tell him that I knew, and that I wanted to get as far away from the manor as possible, for Desmond to start telling me all these crazy schemes he'd concocted to get back at my father."

Silas listened intently. Despite Richard telling Desmond all about Silas's betrayal, his boss had no intentions of quitting his revenge plans on the Morton empire at all.

Figures.

"But I wanted to talk about you," Jessica continued. "So I asked Desmond about the attack. You should've seen his face, Silas. It was completely animalistic. He said that you needed to be taught a lesson, and that's what my father had said too, so I asked why."

Shit.

"I think you can guess what he told me about your current mission." She dropped her gaze to the floor, like she couldn't stomach looking at him.

"Then why are you still here?" Silas asked quietly. "Why did you bother saying you'd come back at all?"

Jessica took a second to think over the question before closing her eyes and taking a deep breath. "Because Desmond also, stupidly, told me that you were so behind on your deadlines, because you were letting your *feelings* get in the way. I think he must've forgotten who he was talking to." A joyless laugh escaped her before she continued, "I didn't believe him, of course. I came to the hospital straight after that meeting, ready to call you a complete ass for lying to me, but seeing you—it was just too much to take in. So I told you I needed time, gave you Desmond's message, and left.

"Call me stupid, but I couldn't help but question everything Desmond had told me. I mean, I know you lied about our first meeting, and you engineered all of those *coincidental* run-ins at the beach and waterfalls…but I just couldn't believe that you'd lie about the rest of it."

Silas's guilt lay heavy on his chest, weighing his weakened lungs down and making it difficult to breathe. "Jess," he started, but she kept talking.

"I've seen enough insincere apologies in my lifetime—from my father, the few investors that still had a scrap of humanity left within them to say sorry. But yours, Silas—that day at the hospital when I came to confront you—it was real. And that's why I decided to give you another chance.

"I really was on my way back to the hospital when Bea told me about your mother, and I did want to help you through that. And out on the balcony, my feelings for you had never been clearer. When I asked if you were out of the con game for good, I *knew* you were about to tell me about the mission. So I let you believe that I didn't need to know."

Silas thought back to that conversation—about how easy it had been. Of course she didn't want him to explain his work to her. She already knew everything.

"But, if you wanted to give me another chance," Silas huffed a laugh before continuing, "then what are we doing here?"

"Yeah, that's where it gets complicated. Desmond said he told you about the mission he gave me?" Jessica asked, and Silas nodded. "I really thought I could handle it. I don't even know why I accepted, but I was in Desmond's office, and he was so *persuasive* that I just agreed to it. It was stupid, reckless, but once I was in, I didn't know how to get back out."

"You should've come to me," Silas said. He knew all too well about how *convincing* Desmond Rose could be.

"I agreed before I decided to give you another chance. I was hurting, and some silly part of me wanted to see if I could hurt you as much as you had me."

Silas gestured to the hospital room. "I think you did a pretty good job."

She looked at him incredulously. Not the time for jokes, then.

"And after I'd realised what a terrible mistake I'd made, I tried to back out of it. But Desmond...he said he'd just have to teach you the lesson in 'other ways', and I was worried what that might entail. So, I decided to keep him sweet. The more he believed that I trusted him, the more information he'd tell me. He called me his 'eyes on the inside', and once the plan had been carried out, he'd get me as far away from my father as possible."

"I could have gotten us far away from them on my own, Jess. I *promised* you I'd do that for us."

She nodded again, wiping her tears with her jumper. "I know. In my father's office, you gave me the strength to get out of that situation on my own. And when you saved me from France, I knew you'd do anything for me." She looked up at him, a hint of gratitude shining in her misty eyes.

"Then I'm still not sure how we ended up here," Silas said again. He *needed* answers.

"Please believe me when I say I tried everything to get us out of this situation, Silas. Desmond gave me instructions to get you to Emsterel Thicket, along with a promise that we'd both die if I didn't." Fear clouded her face as she paused briefly. "I think Desmond sent Barney to meet us outside the thicket to send me a message, that he was watching me. I know I should have told you, but I was scared. I—I tried at the lake…" Silas could've sworn he saw her cheeks blush. "I didn't want to lose you, and I thought that if he believed I was still on his side, I could help get you free." Her words broke into muffled sobs for the last confession, "But I failed."

Silas just watched her for a long moment, turning her explanation over again and again in his head. It checked out. She'd felt betrayed by his lie, and been sucked into the

Desmond Rose trap while at her weakest. Silas knew a little something about that.

"Jess," he said finally, reaching out for her hand. She gave it to him. "Desmond is an evil man. He turns people against each other to get his own way." He stroked a tentative finger down the side of her face, and she didn't pull away. "I am so, *so* sorry for getting you mixed up in this. You're too good for this game, and you're too good for me. For what it's worth, my feelings for you were never anything but genuine."

Jessica sniffled, tears welling in her already-glassy eyes. "You—you said you'd never hurt me, Silas. You told me you *couldn't*."

"I know. And from that day we spent together at Roseding Point and Cirrane, I knew I needed to find a way out of Desmond's clutches," he pleaded, a thick lump forming in his throat. "I don't know how, but I was yours so fast, Jess. Honestly, I was scared."

"How did you even get into this mess in the first place? It's not you, Silas."

He knew that. Despite his feelings towards himself and everything he'd done for his boss, Silas knew that the con game wasn't truly his to play. He'd been swept into it by a bad situation, becoming trapped with no escape.

So he hung his head and explained, "I—I had no choice. You know what Ma went through. Three years of treatments, surgeries, and therapies...I needed to pay the bills somehow. They added up and up and up, and I needed the money quickly." He paused as she paid too much attention to her nailbeds. "I *never* found pleasure in following Desmond's orders, like some of the other men working for him. And I'd never have done any of it without a true cause—like taking away my ma's pain. Saving Maria from Desmond's orders. Keeping you safe—or trying, at least."

Jessica finally lifted her chin. Her eyes were swollen and red. Her skin was blotchy and covered with a thin sheen of sweat. Cloudy tears beaded at the tip of her nose, threatening to drop as she hiccupped through silent sobs. But she looked confused. "What happened to Maria?"

Silas tried to ignore the vision of Desmond's men flashing through his head. "It's not my story to tell," was all he said.

Jessica nodded. "I'm sorry," she whispered.

Silas sighed, shaking his head. "You were only doing what you thought was right for you," he mused. "You have nothing to be sorry for."

And he meant it. Because he'd brought her into his mess; he'd given her the motivation to go behind his back to Desmond. She'd been trying to keep him safe in the dungeons.

Sure, she'd lied. But so had he.

She saved him after Ma died, he'd saved her from her father and his investors.

"I truly did fall in love with you," she squeaked through the rivers of tears cascading down her cheeks. "That wasn't a lie."

He smiled weakly. "I know. You knew I was *special*."

A wet laugh gasped out of her at that, and she lifted her eyes back to his. They held eye contact for a bloated pause, both silently evaluating what had gone on between them. Silence still surrounded them as he squeezed her hand still in his, running a rough thumb back and forth over her knuckles.

A peace offering.

"Damn you, Silas Knight." Jessica sighed before answering his questioning look. "Why did you have to make me fall in love with you this hard?"

CHAPTER TWENTY-NINE

✦

Silas and Jessica stayed up for the majority of the night making up for lost time—and they'd lost a lot since coming into each other's lives. They'd swapped notes on the Conman King himself, as well as devised a plan on how they were going to get out of this one alive.

Jessica was more than willing to answer every question Silas had. "Desmond doesn't need anything from my father anymore. I'm not sure how, but Barney got the incriminating documents from his office and Desmond has been using them to blackmail him and his team ever since. He'd pretty much milked Richard and his investors dry, so his final task was to kidnap you from Emsterel Thicket and bring you back to the office. Desmond gave him one last moment to see you, but...I don't know what happened to him or his men after that."

Silas nodded, finding it difficult to feel any remorse for the man who had captured him and delivered him to his death. And he certainly didn't give a shit what happened to Richard Morton after everything he'd put Jessica through.

"Why were you okay with Desmond enlisting the help of your father, after all he'd done?" Silas asked.

"I didn't know Richard was a part of the plan until it was too late," Jessica mumbled as she picked at her fingernail beds. "I think Desmond's been telling us all something different, making us believe we were the *Chosen One*. He'd tell us one thing then go behind our backs and do the opposite. I never cared about being his *favourite*, but Barney definitely does. Sadly, he still believes every single word coming out of that bastard's mouth."

Silas nodded. Everything she was saying tracked—Desmond revelled in the power his minions gave him. He'd tell anyone anything to get them playing in his sick game.

"Desmond doesn't need me for anything anymore," Jessica continued, eyebrows drawing together in deep thought. "If he knows I've gone behind his back, he'll kill me."

"I won't let that happen," Silas threatened coolly, the strain on his voice box sending rough aches down his throat.

Jessica stopped pacing and looked him up and down. Her throat bobbed as she whispered, "How?"

Silas choked out a laugh at the seriousness of her question. Because it was valid—he bet he looked like shit. But she remained stoic, so he gestured at the private room around them and said, "We're safe here. You'll stay with me at all times while I'm recovering, and we'll deal with that weasel when the time comes."

Jessica's shoulders slumped, covering her face with her hands. "This is all my fault," she said.

"It's not," Silas replied, voice a little harsher than he'd intended. "Desmond Rose is to blame for all of this, and I promise you I will make it right."

Jessica loosened a breath, nodding.

There was no rush to get out of this hospital room. Once Silas was back in perfect health, they would deal with their insufferable boss—together.

Silas fought off exhaustion for as long as he could bear, but the dozens of medicines being pushed into his body finally got the better of him somewhere around 4 am. He fell into a deeper sleep than he'd had in weeks.

☆☆☆

At some point during the early morning, Jessica decided that the chair was too uncomfortable for sleep and had squeezed onto the single bed next to him. They both awoke to a nurse standing in the doorway with her hands on her hips, clearing her throat in a very disapproving manner.

It was bright, the low sunrise reflecting off a sheet of white snow that masked the outside world.

A fresh start.

Jessica jumped off the bed, clearly embarrassed, as the nurse rounded them and started taking his vitals. Silas smirked as she excused herself quickly, murmuring something about getting a coffee.

"I tell you something—I really love that girl," Silas confessed to his nurse once Jessica disappeared, who merely returned another stern look and a raise of the eyebrows. He smiled smugly despite himself.

He was feeling much better—what a world of difference the right doses of antibiotics could make. The nurse seemed to approve of his condition, too, as she nodded at each new vital reading she took.

"Hey, what time are visiting hours?" he called before she left.

"They start in half an hour," the nurse said as the door swung closed behind her.

Shit. That meant they only had thirty minutes before Desmond arrived. Silas was certainly feeling better, but he wasn't ready to go up against his boss just yet.

So, when his not-so-friendly visitors bundled into his small room, he played possum, only opening his eyes when absolutely necessary.

"He's been like this all night," Jessica grumbled, playing the part perfectly. "Pathetic, really."

Another stinger.

"Silas, my boy!" His boss tried to click his stubby fingers in front of his face, but all that came from them was an uncomfortable sound of friction. "You're not being very sociable today."

"I feel like shit, Des," Silas croaked. He might've been playing up the severity of his condition, but his voice was still almost completely gone. "Leave me alone."

"Can't do that, hoss." Desmond's smug demeanour was infuriating. "I know what you'll do. You'll leave out the window and I'll never see you again. And would that ever ruin my plan!"

Silas opened his eyes then, very slightly so he was squinting at the disgusting vermin standing too close to him. "Enlighten me, then. What's your plan?"

Desmond let out a hearty chuckle, holding onto his protruding belly like Santa Claus, but shook his head. Not a complete idiot, then.

"Say, Jessie," Desmond turned his attention to the woman rubbing exhaustion from her eyes in the chair across from him. "Why don't you head off and have a rest? Come back at the end of visiting hours."

"Oh, no. I'm fine thanks, Des."

"You don't look fine," Barney chimed in, earning himself a poisonous darting glare.

"I said I'm fine." Jessica's voice was firm, without a hint of worry in it at all. "I'm not leaving. Drop it."

Desmond raised an eyebrow and looked back and forth from Jessica to Silas. "What's going on?"

Maybe he wasn't as slow as Silas gave him credit for.

"Nothing's going on, Desmond," Jessica drawled, massaging her temples. "I just don't want to see him get away. I'm not leaving his side until we're finished with him."

The sinister tone of her last sentence almost sounded like a threat, sending a silent chill down his spine.

"Suit yourself, princess," Desmond murmured quietly, obviously under the spell of Jessica's charm.

It was an effort not to smirk at how well she played them. It was…hot. But before he could marvel at her some more, a terrifying thought swept through his mind.

"Where's Bea?" he asked urgently, suddenly realising his friend's absence.

Desmond's eyes twinkled. "Oh, the nurse? What would you say, Barn? Probably somewhere at the bottom of a lake by now."

The computer screens around his bed roared into action as Silas thrust himself upright, eyes bulging. No, *no*. This couldn't be happening.

Jessica leapt from her chair and grabbed onto the sleeve of Desmond's bomber jacket. "Are you—" she started before he let out a blood-curdling howl of laughter. Barney joined in nervously.

"Calm down, you two. Your little friend is probably at home, hopefully changing into some cleaner clothes. I let her go but made it very clear that if she were to call the pigs, we'd kill you all. So don't be hoping for any help from her."

"I'm going to fucking kill you," Silas growled, lying himself back down awkwardly as fireworks of pain exploded throughout his body. A nurse came in to check what all the fuss was about and reset his monitors.

Desmond winked at him, and that was the last thing Silas saw before closing his eyes and spiralling deeper into his roaring rage within. He didn't open them again for the rest of the visit.

☆☆☆

Barney and Desmond talked for hours, relentlessly shrill voices burning a hole from one ear to the other through his festering brain. Silas was still vibrating with fury, even hours after Desmond's practical *joke*.

The end of visiting hours couldn't come soon enough. Unfortunately, the day dragged like a half-dead corpse hopelessly trying to get away from its killer.

When Desmond and Barney finally left Jessica alone with Silas, he cautiously allowed himself to perk up again.

"Hey," he smiled as she awkwardly sat on the edge of his bed, using one finger to push a strand of hair out of his eyes. "I missed you, pretty girl."

Jessica smiled at that. She tentatively leaned down to meet his lips with hers, stopping every few millimetres to make sure he wouldn't push her away. They shared a quick peck, but that was all Silas needed to feel himself again.

"I texted Bea earlier," Jessica said, cupping his hand with hers. "She's fine, and so is Maria. I could practically feel the anger radiating from you all day, so I wanted to check."

He blew a sigh of relief, kissing the back of her hand. "Thank you."

She replied by resting her head on his chest, the familiar weight calming his frustrated heart.

He wanted to go up against Desmond, and his body was now raring to go. Every muscle was charged with electricity as he thought of all the ways he could inflict pain on Desmond Rose. The tools he'd use, the feeble cries his boss would whimper, begging him to stop. Oh, he *would* stop—but only once Desmond was dead and gone from their lives forever.

"What are you thinking about?" Jessica pulled him out of his twisted fantasy, jolting him back to his sterile reality.

"That I'm going to kill him," Silas confessed quietly before he considered the fact that she could very well run and tell their boss that information. But any doubt that she was bluffing melted away when he saw her vicious grin radiating from cheek to cheek. It was the perfect balance between sweet and sinful, and Silas knew she was on board.

That was where the conversation ended—for now.

Silas pulled himself out of bed, swinging his legs over the side to slide out from underneath her. His body felt like it'd been injected with cement, each limb heavier than the last.

Jessica looked as exhausted as he felt. She wasn't used to all this lying, manipulating. The stress of the character she adorned around Desmond and Barney weighed heavily on her shoulders, and he saw through the easy smile she was using to mask it.

"Here, lay down. You need to rest," he said, gently lowering himself into the visitor's chair.

Jessica looked uncertain for a moment, but smiled weakly and lay down, closing her eyes as soon as her head hit the thin pillows. Her breathing turned even and slow as he drew small patterns along one of her ankles.

Silas sat in Jessica's chair for an hour or so after she had fallen into a blissfully deep sleep, watching the tiny TV monitor on mute. His nurse came in at one point, face as disapproving as ever, and tried to shoo him back into bed. After a few moments of silent arguing, she gave up and threw her hands in the air before retreating into the hallway.

A good sign.

Yes, he was feeling much better. The painkillers were taking the edge off his open wounds, but he hadn't had a dose in a while and he still didn't feel the soreness creeping back in. The agonising memories from the dungeon still plagued his memory, but they were finally beginning to become a little less terrifying.

They weren't real.

He'd escaped, and he was in hospital.

Safe. He was safe.

Jessica was safe. Bea and Maria, too.

The vivid visions were no longer real.

Silas was just drifting off into a shallow sleep—this chair was the most uncomfortable thing he'd ever encountered—when his doctor pushed through the door. The swift movement cast a breeze around the entire room, startling both Silas and Jessica awake.

"Mr Knight," the doctor stuttered momentarily as she mistook Jessica for the patient. Her blue eyes settled on Silas, and she repeated her greeting. "Mr Knight. I'm Dr Preece, do you remember us meeting?"

Silas shook his head slowly. A corner of Dr Preece's mouth twitched up in a tight knowing smile. Her dark brown hair was tied up with a few deliberate strands left out to frame her face. She had thin square glasses that sat at the end of her nose. "I didn't think you would," she said. "You were completely out of it when you first arrived. Although I'm glad to see you're making a full recovery."

"Thank you." Silas gave her a weak smile. "I'm feeling much better. When can I get out of here?"

"Eager to leave us so soon?" the doctor asked, low voice tinted with playfulness.

Silas let out a small fake laugh. "No, no. Well, yes. I've been here too much for my liking these past few months."

"Yes, that's what I've come to talk to you about actually," Dr Preece said, tone falling flat. "Would you mind stepping out, dear?"

She directed the question at Jessica, who was still rubbing her eyes and trying to fully wake herself from her slumber. She stopped stretching to acknowledge the older woman in front of her, but she couldn't stop her yawn from tainting her words. "Who, me?"

"That's right."

Jessica looked at Silas in confusion and perhaps a little panic. He understood. "Anything you have to say to me, you can say in front of Jessica," he reassured.

The doctor gave them both a stern look. "No, Silas. Unfortunately, this cannot be said in front of your fiancée. She will have to step outside."

Silas could see the offence on Jessica's face clearly, but she swung her legs off the bed and strutted out of the room anyway. She gave Silas a quick glance before disappearing down the hallway. Dr Preece shut the door behind her.

"I'll just cut to the chase, Silas. We can see from your records that you have been here twice in the past year. Last time was for a pretty dangerous attack, and now you're back in—less than four months later—for an infection that almost killed you and some very suspicious wounds."

The doctor offered a pause, but Silas didn't fill the silence. He knew where this was going, but he wouldn't give her the satisfaction of helping her to the point.

An inward sigh. "Last time you were here, you told the police that you couldn't remember anything from your attack. When you came in a few days ago, your fiancée told us that you wouldn't be pressing charges." The doctor pushed her glasses up the bridge of her nose before leaning closer. "But she cannot make that decision for you. I need you to tell me if these attacks were related."

Of course they were related, Silas wanted to shout. He wanted to confess it all, have the hospital and police deal with his twisted boss. But that would incriminate Jessica, who had only become tangled in mess because of him. Barney would be taken away from his wife, and he didn't deserve that—not really. He was just a good guy caught up in a bad situation.

Bea might even be wrapped up in it all once the police investigation got underway. He couldn't risk her job, family, and life for something she should never have been dragged into in the first place.

No, Silas would have to deal with Desmond on his own—and that meant no police.

"Not that I know of, Doc," Silas said, shaking his head. "And Jessica's right, I won't be pressing charges."

"Are you sure?" she asked, one eyebrow cocked in disbelief. She leaned even further forward, forearms resting on her knees. "Silas, you can trust us. We will take care of you."

Her voice was so soothing. For a moment he toyed with the idea of letting all of the secrets spill out, but shut it down instantly. This was something that he had to do alone.

"I appreciate the sentiment, Doc. But they weren't related. I can't remember much of the attacks, but it wasn't Jessica."

Dr Preece straightened, slightly taken aback at how he brought her into the conversation so easily, but nodded shallowly. "I understand. Thank you for your time," she said through tight lips as she stood up. "As for leaving, I have no problem with discharging you tomorrow morning. We'll give you the rest of your antibiotics in capsule form, along with some more painkillers. I know you have a nurse in your close circle—she can redress your wounds when needed. Come straight back if you start feeling worse again, but you're making a great recovery so far. Happy with that?"

Silas sighed a deep breath of relief and nodded. "All good, thank you."

Dr Preece gave him a professional smile before heading out the door and saying, "Take care of yourself, Silas." Her smile didn't reach her eyes.

He let his head fall back onto the pillow as he relaxed, grinning at the thought of his near freedom. Only a few more hours until he was out of this fucking hospital.

Only a few more hours until Desmond Rose was dead.

CHAPTER THIRTY

✦

"Wait, Silas, slow down!" Jessica urged, trying to catch his eye with hers as he darted around the room looking for his missing shoe. "What are you doing?"

"They let me sign the papers while you were out getting breakfast," Silas said, pointing at the small stack of discharge forms on the edge of his bed. "We need to get out of here before Desmond arrives. Do you know where my shoe is?"

"You only came in with one," Jessica murmured, deep in thought. "What's the plan, Silas? Desmond will want you back at the office…I can't let you leave."

Silas fought the urge not to ask her why she hadn't informed him of his lack of footwear five minutes ago when he'd started looking for his damned shoe. "I have a plan, but we have to go now."

She didn't look convinced, so he took her face in both hands and asked, "Do you trust me?"

Jessica nodded slowly, wide eyes twinkling. So he kissed her quickly and took her hand, guiding her out of his room. Visiting hours weren't for another hour, but that didn't mean Desmond hadn't got there early to monitor his whereabouts from afar.

"Do you have a car?" Silas asked as they approached the lift.

"No, I came in Barney's van with you—remember?"

Silas didn't remember anything about getting to the hospital, but now wasn't the time for a memory game. Instead, he called a taxi from her phone as the lift slowly descended to freedom. As luck would have it, the taxi driver was only a five-minute drive away from the hospital, so they were concealed behind the tinted windows within no time.

Silas gave his address to the driver. He needed some supplies from the apartment before he could find his boss, ending this once and for all.

"Silas," Jessica said, voice quiet and nervous. "When Desmond realises you're gone, he'll know that I had something to do with it…He'll kill us."

He knew that, but they were out of options. With any luck, he'd simply reach Desmond before Jessica was put in any danger. He'd already sent out a joint text to Maria and Bea from her phone, letting them know their part in his plan. Silas leaned over and pressed his lips to her temple.

"Don't worry, pretty girl. I won't let him touch you."

Jessica untensed slightly at his touch, even if his words were rough with fury. Her face was still pinched with fear, so he guided her to rest her head on his shoulder. She did just that, remaining there for the agonizingly long drive back to their apartment.

☆☆☆

Silas threw open the doors to his rickety wardrobe. Under the remaining stacks of money, the bottom wooden plank lifted to unveil a plethora of illegal weapons. Firearms, knives, batons and more all lay uncomfortably in the darkest corner of his room.

His collection had been gathered over the years he'd worked for Desmond. Too many *students of the game,* as Desmond liked to call them, had been expecting him. They'd been waiting for him to teach them a lesson, ready with weapons dangerous enough to kill—should they fall into the wrong hands. And if his boss knew that his victims had been hiding illegal weapons, he'd surely have made Silas hand them over.

So whenever he was finished with the job at hand, Silas would take the weapon home with him and hide it. He never told Desmond what he found. He piled money high on top of the casket, never to be touched by anyone again.

Until today.

Silas pulled out each weapon between his forefinger and thumb, trying to keep as much distance between himself and the vicious tools as possible. He laid them all on his bed—thirteen pistols, an array of bullets to go with them, a belt buckle knife, several flick knives, and even a hand claw. Silas winced at the thought of actually using a *hand claw* in a real-life scenario—he wasn't in the business of hunting teenagers in their dreams, after all.

The spread of dangerous weapons laid out in front of him made Silas feel ill. He never wanted to see these things again. But he knew that Desmond would most likely know that he was out of the hospital by now, and therefore be devising a plan on how to kill him first.

Silas pulled on some fresh jeans and looped a belt around his waist, ripping off the old buckle. The belt buckle knife slotted nicely in its place. Two pistols fit in both concealed pockets of his oversized brown leather jacket, and another pointed down in the back pocket of his jeans.

What he wouldn't give to tuck a book there instead and forget all about this fucking nightmare.

The flick knives lay in any nook that hadn't yet been filled, and the hand claw fit Silas like a glove. Looking down at it, he thought he might retch—if only he had the time.

"Ready to go?" Silas asked as he strode through the living space towards the front door. Jessica had been left in the lounge to rest with Ziva, who was curled up with her head on her lap, whining quietly. Jessica seemed genuinely nervous, biting the skin around her thumbnails.

"Go where?" Jessica feigned innocence, biding time that Silas certainly didn't have. He sighed before walking back towards her, placing the weaponless hand on her cheek.

"I can leave you here, but I have no idea if this is the first place they'll check," Silas warned. "Or I can drop you at the café where Maria and Bea are waiting for you."

Jessica weighed her options. "The café."

Silas sped them to the Twinkling Bliss café, on high alert for anything suspicious. It wasn't unheard of for Desmond to run someone off the road, and it would be a simple way to make their deaths look like an accident.

Jessica begged him to walk her the ten steps from the car to the café, tears flooding her warm whiskey eyes.

He'd never seen her so sad; so broken.

So he obliged, weapons still clinking together in his pockets as they walked. Luckily he'd remembered to take off the hand claw before he saw Bea and Maria, who were both waiting by the counter for Jessica with open arms.

Silas gave them a quick wink and a smile as the three women embraced. He kissed the back of Jessica's shaking head, but before he could leave, she spun around to face him.

"Silas," she whispered. "Promise me you'll come back."

Bea leant her head on Jessica's shoulder in a gentle embrace while Maria wiped a tear from her cheek, but she never took her eyes from his.

Emotion caught in his throat as he looked right back at her, the others fading away. He took a step back towards her, pressing his body lightly against hers. Cradling her neck with both hands, Silas angled her face up towards his as he said, "I will *always* come back for you."

Jessica's throat bobbed as she nodded. He leant down to give her a brief, lasting kiss before backing out of the café, taking a final glance at each of the three women. The most important people in his life, he realised.

Silas's final look at Jessica had him wanting to storm straight back into the café and take her with him. To somewhere far, *far* away.

But he needed to do this. *She was in good hands.*

It was a short ride to Desmond's office, and Silas was more than ready for whatever would come next.

He swung the car into his usual parking spot, half hanging off the high pavement. Refitting the hand claw, Silas elbowed his way out of the car.

It was a dark day, thunderous clouds threatening to break at any moment. They blocked almost all light, making it look like late evening rather than midday. Silas took a deep breath of the fresh, crisp air. Savouring the feeling of the cool temperature burning in his lungs, he looked towards the building where it all started.

And to where it would be finished.

Cracking his neck, Silas took a step from the kerb towards Desmond's lair. But before he could take another, his phone vibrated in his front pocket.

"For fuck's sake," he mumbled to himself as he phished for his phone among the weapons in his pockets. He wasn't expecting anyone, but still the name flashing across the screen was a surprise—Artie. He glanced left and right as he waited for his phone to load the words. No one was around.

Don't do this, Silas. Going up against Desmond isn't worth the risk.

He was still hyper-aware of his surroundings as another message buzzed through.

Foolish of you to think I hadn't crept into Dirty Desmond's camera system as soon as I started working for him. And if I can see you, so can he—and he's got a hell of a lot more weapons than your little finger blades.

Silas was stuck in place, a million thoughts racing around his head at once. How else would he take Desmond down? How could he keep Jessica safe from the lunatic encased in metal in front of him? As if Artie read his mind, another text vibrated in his hand.

I'm in the cameras. I have the tapes to destroy him.

Silas considered it. Desmond was dirty, all right. He had women of all ages coming and going from his office, all of which were only drawn there with the promise of a heavy paycheck on the way out. He was the brains behind countless frauds, cons, and unsavoury transactions. If Artie had images of those visits, they surely could get Desmond behind bars.

But the police would want to look through the rest of the camera footage—incriminating the rest of them in the process.

No, Silas had come here with a plan, and he was damned sure going to stick to it.

I know what I'm doing.

Silas sent the text before thrusting the phone back into his pocket and striding purposefully towards the door. It was unlocked, so he silently slipped in.

The storage containers were as cool and dark as they always were, but an unsettling air hung thick around Silas as he moved through them. The concrete floor pattered underneath his heavy boots, slow and meaningful steps pulling him closer to Desmond's office. Silas had been there so many times he could guide his way through blindfolded, but something was different this time.

Out of nowhere, he heard the violently loud laugh of Desmond Rose. It was coming from another shipping container adjoining the one he currently stood in, but his boss was still close.

Silas quickened his pace to the office, shutting and locking the door behind him. Desmond's office looked the same as it always did—whiskey glasses and a full ashtray strewn across his desk, plenty of papers and not-quite-legal contracts in folders lining the blue metal wall behind his chair, stacks of hush money piled in the corner for anyone to take.

His phone had been vibrating in his pocket relentlessly during the short trip to the office, and he took it out to turn the damn thing off. Before he could, a message caught his eye from Artie.

You're all over the cameras, idiot!

I can see Desmond, he's in the room next to yours. With a small ginger guy. And lots of weapons.

Not in the office! They are through the door right in front of you!

Silas looked up at the door in question, leading to his soon-to-be-dead boss. Through the frosted glass panel, he could see shadows moving.

Cheers, Artie. I'm going in.

What followed was a flurry of vibrations, but Silas ignored every one of them. Instead, fury distorting all sense, he burst through the unlocked door. But the silence halted him from moving forward—he was all alone in there.

A cackle, like that of an evil clown, rattled through the walls. They were toying with him. There were two doors in front of him now—one that presumably led back to the entranceway storage locker, and another that would take him further into the steely pit.

A deep breath and a roll of his tension-frozen neck later, Silas took the door that would lead him back to his personal hell.

Once again, Silas was left alone in the new box. And again, the laughter came. Frustration rose as adrenaline coursed through his limbs, desperate for an outlet. The buzzing on his thigh only made it more urgent.

Take the left door, through to the right. Left again—there's your guy.

Finally, a bitter smirk snarled out of him. Silas followed the instructions, not being so careful with his footing anymore. He threw the final door open, meeting the manic eyes of his old boss. They twitched as Desmond's laughter screeched through the room.

He had something shiny in his hand.

But before Silas could process it, or the other man standing in front of him, Desmond threw the twinkling object into the empty space between them, dodging out another open door and slamming it closed behind him.

There was no time to react before the black ball of ammunition exploded mid-air, echoing the crackling light throughout the small room.

CHAPTER THIRTY-ONE

Silas groaned, the cold wall behind him a stark difference to the room before him, which had instantly turned stifling since the explosion. The impact had thrown him backwards into the wall, ricocheting him off the unforgiving metal.

The lights had also been knocked out, so when he came to an unknown number of moments later, Silas was in complete blackness. Floating dust settled on his skin as he lay slacken in the corner of the room, silently considering his next move.

Eerie sounds chased each other around him as he gently rose to his feet, the sticky air now tinted with the scent of burnt flesh. Someone was whimpering in the far corner of the storage unit, but from the swirling cackle getting further away from him, Silas knew it wasn't Desmond.

Silas cursed him out quietly.

Taking his phone out of his pocket and illuminating the small screen, he angled it towards the moans.

Barney lay on the cool concrete, dust gravitating towards a river of blood oozing from a wound running along his entirety of his stomach. He tried to contain the liquid, but the blood just bubbled wickedly around his fingers. He looked in Silas's direction, whines now becoming muffled by the pooling blood dripping from the side of his mouth.

"Help…me…please."

Silas looked from Barney's pitiful eyes to the wound, then back again. He snarled under his breath as he knelt next to Barney's head, grabbing his shoulder slightly rougher than intended.

"I'm—I'm sorry, Silas," Barney choked out around his own blood. He took one of his hands from his wound, seemingly giving up all attempts at saving himself, and placed it over Silas's. It was warm, sticky. Blood squelched between his knuckles, forcing Silas to choke down a retch.

"Why'd you do it, Barn?"

"He threatened Marlene, man. He said he'd tell her about how bad my gambling had gotten." More blood spluttered through the confession. "And…he paid off my debts, told me what you'd done to me the past year. I'm sorry, Silas. I was angry, I thought I wanted revenge."

The dim phone light reflected off the guilt and embarrassment pooling in Barney's eyes. Silas believed every word. Kidnapping and intent to kill someone wasn't what he would equate to a gambling secret being confessed, but he'd been around Barney for long enough to know the truth—been forced into the position of *confidant* enough times to hear it from the man himself. Marlene was his entire world. If he lost her, he'd lose absolutely everything.

Silas blew out a thick sigh and threw him an understanding nod. Barney wasn't the evil here, he was just a guy caught up in something terrible. Maybe he'd still have a life to live if Silas hadn't been so quick to con him with that fake jewellery. Desmond wouldn't know of him, and Barney would be at the betting shop right now riding a winning high.

A small wave of grief washed over Silas, but he shook it off quickly.

Barney was fading fast, a pool of his blood expanding around them. "Will you tell Marlene—" Barney's voice was deathly quiet, words jutting out sporadically, eyes flickering. "—Tell her I love her?"

Silas ran the bloody hand over Barney's forehead, pushing his red hair away from his eyes. His skin was both molten hot and freezing cold all at once. All he gave him was another nod, but Barney's mouth twitched into a smile before he gave out, his eyes closing and head lulling to the side. Blood still jerked from his wound, but there was less fight behind each spurt.

Silas stood, wiping his hand on his jeans. He picked his phone up and, after giving Barney one last mourning look, locked the screen—plunging them back into complete darkness. He stepped over Barney's limp body on the way to the door Desmond had escaped through.

This new room was blindingly bright in comparison, with LED strips running along each metal ridge on the ceiling.

The new room was free of Desmond, but that was the only similarity it had to the others. The walls were painted white instead of the same midnight blue as the other containers, the colour flaking off the metal in some places. The floor was covered in a soft pink rug. The cool lights made it look too bright, too *creepy*—like a bedroom in a dollhouse. There was a small bed in the corner and a bucket in the other.

The door in front of him swung open, landing Silas directly in front of his target. Desmond swaggered in, allowing the thick door to creak closed behind him.

They remained on either side of the room, staring at each other expectantly. It was just the two of them, standing one on one, waiting for the other to make his move.

"Well, look who we have here," Desmond crooned with a soft smile. "Mr Knight, the one and only. I'm starting to think you're indestructible. It's just everyone around you that dies."

Desmond kissed two fingers before pointing them up to the ceiling. Silas felt his stomach churn in disgust. "Don't make a mockery of Barney like that. You killed a good guy."

"Oh, now why would I do such a thing?" Desmond feigned hurt, hanging his head and caressing his heart. "I loved Barney, he was a top fella."

"You trained him to die."

"I did not. *You* are the one that left me—I had to find someone else!" Desmond's tone was too reasonable, like he actually believed there was innocence in what he was saying. "Perhaps *you* killed him, Knight."

His vision flickered crimson, but Desmond just smirked. "All of this comes down to you. Whatever I've done, whoever I've enlisted to help me, it was because of *your failure*. All you needed to do was ignore those silly little feelings of yours, and the others would have been none the wiser."

Desmond either felt his seething anger radiating from Silas, or grew bored with the blame game, because he straightened and motioned to the room around them. "Do you like what I've done to the place? I tried to make it fit for a queen—or at least someone used to living in such an impressive manor."

Wait…*what*?

The look on his face must've asked the silent question, because Desmond chuckled and answered, "You didn't really think I could let her go, did you?"

Silas's blood ran cold. "You locked Jessica down here too?"

Desmond scoffed loudly. "Come on Knight, of course I did. I *had* to. She tries her best, but you know she's too forgiving. I mean, just look at how she went running back to you. Who knows who she would have blabbed my plans to if I'd let her go."

"Since when?"

"Only after Ricky's lackeys had you brought here. I made it very clear that I had a room for her from the start, should she want to get away from you or her father—such *filthy* liars, both of you—but she was adamant that she wanted to help you mourn your mother." Desmond rolled his eyes, but added casually, "My deepest condolences, by the way."

"Fuck you," Silas spat.

Desmond snickered. "See, that's the problem with you, Knight. You can never see when I'm trying to help you."

"You gave the orders to have me killed. You convinced Richard it was a good idea to kidnap Jessica to teach me a lesson. When, exactly, do you think you *helped* me?"

Desmond grinned, but his eyes had darkened. His voice lowered into a growl as he said, "All I wanted was for you to realise you're nothing without me. We've been working together for years, Knight, and you threw it all away—threw me under the bus—for some girl you barely know. I wanted to show you that she was nothing more than a selfish bitch who was only looking out for herself, and what do you know? She went behind your back and played you like a fool. I needed you to see that she didn't belong on the pedestal you put her on." A noncommittal shrug. "But somehow, you were both stupid enough to forgive each other. So now, it really is *game over*."

Desmond pulled a gun from the waistband of his jeans, ready to strike, but Silas got there first. He lunged forward, hand claw thrusting out in front of him as he swiped towards his boss, connecting with anything he could with his five finger blades. The metal sliced through skin and material with ease, and Desmond staggered back like a drunken fool.

"What the—"

As he fell away from the blades, Silas could see the damage. Five long gashes across his chest and face, all taking a moment before splitting with cascading streams of blood. The blades weren't long enough to do any lasting damage, but they had surely knocked the old bastard down a peg or two, and Silas used it to his advantage.

Heading straight towards the wounded animal, Silas reached for a blade in one of his pockets. He wanted to savour this, enjoy every second for what Desmond had put him and his friends through. He flicked it open with just enough time to sink it into Desmond's kidney, eliciting a guttural cry. The gun clattered to the floor.

Their faces were close enough that Silas could feel his victim's the staggered wet breaths on his cheek. He stared into Desmond's horrified eyes as he twisted his face into a bitter grin and rotated the knife.

Oh, how sweet those screams of pain were to his ears.

"Silas, please," Desmond gasped as the blade minced his organs like they were nothing more than scraps on a butcher's floor.

"I'm going to enjoy this, Rosey boy," Silas snarled into his ear.

"Please, Sy. I'll give you whatever you want."

Silas drew back slightly at the pleading in his tone, but only enough for him to generate more force to plunge the knife deeper into his boss's stomach.

"Whatever I *want*? Oh, that's awfully kind of you Des. Okay, let's see, shall we? I would like—" Another squelching stab forced the slimy man to keel onto his knees,

"—the last three years of my life back. I'd like Jessica and Barney to not have their lives ruined at the hands of your sick *fucking* games." Silas yanked Desmond's slick hair back so they were facing each other. His boss was drained of colour, beads of sweat running down his brow profusely. He held the crimson knife up to Desmond's throat, pressing the blade in, in, in. "Can you do that for me?"

The man's face contorted in anguish, thick sobs ricocheting through the room.

Too much. *Was he acting?*

That hesitation was all Desmond needed to thrust himself towards Silas, stabbing him right back with a knife he'd pulled from his pocket. Immediate searing pain radiated through Silas's stomach, dropping him back to the concrete. The knife was still nestled into his stomach, the coppery smell hitting him instantly, coating his tongue and turning his vision red.

"Oh, Silas..." Desmond sneered, despite his own wounds bleeding him dry. "How did you think you'd best me? Even with your little knives, you cannot beat the Grand Master."

Grunting over the smug words, Silas scoured his brain for what to do next. But the pain from the cool blade—noticeably longer than anything he had in his possession—was flashing throughout his entire body, shaking any coherent thoughts from his head.

"Such a shame. Really, it is." Desmond knelt over him, looking hungrily at the knife handle like it was a piece of meat and he was a prowling tiger.

That knife was the only thing keeping the blood inside his body—the only thing keeping him *alive*.

"You were one of my favourites, Knight. It's a real pity you have to die now. But don't worry, I'll keep your little plaything company. I think she has some apologising to do."

Desmond reached for the handle as vengeful energy coursed its way through Silas's bloodstream.

But before he could use the last of his energy to reach the gun in his pocket, the door swung open with a piercing wail. Jessica ran in, coming to a halt as she took in the scene before her.

"Jessie?" Desmond sneered, suspicious eyes darting from her to Silas, then back again. "Come to rejoin the winning team?"

Silas squinted to look up at her, trying to catch her eye. But she was too focused on Desmond. "Whose side are you on, sweetie?"

Silas watched as her eyes shuttered, probably regretting coming here at all. *What was she doing here?*

"Get away from him, Jess," Silas whispered, pain ripping through his stomach and dicing his words. She still didn't look at him.

"Now now, Silas. Jessie's a big girl, she can speak for herself," Desmond gasped. One hand was still pressed to his wounds, but the other had somehow found the gun it had dropped earlier. The gun that was now casually being angled towards Jessica. "Who are you here to help, dear?"

"The man who would never hurt me," was all Jessica replied, eyes flickering to the gun Desmond was holding. "That's you, right Des?"

His boss perked up at the sweetness in her voice, although Silas couldn't ignore the shakiness of her breaths.

"That's right, Jessie. I would *never* harm you." Desmond's eyes slid to Silas, eyebrows jerking up as if to say *you lose*. But Silas looked back to Jessica, who was slowly closing in on Desmond.

"How lovely it is to hear those words from you." She gave him a siren's smile, beautiful enough to lure anyone in. "Why don't you let me take the final shot? I think I've been through more than enough to deserve it, don't you?"

Desmond's eyes gleamed. "By all means," he said, bowing as he flicked the gun around and extended the handle to her.

She hummed, accepting it and weighing the weapon in her hand. It was then that she finally met Silas's stare, sharing a silent secret. Desmond now lay on the floor, defenceless.

The spell of Jessica's charm, indeed.

"Thank you for this gift," she said. "Only, I did want to get your opinion on something before I take it."

Desmond's snide smile fell as her tone grew bitter. He looked at Silas, then at the gun.

"See, I realised that we never talked about the whole hostage situation. Where you wanted to take me and sell me back to my father? That doesn't seem all that *harmless* to me."

Desmond chuckled awkwardly. "That was a before I knew you, Jessie."

"And what about keeping me locked in this room while you waited to take Silas to hospital?" Her voice was low; lethal.

"I had to protect my investment, sweetie. And you had nowhere else to go—Richard wouldn't take you back, this one was rotting away in one of my boxes. Who else would've taken you in? I was *helping* you."

A loud laugh burst from her at that. "Really? You were helping me by holding me hostage, feeding me lies about Silas, my family, and everything I thought I knew?"

Desmond's skin had turned a horrid mixture of pale yellow and grey. "Don't lie, Jessie. You liked the game; I know you did. I couldn't keep you away when we had Silas strung up like game meat down the hall."

"She was looking out for me," Silas interrupted slowly. He wasn't feeling so great, either. Jessica glanced at him sidelong, understanding the urgency of his condition.

Desmond spluttered on a laugh. "Go ahead, blame me for your actions. But you," he pointed at Silas, "needed the money and *I* funded your mother's treatments. And you," a jab at Jessica, "wanted to get away from your father, and I gave you an out. What did you expect, for me to grant your wishes for free? You both owe me—it's not my fault that neither of you understand the con game. I've taken back nothing more than I was *owed*. Perhaps you should both take a long, hard look at yourselves before blaming me for your wrongdoings." Desmond coughed and spat a wad of bloody saliva on the floor between them. "You might even find that you're no better than me."

Silas snarled, but Jessica looked uncertain, guilty. *No,* Silas silently urged, *don't believe him.*

"We're nothing like you, Desmond. You prey on people's desperation and use them for your own personal gain. You—" Silas was fading fast; his words were failing him. "You trained us to be killers and forced us to do your dirty work. We're *nothing* like you."

"Is that right? Then tell me, how did the families of the people you've conned react when you gave them all that money back, Knight?"

Silas growled, "You really do have an answer for everything, don't you?"

Desmond shrugged coyly, mistaking it for a compliment. "I really do. And when you two get into your next sticky situation, you'll be wishing you still had Desmond Rose to come bail you out." He sneered. "Don't forget about what happened at the café, son. You'd be in prison if it weren't for me."

Jessica looked up at that, knowingly. Perhaps Maria had told her. Something snapped within her then, and Silas saw it. She drew then gun up in front of her, snarling, "Go to hell."

Silas dared to watch as she pulled the trigger and the blaring sound recoiled off the walls in all directions.

Desmond Rose fell with an almighty crack.

And then Jessica was next to him, kneeling as gentle hands kneaded the skin around the knife still embedded in his stomach. But Silas couldn't look away from her face, panic twisting her features as she whimpered at the sight of him. She grabbed her phone from her pocket and hit the screen a few times.

"Can you come in here please?" she whispered through the phone, not bothering to wait for a reply as she hung up and turned back towards him.

She still wouldn't meet his eye, so Silas lifted a shaking hand to her chin and guided her to face him. She looked peaky, like she could throw up at any moment. She didn't return his feeble attempt of a smile as she said, "What did I do?"

His reply was interrupted by a chorus of gasps from the doorway. Silas craned his neck upwards to see Bea rushing towards him. Maria was frozen in place, hands over her agape mouth as she took in the scene.

Desmond's dead body collapsed in a crumpled heap on the concrete. Silas lying with a knife buried in his stomach on the rug, which was now a disgusting shade of murky red.

She was further away from this than any of them. Bea and Jessica had both been in the dungeons before, but it was all new to Maria. He made a mental note to talk her through it, if he made it out of here alive.

"Call an ambulance!" Bea said to no one in particular as she took off her flannel shirt and wrapped it around the knife handle, attempting to stem the blood still oozing around it. Silas clamped his teeth together at the immense pain of the blade shifting in his stomach. Jessica grabbed his hand in hers and squeezed, meeting his eyes as if speaking to him silently.

You will be okay.

He squeezed hers back. *So will you.*

Maria ran back into the room shouting, "The ambulance is on their way." He hadn't even noticed she'd left.

Bea tore Silas's attention away from Jessica as she leaned to hover further over him. "Silas? Can you hear me?"

He nodded a fraction. "Good. The ambulance is on its way, and they'll get you patched up. You just have to hold on for a few more minutes."

Silas nodded again and turned back to Jessica. The searing pain made it seem impossible to hold for even another second, but her face—the flushed cheeks, her glassy eyes, the lines of worry creasing her brow—made him willing to try a little while longer.

She'd come to save him—she came back. Who knows where he'd be right now if Jessica hadn't turned up with a plan of her own.

"One last con," he croaked.

She smirked half-heartedly. "Never again."

CHAPTER THIRTY-TWO

✦

Silas had become far too well acquainted with the bare hospital room he opened his eyes to. Jessica, who had apparently not left his side, told him he had been under sedation for two days to help him recover from the surgery.

Bea gave him a familiar smile of relief, with a tiny hint of humour. They had been down this road together one too many times.

"I've heard they're in talks to name the whole floor after you," Bea said dryly as she gave him a kiss on the cheek. "The Silas Knight centre has a nice ring to it."

He laughed, eyes crinkling as the movement nudged his stitches.

Jessica was an emotional wreck, blubbering all over his paper-thin sheets. She hadn't found any part of it *funny*.

Through the next few days, Silas was visited by a number of officials. The first were two policemen, asking for his account of the story. Jessica had already given hers, and once they were happy that everything matched the security footage that an anonymous source had given them—spliced to fit the narrative that it was strictly a defensive killing—they left them alone and closed the case.

Silas made a mental note to thank Artie once he got his phone back.

Doctors swarmed his room at one time or another, asking for bloods, tests, and more scans. He'd been rushed into surgery as soon as he'd arrived, and it had gone well, but he'd lost a lot of blood and needed to be closely monitored due to the extensive injuries to his abdomen.

Bea came and went whenever she had time to visit around her busy schedule. Maria popped in once or twice, but she wasn't a big fan of hospitals. Silas practically ordered her to stay away. He'd be back in the café soon enough.

Jessica spent each night huddled next to him on the small bed, barely keeping a tiny distance between them. He stroked her hair as she struggled to fall asleep, and she calmed him down when the night terrors came to claim him.

"We're okay," she whispered into his ear one night, hand over his racing heart. "We're safe, and we're together."

That became their constant, their lifeline. Whenever one of them was flanking, their memories threatening to pull them deep beneath the surface, the other would repeat those exact words.

Okay. Safe. Together.

Dr Preece had been in a few times, not as Silas's doctor, but as a second opinion. She'd been told their story, and she wanted to offer both of them a free referral to the hospital's counselling department. They both swiftly took her up on it.

Silas's therapist came to his room to conduct the sessions, but Jessica had hers in the official offices in the hospital.

Today was her third appointment. She kissed him on the cheek, lingering for a long moment as he whispered those three words to her.

She wore a baby blue sundress despite there still being a chill in the crisp February air, with white pumps and a matching ribbon tied in her untamed hair. She looked as gorgeous as ever, but her eyes were tired. Her smile was strained.

Before she could slip from his grasp, he pulled her gently towards him. Letting go of her fingers, he cupped her face and stared deeply into her eyes.

"When I was younger, Ma and I would camp out all night to spot shooting stars." Jessica's face broke into a soft smile. "I'd always wish for silly things, you know? Cars, the best toys, my favourite TV shows to release their new seasons early," he continued as she giggled. "But my ma would always wish for the same thing—for me to be happy. I'd think of that from time to time, assuming it never came true because she told me what she wished for. But you…I think you're what she wished for me. *You* are my happy wish come true."

Jessica didn't resist the tears spilling over her lashes, and neither did he.

"I love you, Mr Knight."

"I love you too, pretty girl."

She leaned in, lips slightly parted to offer him a longing lover's kiss. She hummed softly into his mouth, and he wished he could pull her down onto this bed and spend the rest of the day with her. But she tore them apart, and then she was gone.

To occupy the mind-numbingly long silence, Silas sent a text to thank his saviour.

> *I realised I never got to thank you. For the CCTV footage—for saving my life, really.*

Within a few seconds, the phone chimed with a reply.

> *Which time? Kidding! Don't mention it. Oh, and don't ever do something that dumb again. I can't be looking out for you 24/7.*

Silas huffed out a small laugh, wincing at the burning pain from his still-fresh wounds. Still, his elated mood didn't waver. Since the news confirming Desmond had remained dead after Jessica shot him, Silas had been on top of the world.

> *No need to worry about me, Arth. I reckon I'll be keeping it lowkey from now on.*

Silas placed the phone down on the plastic table next to his bed and relaxed into the pillows, closing his eyes for a moment's rest. A small smile tugged at the corners of his mouth as he did so.

☆☆☆

Judging by the sunset casting a soft orange glow over the plain hospital room, Silas had taken a little more than a *moment* to rest. He woke up groggy, the painkillers a nurse had offered him earlier finally wearing off. Jessica was sat in the visitor's chair, legs hanging over one of the armrests as she read her book.

"Hey," he croaked before trying to clear his throat. "How was your session?"

"Hi, you. It was good—really helpful," Jessica said tightly, putting her book down. "The doctor says it's important for me to recognise that it wasn't my fault, what happened to us."

"It wasn't," Silas agreed.

Jessica nodded, nibbling at her lip. "And that's what I have to come to terms with. What's done is done and I can't change it. It's going to be difficult…but I'll get there."

Silas patted the empty spot next to him on his thin bed, and she lay down next to him. "For what it's worth, I don't blame you," he murmured into her hair. "For any of it."

"Thank you. And I don't blame you," she said just as quietly.

That was something Silas was having to come to terms with, with his own therapist. And something they'd both be working on for a long time to come. But he could hear the truth in her words as she reassured him, and now they had nothing *but* time.

All the time in the world.

Everything they had been through in the past year was over. Desmond was gone from their lives forever, Jessica was safely removed from the Morton manor and away from the family's investors, and Silas was no longer plagued by the thought of his next heist.

After the longest con of his short career, Silas Knight was free. Free to live the life he'd been dreaming of with Jessica, without danger threatening their future.

Because they were *okay*.
They were *safe*.
They were *together*.

EPILOGUE

One Year Later

✦

"Come on, honey! We have to get ready for the party!" Jessica squealed as she came up behind where he sat on the sofa, almost clipping him with the box in her hands as she leant over to kiss him on the cheek.

Silas groaned, resting his open book over his eyes in a bid to hide. "I don't want to get ready," he said in a pathetic-sounding voice. "Can't we just go to the café?"

He heard Jessica come to a halt, her voice getting louder as she walked back through from the bedroom. "You want to have our leaving party at the Twinkling Bliss *café*?" she asked, falling into his lap. Silas made an *oof* sound at the surprise and removed the book from his face. She was looking back at him with those wide, warm whiskey eyes. "Am I understanding that correctly, Mr Knight?"

He hummed in agreement, nodding. Jessica rolled her eyes and wrapped her arms around his neck as his fingers drew lazy lines up and down her thigh. She gave him a knowing smile, kissing him deeply. The air between them heated, and his hand travelled higher, a silent question.

But she broke them apart, swinging her legs away and standing, picking up another box. "Nu-uh. There's too much to do. Come on, grab a box—quickly! We need to get the rest of this stuff packed before the movers get here tomorrow morning."

Silas took a long, calming breath before following her orders and picking up a half-full box labelled 'lounge'. Ziva jumped onto the sofa and lay in his seat, snuggling into the warm cushion.

"Lucky,' he murmured at the dog, and Ziva's eyes twinkled.

Silas carried the box over to the shelving unit, still full of little trinkets and photo frames. Allowing himself a second to look over his ma's ornaments, a smile graced his lips. He knew Ma would be so thankful that they were getting out of Fayette Bay together.

"Here," Jessica handed him some old newspaper. "I'll help wrap." She took a ceramic teddy bear holding an S from the shelf, smirking at it as she wrapped it tightly in paper. Silas had painted it for Ma when he was five years old, and it wasn't his finest work. But she'd loved it, never allowing him to throw it out.

He picked up another—a multicoloured glass dog—wrapping it and tucking it in the box. They finished the ornaments together slowly, Silas telling her the backstory of why his mother collected such obscure trinkets.

Then he grabbed the first framed picture—one of Ma, bundled in winter clothing as she sat on a darkened beach, grinning widely as the stars twinkled above her. Silas had taken it when he was fifteen, when Ma had woken him up in the dead of night to watch a meteor shower. It was one of the only trips to the beach he'd actually enjoyed.

The next picture was a polaroid of Jessica in a yellow sundress, her silhouette shining against the blazing sunset. Even though her face wasn't showing, her happiness still radiated through the print. Silas had taken it back in July, one of the first times he'd ever seen her feel free.

"Remember this?" he asked, showing her the print. She beamed, resting her head against his arm.

"How could I ever forget?" she returned fondly.

Their picture together from the same day joined the collection of frames, along with the memory he had captured of Jessica and the deer at Emsterel Thicket.

Looking through the pictures now, Silas felt a surge of emotion build within his chest. He looked down at her, her eyes glassy as they packed away their memories together, getting ready to make many, many more.

"I love you," he said, leaning to give her a peck.

Jessica had been a ray of sunshine in his too-dark world. Her smile, her laugh, her love. She'd blindsided him in the best way.

"And I love you," she hummed as he pulled her into a tighter embrace, wrapping his free hand around her neck and smelling her inky curls. "But we *have* to get ready for this party!" she added, lightly hitting him on the chest. "Let's go—rally!"

Silas rolled his eyes dramatically, but obeyed.

A few hours later, they were sitting around the foldaway table Artie had lent them, playing cards with their closest friends. Silas nuzzled Jessica's neck as Bea called "Bullshit!" for the tenth time that round.

The guests groaned, and Artie tried to hide his smirk. Bea's cheeked flushed as she pushed the middle pile towards him, not meeting anyone's eyes.

The game finished and Silas guided Jessica over to the sofa before they could get roped into another round. Maria had burst in a few minutes ago, and she was keeping the guests entertained with the extra alcohol and board games she'd brought to play.

"Hey," he said quietly. Jessica turned to look at him, their noses almost touching with how close they were. "Are you excited?"

"To get out of here?" she asked. He nodded, and she huffed out a little laugh. "It's all I've ever wanted. A wish come true."

"Are you happy?"

Her face broke out into a wide grin at that. "Of course I'm happy," she said, looking down at the twinkling clear diamond sitting on her ring finger. "I don't think it's even possible to be any happier than I am with you."

Silas slid his hand underneath hers, folding their fingers together and bringing the ring up to his lips. He kissed it lightly. "I can't wait," he confessed.

And no truer words had ever been spoken. One whole year of freedom had shown Silas everything he needed to be happy. And he'd never been more certain that this was it for him—*she* was it. The stars in his darkest moments. The sunshine in his new world. And he couldn't wait to explore it with her.

"I love you, my pretty girl. It's just you and me now, forever."

THE END

ACKNOWLEDGEMENTS

Wow. Let me start off by saying that I didn't think this book would ever get through its first draft, let alone end up on the market as a self-published book. So typing an author's note is just a little surreal right now!

I would like to begin by acknowledging everyone who helped me persevere with my passion for writing and pushed me to tell Silas and Jessica's story—anyone who I've ever mentioned my book to and who has continued to cheer me on from the sidelines.

Endless thank yous to my mum, who has always believed in me no matter what I put my mind to. I would not have been able to write my book without your constant unwavering support and love. Please accept these words as payment for the first 18 years of my life.

Thank you to Brandon, who has watched me write, edit, proof, rewrite, and fret over this novel for three long years. You've always had my back and believed in me, even when I was ready to forget every single word for good. Thank you, from the bottom of my heart, for everything you have done for me, our family, and this book.

I couldn't write my acknowledgements without mentioning my wonderful son Albie, who has spent the last two years teaching me that I could do absolutely anything, even when I was convinced I couldn't.

And to Polly and Pirate, who offered moral support while they slept and walked over the keyboard a million times. Any typos are accredited to only them.

Thank you to my beta and advanced readers for their kind words and helpful criticisms. You were an excellent confidence boost and all lovely to work with. And thank you to Bia Shuja for designing this wonderful cover.

Finally, I want to extend my deepest gratitude to anyone who picked this book up and gave it a chance. The fact that my words are in your hands right now means more than you'll ever know. So thank you!

ABOUT THE AUTHOR

GEMMA NICHOLLS is a professional writer from sunny South England, now residing in rainy South Wales. She's always been passionate about writing, creating stories, and finding new worlds to take her away from reality for an hour or two. She loves rom-coms, fantasy, and any book where the love interest leans against the doorframe in *that* way.

Gemma lives with her wonderful boyfriend, their son, and their two wild tuxedo cats. She drinks far too much coffee for her own good and hopes that her books will put a smile on people's faces, giving them a safe space to escape reality for a little while when they need it most.

For latest information on new releases and other fun stuff, come say hi on Instagram:

@gemmanichollswrites

Printed in Great Britain
by Amazon